I dedicate this book to Betsy Roebuck Cratch, my wife of 55 years. Mathematically speaking, I never fully understood how two could become one and then make three, but we did it. Thanks for the memories and especially for the three wonderful daughters. I love you dearly.

FOREWORD

I have pondered of late, why an eighty-one-year-old man in his right mind would take on the task of writing a novel. The answer would probably come more easily if I could confess to a childhood dream to be a writer or the desire to model the life of an admired teacher or professor. But such is not the case. In fact, I do not recall ever having such a thought or desire until recently. The genesis of this project began with my attempt to write my memoirs for my extended family: three daughters, their spouses, 23 grandchildren and 6 great-grandchildren. When I began to record family stories of the old days, and as they came to mind, I shared some of them at family gatherings. Someone said, "Oh, Grandy, you should write a book."

My response to the pondering was, "You will never know you can if you do not try." Once the decision was made, the ideas, the plot, and the flow came so quickly, I had difficulty jotting them down before another thought demanded attention. The notes were easy, but putting them into a form I hoped readers would enjoy was not nearly as easy. I have woven several events from my life into the story to give it vibrancy. I wonder if you will be able to detect reality from fiction.

Brody James Edwards and every character in this book is a figment of my imagination. There has been no intention to portray real people in the story. I have, however, given to some of the characters names of real people I have known and whom I wish to honor in this way. So, if you see your name or something close to it, you will know I was thankful for having known you. I hope you find Brody's story captivating as he deals with the ups and downs of life, loss of dreams, horrors of war, injury, healing, hate, guilt, love, redemption, a new career, and an ending I hope will make you think, "Wow! I didn't see that one coming."

The voices Brody hears are real to him, therefore they deserve to be in quotes. Be advised that Rage always speaks in **bold** print, whereas Reason speaks in *italics*.

To the residents of Chocowinity: I hope you are not disturbed by my placing Ye Olde Sweet Shoppe in the location you know as Hickman's garage. It was the place where my family owned and operated the Chocowinity Drive-in Grill from 1949 until 1952 and is therefore special in my memory.

Blessings to all who read this.

Geoff Cratch

Shrink AKA Josephine Mandino, CMDR, USN, PHD and maybe some other titles I'm not privy to, asked me, "These voices that speak to you, are they voices you recognize, like someone from your past?"

"No, ma'am, definitely not people I recognize or remember."

"Brody, do you think you actually hear them or just think you hear them?"

"Umm, that is hard to say. At times they are so real that I respond verbally without thinking and am embarrassed when I see others looking around to see who I'm talking to. Other times, I respond with a thought, as real as if I had verbally expressed it, almost like I'm reading a book and I'm one of the characters."

"Very interesting."

"Typical psychiatrist."

"Shush."

"You heard a voice, didn't you?"

"Yes, Ma'am."

"What did it say?"

He thought your response of "Very interesting" was, "Typical psychiatrist."

She chuckled. "I see."

"I see, too."

"Shush."

"I will not even ask. I should have seen that one coming. Do you have any idea who these voices are?"

"I'm beginning to see one of them as probably my alter-ego. At least we're a lot alike. That voice is like an out-of-control me. I call him Rage."

"Now, I find that interesting," she chuckled. "And I want to ask you some questions about yourself rather than the voices. Reports from your doctors and your nurses say that you are always angry, ready to express your frustrations instantly. I would like to hear your explanation for such behavior, please."

"Well, let me begin by saying, it's not fun to awaken from a nightmare so real that your first conscious thought is, "He is going to kill me!" Then, after coming to the realization that it was a nightmare, to realize you do not know where you are, and that gets compounded by the fact that you do not know who you are. That's just the beginning. To hear someone tell you that you are Lance Corporal Brody James Edwards and you've been seriously wounded in a combat situation in Afghanistan, and not remember any of that, well it really made me want to scream."

"Did you, or have you? Screamed, that is?"

"No ma'am."

"Give it a try. It might make you feel better."

"Are you serious?"

"Yes, give it a shot!"

"Ahiahiiiee."

"You can do better than that, let it all hang out!"

"Ahiahiiiee!"

"That's better. Do you feel any better?"

"Umm, I don't know. But that's just the beginning. It really pissed me off – oh excuse me – I mean it made me mad, when they began telling me, "You are six-foot-one, 185 pounds, have reddish brown hair, blue eyes and a square cut cleft chin. I mean they do have mirrors in this place. Give me a break, I'm not an idiot!"

"No, you certainly are not. Have things started to become clearer for you in the last few days?"

"Yes ma'am, I was confused when they said I enlisted in Monterey, California, but when they told me I was from Chocowinity, North Carolina, that was like a curtain opening up to allow memories to come at me pretty rapidly. I'm gradually fitting the pieces of my life back together, so slowly as to be frustrating, but definitely better than it was."

"Good. Now let's get back to the voices: Any idea about the identity of the other voices?"

"I'm working on that, Doc. I have a question for you. I've been conscious for about a week now, but these voices seem to have been present for longer than that. Is it possible that we have been conversing during my month-long coma?"

"Brody, that's a question you should pose to your neurologist. He could give you a better answer than I can. I just don't know. It seems unlikely, but with brain injuries, who knows? Volumes have been written on the affects and effects of brain trauma, and I certainly haven't read them all. I will say that your case is very interesting," she chuckled. "I think I can help you. Are you willing to work with me?"

"Yes, I definitely need help. I have to admit that I'm beginning to enjoy the friendly banter with the voices, and that bothers me."

"I don't think you should let that bother you. Here is what I would like you to do. Try journaling your thoughts and conversations. It might help you to clarify your thinking and deal with those voices. It will surely be helpful to me to see the situations that bring on these events. I have journaled every day for the last six years, and it has proven profitable as I often go back to check events I recorded."

So, there I sat in the day room of Building 19 of the Walter Reed Medical Center in Bethesda, Maryland, staring at this laptop computer, and the only thing I could think of was Snoopy sitting on his dog house with his little typewriter in his lap, trying to write the Great American Novel. All he can come up with is, "It was a dark and stormy night."

Well, come to think about it, my current nightmarish situation did begin on a dark and stormy night. At least that's when I came out of what I've been told was a month-long coma. I still don't know if it was the clap of thunder or my screaming that brought me to consciousness. I can tell you this, if the nurse hadn't turned on the lights in my room, I'm convinced that what turned out to be an IV apparatus would surely have cut off my head. Okay, I know that sounds ridiculous, but to me it looked like Ali Baba was swinging his scimitar right at me. Oh, Ali Baba, that's grunt speak for a bad guy. Feel better now? God, I hate those rag heads!

"Good morning, Jarhead."

"Well, Rage, you decided to show up after all. I was beginning to worry about you."

"**Bullshit. We're too much alike for you to worry about me. Besides, you have every right to hate that guy. I mean he did try to piss on you, didn't he**?"

"He came mighty close. Thankfully, he didn't know I was there. I could smell him. If I had been three feet closer and had his scimitar, he would have one less head and I wouldn't be able to refer to him as that uncircumcised prick anymore, heh-heh. Hey, that's the first time I've laughed since being here. Maybe this journaling thing will be helpful after all."

"Okay, Jarhead, why don't you get to work and put it down just as if you're talking to me and not to Shrink. Show it to her at your next session so she can see how much progress I've helped you make."

"Hey, Rage, no conceit in the family I see, but maybe you're smarter than you look, heh-heh."

Well, here goes:

I landed at Kandahar on July 16, 2011 and was driven to Camp Delaram, which is a Forward Operating Base whose mission is to help Afghans bring their life back to normal after an attack by the Taliban forces, and to prevent further attacks if possible. My first look at the base made me think I was watching TV reruns of M.A.S.H. Tents for barracks, tents for showers, plywood floors, wood stoves, metal lockers, boy it's not the Hilton! We three new arrivals were introduced to the Commanding Officer, Major Anthony Longmire, who briefed us on our mission and told us we would each be paired with a veteran for training purposes.

My trainer was Sgt. Mike Ball from Sterling, Virginia, a nice guy who had about two years on me in age and length of service. We spent the next two weeks going over maps, briefings on previous missions both successful and some not so successful. In the ensuing months, he and I became buddies, with him telling me of his football exploits and me responding with my baseball stories. He did a good job showing me how to use my security training out in communities in ways that did not offend the natives or, in some cases, let them even know we were their protection. He was very effective in using humor to get across a point. I remembered a time when, to make sure I knew how vulnerable we were out in the various communities, he said, "Do you know why there are no Walmart's in Afghanistan?" I admitted that I didn't.

"Because there is a Target on every corner. And don't forget that the company logo is emblazoned on the back of your uniform."

"What do you call an evil Afghani?"

"I don't know, Rage, what?"

"Mu Ha Ha Ha Med!"

I almost admonished Rage to be quiet, when the thought hit me that indeed humor played a big part in making life in that place more bearable. The constant urge to look over your shoulder to see if someone was aiming at the Target logo on your back did create tension that was eased better by humor than any other way I knew of. Fortunately for both Mike and me, there was a guy in our hut who kept us in stitches. Picture this: six of us in the hut, lights out and almost asleep, then Joel Connors, from Piney Flats, Tennessee, would tell a joke. He only did one a night, but he seldom failed to do one. Here are a few that come to mind.

"What did the suicide bomber's mom say?"

"My Allah! They blow up so fast."

"What's the difference between a microwave oven and an Islamic extremist?"

"A microwave doesn't blow up every time the timer goes off."

After the first night or two, no one even tried to answer his questions. We just waited for him to provide the answer and that would be the last spoken word except for an occasional yuck or a mumbled good night.

It's strange that such memories would be the best of my entire time in Afghanistan. My next thought was the doctor's admonition to focus on the issues at hand and not be so easily distracted. "Back to the task at hand," I thought.

The first six months went smoothly. Then in early March 2012 an Intelligence Report came in citing the likelihood that the Taliban might make a strike on a village about 25 klicks to the northwest. Mike and I were given the mission of spotting for their arrival and calling in air support to take them out before they reached the village. We both were issued four-wheelers loaded with enough Meals Ready to Eat (MREs) to last several days, and a bed roll with a sheet of water- repellant tarp for cover. I had my M16, and Mike had his M240B machine gun. We planned to arrive on site at about 0300 hours, secure our bikes, catch a few winks and set up watch, one on either side of the village. He had mapped out vantage points for both of us, showing me in a ravine containing a large evergreen tree. I could see that it provided good access going to and from our bike site. The villagers would not be aware that I was present. Mike had stressed the importance that they not know we were present, because we simply did not know if everyone there could be trusted.

Things started hitting the crapper immediately. When I climbed up the dune to look out from beneath the evergreen, the Taliban were already there. They must have arrived while we napped. There were two pickup trucks, both with mounted machine guns, and I saw what looked to be fifteen to twenty ragheads yelling at frightened villagers.

I noticed a fast-approaching storm, with very dark clouds and lightning coming at us from the west. The leader was walking right toward me while unbuttoning his pants. It was obvious he was going to take a leak down the ravine and probably on the tree I was using as cover. I could smell him and his urine, and I was trying to hold my breath to avoid the smell and to escape detection. He finished his business and turned and walked away, so I took a quick peek to check the situation. To my horror, I saw three ragheads dragging Mike toward the gathering. His helmet was gone and I could see him bleeding from a head wound, probably from a rifle butt. They tied his hands behind his back, ordered the villagers back inside and began to interrogate Mike. Ali Baba spoke fluent English, and I thought, "Yeah, he probably went to Harvard or Yale." A quick count confirmed my previous estimate to be in the ballpark, as I now knew there were nineteen of them. I thought, "There's no way I can get all of them before they kill Mike."

"That SOB is going to decapitate him."

"But what can I do against nineteen to one odds besides get myself killed?"

"Semper Fi, Marine."

Shaking in my boots, but determined to give it my best shot, I moved out from under the tree and climbed up the dune to assume a prone firing position; things continued downhill, literally, as the sand gave way, causing me to slide to the bottom. By the time I scampered back up top it was too late. The most horrible scene I hope I will ever see was that of Ali Baba, one hand holding his scimitar and the other holding Mike's head, screaming, "Allah Akbar!" followed by a blood curdling trill of a yell that caused me to lose all sense of caution.

I rose and drew a bead on his forehead. Again, the sand betrayed me as my foot gave just enough to cause a miss. The shot – I so desperately wanted to hit him between the eyes – actually hit the hand holding the scimitar and I saw a finger or two fall to the ground along with the scimitar. Things seemed to stand still, as if I were looking at a photograph.

Ali Baba was holding his injured hand while running toward the trucks. The next instant, all the others turned their focus toward me. This time I didn't wait for the sand to cause a fall. I dropped like a brick to the bottom of that ravine. I hit the bottom, breath knocked out of me and dazed. I tried to get up and run but didn't because I felt a surge of static electricity. Every hair on my body did a little dance, then a flash of lightning followed by a tremendous clap of thunder. Shaken from the fall but not severely hurt, I grabbed my rifle, expecting to see heads peeking over the rim above. When none appeared, I made my way once again to the top.

Bodies of the Taliban were lying everywhere. One of the trucks was gone so I guess Ali Baba made it to the truck before the lightning struck. Then several men came from the village and went from body to body. It was not pleasant to see them cut the throats of three who were evidently not yet dead, but it was prudent for them to do so.

They greeted me warmly, thanking me and clasping their hands together and bowing. I asked if anyone spoke English. I had no ability whatever to converse in Pashto or Dari. One man said, "Little bit," pointing to his head, "Speak not good." I showed them where to place the truck to set up an ambush if the Taliban returned, and I assured them I would send replacements soon. I tried to contact the base but the lightning strike had killed the signal so the call did not go through. With the camera on my cell phone, I snapped a picture of the bodies for evidence.

"You are one lucky Leatherneck. You do know that, right?"

"In your vernacular, damn straight."

Two villagers helped me carry Mike's body back to the bikes. I used bungee cords to secure his legs to the gas tank, to keep them out of the way of my shifting gears. It was not pleasant securing his head to the back of the bike, but it had to be done. Pulling his torso close to my body, I experienced the distinct smell of death. Gagging several times but not throwing up, I gave it the gas.

After about fifteen minutes of riding as fast as I dared, I noticed my stomach was growling from hunger and nausea. I slowed to a stop and got off the bike. Grabbing a package of MRE's, I walked some thirty yards away from the bike, trying to get away from the smell. MRE's don't taste great even when you are as hungry as I was, but they are disgusting when you must swallow every bite multiple times to get them to stay down.

It was almost 1400 hours as I mounted the bike again, hugged Mike's torso to me and took off. As we approached the base I became wary, knowing the Taliban spied on us. Seeing the last place that offered any cover for an ambush, I stopped the bike, got Mike's machine gun and my M16 off my back and secured them by placing the barrels on the handle bars and under Mike's arms. Knowing I had to crash my way through whether they were present or not, I experimented with revving up the engine while squeezing Mike's right hand around the throttle to see if we could maintain speed so that I could fire both weapons. Satisfied that it seemed to work, I started for home, my right hand over his, with the intention to keep it there unless I had to start firing my rifle. I remember seeing some movement as we neared the rocks, and I reached for my rifle.

That's the last thing I remember before finding myself here.

Having spent the weekend doing online research to try to get a better understanding of why those freaking Arabs act like such idiots, I approached Shrink's office with mixed emotions. I was still angry and upset, but feeling like some progress had been made in that I have a grip on what had happened to me up to a point. Yeah, and I must admit, Shrink didn't hurt the eyeballs, you know what I mean. She would make any male take a second look. So, at 0900 hours I rolled that wheel chair into her office, feeling good for a man with three gunshot wounds in his body.

Wait a minute, you don't know about my injuries yet, do you? Well, let's get that out of the way before she calls me in. The one in my left shoulder is just a flesh wound. The bullet passed through cleanly without touching a bone, so the muscle should heal nicely, they tell me. The one in the right leg is more serious, since it shattered the bone, but the pins should allow me to walk in a few more weeks and hopefully without too much of a limp.

Now, the one to the head is a different matter. Actually, the bullet did not enter my head but rather bounced off the front of my helmet, causing enough blunt force trauma that they had to remove a chunk of skull to allow the brain to swell. So, old pretty boy will be dealing with a horseshoe shaped scar in the forehead, as well as three other scars where screws holding the device to keep my head immobilized have left their mark. Most of it might be covered by hair growth, and I don't have a movie contract, so what the hey. Got to go, Shrink is calling.

After the usual pleasantries, I handed her the printouts of my first day's work and said, "After reading this, you might be able to understand my anger issues better." Then I eased back in my chair to watch her reactions. Ah, did I detect a slight smile? Definitely a nod or two. And then she looked at me with what I felt like might be more respect. I must admit to being a little puffed up. This journaling thing just became a priority in my life.

"Brody, I am really pleased. This proves that you're making progress. I can also vouch for the accuracy of your account of things."

"Really, Doc, I had no idea you knew anything about my past!"

"Oh, yes, your history preceded your return to reality. Major Longmire had sent us a report of your service under his command, so I may know more about you than you do."

For some reason, I could feel my face turning red at that remark. I think I wondered if she knew my reaction to the way she looked in those tightly fitted and well creased navy trousers. I may have stammered as I began to explain that I had spent the weekend on the internet researching Islam and was going to try to put my thoughts together about that before our next session.

She liked the plan and walked with me out to the reception area to set our next appointment for that coming Friday.

"By the way," she said, "I have good news for you. Major Longmire called and said he would be stopping in to see you tomorrow."

"That is good news! I hope he doesn't expect me to pop to attention, with this leg still stretched out and in a cast."

She reached down, rubbed my shoulder and gave me a pat or two, and said, "You know, we don't pay that much attention to protocol around this hospital." As I looked up at those baby blues, I couldn't help but think how nice it would be to be looking down into them.

As I rolled down the hall, I heard, "*Twenty-three-year-old Marines tend to think with organs not known as brains*."

"Hey, who the heck is this?"

"*Listen up Corporal Edwards, the more you hear from me and the more you listen to me, the better off you will be. You can call me Reason if you must have a name, but my first advice to you is to start using your brain for thinking, not that thing below your belt. The chasm between a Navy Commander and a jarhead LCPL is too great to span without major difficulties*."

"Yes, ma'am, I hear you, and of course you are always right – just daydreaming. Yeah, just daydreaming."

Miss Direction — Chapter Three

After my appointment with Shrink, I went back to my room and stretched out on my bed for about thirty minutes. Then I grabbed the laptop and headed for the day room. Upon opening the screen, a new voice spoke to me before my fingers could get to the keyboard.

"Hello, Brody. Or should I just call you Good-looking?"

"Before we get too familiar, who the hell are you?"

"Most people call me Miss Direction. You can, too, unless you want to call me Sweetie Pie."

"A suspicious name if I ever heard one. What's on your mind?"

"Did you watch the President's speech on TV last night?"

"That's a joke. I don't have the stomach for his politics nor his rhetoric."

"But he's so smart, and he always tries to improve our relations with the Middle East. I especially liked his remarks about Islam being a peaceful religion."

"Well, there goes another relationship. You can hit the road, Miss. I don't have time to deal with stupidity. If brains were dynamite, you wouldn't have enough power to blow your nose. Wait, before you go, let me tell you some facts. Here are two quotes from the Hadith, i.e., Sayings of the Prophet: 1. Mohammed said, 'I have been made victorious by terror.' 2. He also said, 'There will come a day when the very stones behind which a Jew is hiding, will cry out O Muslim, there is a Jew hiding behind me, so kill him.' Are you listening? Islam was founded by a self-proclaimed terrorist; his followers have been killing people for over fifteen-hundred years, just because they will not submit to Islam. It is not, nor has it ever been, a peaceful religion! So, put that in your pipe and smoke it, and stay the hell away from me from now on."

"**A peaceful religion, my ass.**"

"Right on, Rage. You had to get in on the act, too, eh?"

"**Why the hell don't we have the smartest people available looking into why these idiots are acting the way they do? We will never solve the problem of global terrorism while chasing symptoms of the problem rather than the problem.**"

"Rave on McDuff! I couldn't have said it better if I tried!"

"**The problem is not radical Islam, it is Islam itself. They all worship out of the same book, the Quran.**"

"I hear you. Tell it like it is, brother."

"Read the book and you will find that those we call radicals are just devout Muslims, doing exactly what the Quran tells them to do."

"Hey, Rage, take a break. I'm afraid you're going to blow a gasket. You are preaching to the choir. Remember, we think alike. You know, I counted over fifty verses in the Quran that tell Muslims to cut off heads, cut off fingertips, cut off a hand on one side and a foot on the other side of the body, not to take prisoners until they 've slaughtered many and to keep on doing those things until all submit to Islam. Sounds more like a killer cult than a religion to me. How about you, Rage?"

"**Damn straight! Wake up, world! Aiiiiiheeeaiii**."

"That was a piss-poor rendition of Ali Baba's yell, Rage."

"**I gave it my best shot**."

Presentation of Purple Heart Award **Chapter Four**

Major Longmire arrived in my room at 0900 hours sharp, and it was good to see a familiar face. I told him so, as well as how nice he looked in his dress uniform. I had never seen him in anything but field gear cammies.

"Brody, to tell you the truth, you look better than I expected to find you. You've been through quite an ordeal."

"This is beginning to sound like a mutual admiration society. Could you fill me in on what happened just before I reached base? I don't remember anything after I opened fire with both guns."

"We heard the gunfire and I quickly dispatched the helicopter, with a spotter and machine gunner, to assess the situation. They spotted the two of you and the bike stopped just a few hundred yards past the ambush spot and called for a rescue team. The rescue team called in a medevac to take you to Kandahar for immediate transport to Germany. I believe the bullet wounds and surgery on your leg were addressed there. When you didn't regain consciousness after surgery they rushed you here to Walter Reed."

"Well, that gives me some questions for the medical staff here. Thanks, Major, I really appreciate your coming."

"Let me finish. The air crew spotted several bodies in the rocks, and their assessment was that it was safe to land. They found six dead and one with multiple bullet wounds but still alive. He was, according to the translator, mumbling about a headless man killing all his buddies. I might add that when we arrived on scene you had fallen back so that your body was lying on the rack, covering Mike's head. So, I can understand his mutterings. Now, let's get down to business. I'm in Washington for several reasons: first, to give my annual report to Headquarters, and second, to walk paperwork through HQ on my nomination for you to receive the Congressional Medal of Honor."

In utter amazement, I stammered, "I – I'm not a hero."

Unfazed, he stated, "My third purpose is to personally pin on your Purple Heart Award which has already been authorized."

"But Major, I didn't kill any of the eighteen fighters at the village." I told him about the lightning strike and the villagers killing the three survivors.

"Edwards, I personally interviewed village leaders who assured me that you had killed all eighteen of them. I even have an image from your phone that shows a body count of eighteen."

"What about evidence that they were killed by rifle fire or lightning?"

"No. By the time I got there they had taken the bodies out into a desert area and buried them so the Taliban couldn't prove their village was involved."

"Don't you see, Sir? That's why they credited me with the kills. I'm sure they were afraid of Taliban reprisal."

I could see him pondering that new information. So, I threw in the fact that I was not sure I killed any of the others either. "They may have killed each other in a crossfire, as far as we know. 'I am not a hero,' I remember thinking as I gunned the engine on the bike, 'I'm scared shitless.'"

"Nonsense Edwards, both of your weapons were empty when we found you. What you've just told me is the essence of heroism: being afraid but having courage to do what must be done anyway." He looked at me with a wry grin on his face and said, "Edwards, we all get some bad breaks and you've had your share. This may be a lucky break for you, because I'm not going to pull the recommendation. Obviously, I need to do some rewording on the nomination certificate, but I will accomplish my other purpose in being here today. Be in the day room by 1025 for the presentation of your Purple Heart Award."

"Please Major," I begged, "Do not make it a big issue. Just pin it on right here in my room."

He reluctantly agreed and proceeded to remove the medal from its box. "On behalf of the Commandant of the Marine Corps and a grateful nation, I am proud to pin this Purple Heart Award on you." As he pinned it to my hospital robe, I thought I saw moisture in his eyes. I know there was some in mine.

Now ready to leave, he advised me to remain silent about the Congressional Medal of Honor award until he had time to redo the paperwork and run it back through Marine HQ.

"Yes, sir, and thanks for not making a show out of the Purple Heart thing."

"Well, I assure you that you will not so persuade me if I get the other award approved by MHQ. Keep improving, Brody, and I'll see you again before I leave for Afghanistan."

I finished capturing all this in my journal, and I think I dozed off, when suddenly:

"Wake up America! I'm mad as hell and I'm not going to take it anymore."

"Rage, don't yell in my ear like that."

"This isn't Rage."

"Sounds like him."

"No, take a guess."

"No way."

"Come on, I'll give you a hint. MM."

"Marilyn Monroe?

"No. Ok, one more hint, Moral. . . .?"

"Moral Majority."

"No, they must have left town when Jerry went to heaven. It is the Moral Minority now, and it really makes me mad that Christians can't pray in school

or before a ball game, but those ragheads can block traffic on streets of New York City and pray with the police guarding their right to do so."

"Oh, come on, Rage, I knew it was you all the time."

"**But you have to admit, life around this hospital would be a whole lot duller if I weren't here to yank your chain every now and then**."

"No doubt about that."

Perks for a Hero — Chapter Five

After breakfast the next morning, I was looking at my schedule of doctors' appointments, trying to work out how to get in some journaling time, when the realization hit me that I indeed was hooked. This process of directing one's thinking toward capturing and storing brain activity was really cool. Seeing I had an hour before my appointment with the neurologist, I grabbed the laptop and headed for the day room and began to set up on a table with a view out toward the west. No sooner than I was pulling up my files, the voices began to speak and my fingers began to fly over the keyboard.

"I thought you said you weren't a hero."

"That's right, Rage, I certainly did."

"Well, what's with the stupid smile on your face?"

"Go away, I'm busy."

"Yeah, give me time to get in a word or two."

"Well, Reason, it's good to hear your voice. You may be the reason for that smile Rage referred to."

"I hope so. You do realize this hero thing could prove to be a real financial boon for you, don't you?"

"What makes you think so?"

"Hey, Congressional Medal of Honor winners get great benefits."

"I don't know anything about that."

"Well what about these? Just to whet your appetite: A monthly pension from the Department of Veterans Affairs of $1259.00, and that, big boy, is on top of your military pay or pension; how about a special ID card that gives you space-available travel on military aircraft? And your children will not be subject to quotas if they qualify for the military academies. So, what do you think about them apples, Grunt?"

"So, okay, you are appealing to my base nature."

"Hey, don't forget about book rights to your life story or movie contracts. I think if you put on a hat to cover that scar, you would be a great cowboy."

"Even better than Clint Eastwood?"

"Now, don't get carried away – although I have to admit you and your big head would fit in nicely with the Hollywood crowd."

Post-Traumatic Stress Disorder — Chapter Six

"I'm cutting it too close for comfort," I thought, as I rolled that wheelchair to maximum speed. I detest being late for anything, much less such an important thing as an appointment with my neurologist. Barging into his office and breathing hard, I saw the receptionist who quickly assured me it was okay, as he was running behind schedule by at least thirty minutes.

Picking up a copy of National Geographic that looked at least a year old, I began flipping pages. Unable to concentrate on the magazine, I tried contemplating my future. A sense of insecurity surfaced and I found myself getting angry and sweating, even though it wasn't hot in the office. I heard a very loud noise in the hallway directly behind my chair.

"Incoming! Hit the deck!"

I responded automatically and fell out of the chair onto the tiled floor. The receptionist ran to offer aid and what turned out to be comfort. The doctor either heard the noise or the receptionist's scream and ran out to find me humiliated and very frustrated. I have to admit to liking the way she gently rocked me back and forth. Helping me back into the wheel chair, my doctor went and opened the door to the offices, and she went back to her desk. I rolled past her, mumbling my appreciation.

As I rolled through the doorway, I looked up at the doctor and saw a smile and sensed a caring heart. "I think that's why he's a doctor." He began by taking my vitals and noting them on charts. Then he sat down behind his desk and clasped both hands together, tapping his fingers to the desk.

"Brody, I believe you're making good progress as far as your brain injury is concerned. So, let's review your situation to ensure you have a grasp of what you've been through and address what you can expect in the future. The bullet hit your helmet at the perfect angle, so it was deflected rather than penetrating your skull. But the impact was equivalent to being struck in the forehead by a large hammer. It resulted in what we call intracerebral hemorrhage or a cerebral contusion, which really means bleeding inside the brain. Some might refer to it as a bruise to the brain tissue. In your case, the swelling or edema was so severe that we had to do emergency surgery to remove a portion of the skull to allow room for your brain to swell or expand. It took two weeks for the swelling to recede to the point that we could put you back under anesthesia to replace the skull.

"You remained unconscious for four weeks, some of the time medically induced, but most of the time for reasons we don't understand. I think it might have been very good for you that the coma lasted as long as it did. I say that because the headaches and minor confusion you experienced upon exiting the coma could have, in fact, been far worse."

I nodded in agreement as he continued.

"I'm encouraged that you've not experienced blurred vision or hearing loss, as some patients do. If you remember, there was some weakening in both strength and reaction time on your left side, but that seems to be clearing up nicely from the looks of your physical therapy reports.

"Now we need to talk about the classic symptoms of PTSD you're exhibiting. Based on these symptoms, which obviously you're aware of, I need to inform you that you have been officially diagnosed with Post-Traumatic Stress Disorder. The diagnosis is fully supported by every doctor who has treated you here at Walter Reed. The anxiety, frequent nightmares, anger outbursts, sleeplessness and difficulty concentrating are well documented in your files; not to mention the way you react to loud noises, like those in the hallway a few minutes ago. These are all classic symptoms of PTSD. It's my professional opinion that a Medical Evaluation Board, which will have to convene before you can return to active duty, will declare you unfit for active duty in the Marine Corps."

In a state of shock, I couldn't speak, and could hardly breathe, for that matter. I said, "Doc, that had not crossed my mind."

"I strongly suggest you think seriously about it in the coming days. In fact, channel your thinking toward what you would like to do with the rest of your life, which almost certainly will be spent as a civilian. I believe a Physical Evaluation Board, which follows the Medical Evaluation Board, will rate your situation somewhere between 50 and 100 percent disability, which means you'll receive a medical pension rather than two months' separation pay. Now, if you receive a disability rating, as I suspect you will, of say, 50 percent, you'll receive a monthly pension of around $1,000.00. If it comes to that, you'll be advised of your rights, and they will explain the formula used to determine the amount of your pension."

"Doc, I can hardly get by on full pay, and they give me free room and board. Guess that means I better find a good job."

Back in my room, I was relieved when a phone call came in to advise me that the orthopedist had been called in to surgery, and I was rescheduled for tomorrow at 0900 hours.

Ouch! That Hurts! **Chapter Seven**

On the button at 0900 I was in the office of my Orthopedist, Dr. Williams. He advised me that he was going to remove the cast, and he thought I could get by with a hard shoe which laces up calf-high, and of course I would use crutches for several weeks. He reminded me that they had not bothered to place me in a cast while I was in the coma, so even though the leg injury had two months of healing, I'd only had to endure the discomfort of a hard cast for one month.

"Thanks a lot, Doc."

He proceeded to use his little vibrator which he called a saw to remove the cast. When it was off, I thought I would scream. The air flow against my skin created an unexpected pain. I had envisioned how good it would feel to be free of that thing, and now I felt like crying.

He assured me that my sensitivity and thought process were very typical and I would feel much better is just a little while. A nurse came in and began putting lotion on my skin, which now looked like fish scales. She washed my leg with warm soapy water and that felt pretty good. Next the doctor began to gently bend my ankle and knee joints which had been immobile for two months. Let me just say it this way: It hurt like hell!

He put my new hard boot on over my pajama leg. Then he gave instructions on training, which would begin the next day, on how to gradually put weight on the foot, the proper use of crutches, etc.

To end on a positive note, "Boy," I thought, "It's going to feel great to get out of this wheelchair!"

Can I Go Home? — Chapter Eight

Back in my room, I saw the message light on the telephone and checked in with the front desk to find that Major Longmire had ordered me to be in the day room at 1100 hours the next morning for a meeting. I began thinking about my future. Could I go home again? Dad had been so upset that I'd dropped out of school, he'd threatened to disown me. I had left home with no particular destination in mind and caught a Greyhound bus to Raleigh, then to Saint Louis. I remember hitching the rails like a hobo for a while. Working for food and sometimes a place to sleep had not been fun or rewarding. Eating too little and drinking too much took its toll, and I literally found myself in the gutter, despondent, and dejected to the point of contemplating suicide. I cried out for help.

It was in Monterey, California that a wealthy lady saw me sitting on the curb, head in hands, crying, and she stopped to give me help. I never learned her name, but she had her chauffeur buckle me in the right front seat and drive me to the YMCA. There she gave the manager her credit card and instructed him, "Sober him up, clean him up, dress him up, feed him, and try to get him to a Marine Recruiting Station. Maybe they can make a man out of him again." She will never know how grateful I am for her help. With that thought I drifted off to sleep.

Awake again, the idea of going back home returned. I knew my dad would forgive me and most likely welcome me with open arms, just as in the Bible story about the Prodigal Son. Certainly, I needed to repair our strained relationship. What other reason(s) could there be? Barbara Jean Woolard, why, she would probably spit in my face, the way I left her. Shame engulfed me. I finally got what I'd wanted so badly, and when the stuff hit the fan with the blowout of my pitching arm, I split town like a fool. "She's probably married with two or more kids by now. What about Aunt Hannah? Now that's worth thinking about. She may well be the only woman on earth that I know beyond a shadow of doubt loves me." It hit me then, not only could I go back, I needed to go back. I wanted to go back.

My father, a tobacco farmer like many in eastern North Carolina, worked hard and drank hard. Maybe that was an inherited kind of thing, because many in his family tree were the same. He was somewhat reclusive after my mother's early demise. I never knew him to pay much attention to any other woman, romantically speaking. He worked the farm for two years after Mom's death, then moved to the small town of Chocowinity where I grew up. I went through all grades of school there. He became a writer of sorts – maybe that's where this urge comes from – doing editorials and political commentary for the local newspaper. His stuff was sometimes picked up by the major news services. I don't think he had to go anywhere to work; he just chose what he wanted to write about and did it all from his office at home or from the front porch overlooking NC Route 33. He was never overly demonstrative with his affection, but I knew he loved me. It was going to feel good to hug him again.

Why he told people that he was the kid and I was the old man in our family, I don't know. It pleased him to kid me about what he referred to as my food eccentricities. He claimed he could always tell the waitress what vegetables I'd want, as well as what my drink order would be, based on what entrée I ordered. He also claimed to know what I would order at every restaurant we went to. That used to bother me until I realized that I tended to order the same thing each time I visited a particular restaurant.

Now to a more pleasant subject. Barbara Jean Woolard, a pert little brunette with brown eyes that sometimes looked as if they might turn golden like wheat, moved to town the summer before ninth grade. I first met her at the Chocowinity Drive-In Grille. For me, it was love at first sight; she took some convincing. We were exclusive all through high school. At first, I thought she was shy, but once we became close, I found out she was anything but shy, maybe even aggressive, or at least very competitive. She was a very good infielder on the girls' fast-pitch softball team. At times, she would don a catcher's mitt and tell me to 'bring it on, big boy!' She could handle my three-quarter speed stuff as good as any guy in school. It was when I took her fishing that her aggression came to the forefront. I made the mistake of asking her if she wanted me to bait her hook, thinking she might be squeamish about handling worms. Boy! She took offense. And that seemed to set the stage for fishing being both super-competitive and, usually, fun.

Like me, she was an only child. But she was the product of a broken home. Upon realizing that their daughter was pregnant, Barbara Jean's grandparents decided it would be better for the couple to marry, even though they were not in love. Her young parents did try to make a go of it, but after ten years they divorced, and her mother moved back home to Chocowinity to help take care of her aging parents.

Barbara Jean never liked to talk about her home life, and she probably spent as much or maybe more time at my house than she did at her own. My dad loved her like she was his own daughter. Once she rushed in the front door without knocking, as was her custom. She was crying, and rushed right past me to my dad, and he held her while she cried even harder. I was upset at that and ran into the back yard, kicking and throwing acorns at the garage. When I calmed down and returned to the house, she was sitting on the hassock at the foot of his recliner, smiling and looking at him as if he had hung the moon. Seeing me, she jumped up, gave me a kiss and said, "Don't worry, I love you almost as much as I do him. Now let's go get some ice cream." Things were back to normal, just that fast. I began pressuring her for sex in the tenth grade and never let up. She was still a virgin when we graduated from high school. And that's all I have to say about that at this time.

There is another memory which involves both my dad and Barbara Jean. Dad was a huge Chet Adkins fan. I mean, he idolized him. Chet Adkins was a guitar virtuoso who used all fingers to pick the strings of a guitar rather than to strum it. That was the most awesome thing in my dad's mind, and he spent hours learning to play the guitar that way. I always thought it rather strange that he loved to do it so much but had no desire whatever to play or perform in public. In fact, I doubt that hardly anyone other than Aunt Hannah, Barbara Jean and I knew he could even play the guitar, much less that he was pretty good at it. He would sit forward in his rocking recliner, gently rocking and picking the guitar while Barbara Jean sang. He introduced her to country music, and together they were good enough to be on television. It has crossed my mind many times how much different lives might be if people with talent also had the desire to be performers, too. I do believe that either of them could have made a career performing if they had chosen to do so.

My thoughts turned to Aunt Hannah. I think it necessary to describe her as black, not because you need to know her ethnicity, but because her skin is so dark it shines like an expensive leather coat or a freshly polished saddle. I mean so beautifully black that if she took off her ever-present white apron, leaving on her usual black dress, you could walk by her at night and never know she was there. I have no real memories of my mother; I was five when she passed away. My memories of a mother are all about Aunt Hannah. She was always there for me. She bathed me, she rocked me, she kissed my booboos, and she disciplined and scolded me as needed, always with loving care. I used to think she was the tallest woman in the world, standing a stately six feet tall, never stooped even in her seventies. She was my protector with the bigger kids in the neighborhood and with my father, always respectful towards him, but not fearful of crossing him if I was involved. The church doors never opened that Aunt Hannah wasn't present, whether it was Sunday morning, Sunday evening or Wednesday night prayer meeting, she was there. She never told me about her schooling, I just know she was plenty smart and she could quote scripture, giving you chapter and verse to fit any situation. I do remember, I think I was in the tenth grade, she caught me looking at Barbara Jean's cute little butt all bent over in those jean shorts, and she said, "Proverbs 27: 20, Death and destruction are never satisfied; neither are the eyes of men, Proverbs 27:20." She always gave the citation of a quote both before and after. Then she scolded me, telling me to keep my eyes where they belonged and to give Barbara Jean more respect. Sometimes Aunt Hannah would call both of us B.J. We got to the point that we called each other that but usually only when we were irritated with the other one.

Later that afternoon, I had physical therapy which involved learning how to use the boot and the crutches, in addition to manipulating the long unused muscles in my leg. By the time I got back to my room, I was pooped.

Shortly after returning, a nurse came in to inform me that Major Longmire had set up a meeting in the day room at 1100 hours tomorrow, “And you are ordered to be there ten minutes prior, looking as sharp as possible, he emphasized.”

Congressional Medal of Honor Nomination Chapter Nine

After breakfast, I decided to review my journal to make sure I had recorded things as intended. I was shocked at how much editing was necessary to add or delete letters to correct tenses, those kinds of things. But generally, I was pleased with the work so far.

Then I began paying attention to getting ready for the meeting. Most of my uniforms were still in a duffel bag, delivered I assume by Major Longmire, but there was a set of cammies with boots in my closet, so I put them on. I thought, "Not bad, but the one suede boot and the one black and blue walking boot don't match." I decided that a hat wasn't in order and made my way on crutches to the day room.

When I entered, I was totally shocked to see the day room full of people: patients, doctors, visitors and even several Admirals and one General Officer, I suppose from Medical Headquarters staff. Now I was really nervous and totally unsure of what to expect. I was motioned to the center of the room by Major Longmire. He announced that his purpose in being there was to inform all present that he had nominated Lance Corporal Brody James Edwards to be the recipient of the nation's highest military award, the Congressional Medal of Honor. The Commandant of the Marine Corps had already given his approval and the nomination would proceed through channels in the coming days, weeks or months until it was approved or denied by the President of the United States. Then he called out loudly, "Attention to Orders," and began to read from a fancy blue hardback folder.

"Citation: Lance Corporal Brody James Edwards distinguished himself by extraordinary acts of heroism at the risk of his life, above and beyond the call of duty, while serving as a forward observer in the Delaram District of Afghanistan. Upon arriving at his designated lookout post, he found himself within a few feet of sixteen Taliban insurgents who were in the process of harassing and interrogating village leaders. Almost immediately three more Afghani fighters came into view, dragging his partner who had been at another lookout post on the opposite side of the village. In an effort to save his friend, he left his cover and climbed up a steep ravine to try to kill as many as possible and hopefully to lay down covering fire for his partner's escape. Because of the steep terrain and slippery conditions, he was unable to reach the top in time to save his partner from decapitation. Spurred by fury at seeing the Taliban leader holding his friend's head aloft while screaming, 'Allah Akbar,' Corporal Edwards initiated firing. His first shot missed the leader's head, but did hit the hand holding a scimitar above his head. The wounded leader was able to escape in one of the two trucks they had arrived in. With uncanny accuracy from a prone position Corporal Edwards proceeded to pick off the entire group of enemy fighters. Corporal Edwards proved that the Marksmanship Medal he won in boot camp was well deserved. Village leaders have verified the kill count of eighteen, and we have a picture taken by Corporal Edwards' damaged cell phone as further verification as to accuracy of the kill count. Unable to contact base operations due to faulty equipment, Corporal Edwards mounted his Fallen Angel in front of him on the four-wheeled motorcycle and began the fifteen miles back to base Camp Delaram. Approximately one mile from base operations, he was ambushed by enemy fire. Due to his keen sense of danger he was prepared for this possibility and now had both his partner's and his own weapon braced on the handlebar of the bike. Crashing right through the ambush, he fired both weapons until empty. The result of that brave action left six more dead fighters with one other severely wounded. His total count for the one day's action amounts to 24 kills and 2 wounded enemies, with only one escapee. Corporal Edwards' extraordinary heroism and selflessness above and beyond the call of duty are in keeping with the highest traditions of military service and reflect great credit upon himself, his command, and the entire United States Marine Corps.

"Ladies and gentlemen, please join me in giving this fine young marine our applause in recognition of his brave deeds, as described in this certificate."

The applause was loud and long. I did get choked up a little, and I used that as an excuse when several called out for me to speak. I gave the old sign of hand to the throat to signify that I was too choked up to speak. Actually, it was more like too embarrassed to do so.

Refreshments were available for all after they went through the receiving line to congratulate and greet me. I had never shaken hands with generals and admirals. It was a weird experience, feeling proud yet embarrassed because I knew I didn't deserve such recognition. I suppose by design, Commander Mandino positioned herself last in the line, and she gave me a very firm hug while whispering how proud she was of me. I don't know if it was the tension of the past few minutes or the realization that my daydreaming of her, pressed against my chest, was nothing compared to the real thing, but I began to tremble. She may have thought I was crying and needed comfort so she hung on longer than she should have. Finally, I cleared my throat, signifying that I was okay, and she backed off.

That afternoon, I received a very pleasant surprise visit by a man and woman and their teenaged daughter. The moment they walked in, I knew they were Mike's, my deceased partner's, folks; he looked so much like his dad. By the time I made it to my feet, we were all crying and hugging. It was a most enjoyable, though emotional visit. I asked if they knew what had happened, and they assured me they were all too familiar with the details. The lump in my throat wouldn't allow me to respond at that moment, so I just nodded.

Finally recovering, I told them of bringing Ali Baba's scimitar back to the base with me with the intention of spending the rest of my tour, if necessary, to finding him, and then using it on him. "Since I now don't see how that could ever happen, I feel obligated to offer it to you, if you'd like to have it." They responded with an immediate and firm "No," but expressed their hope that I might one day use it just as I'd intended.

Mike's mom seemed so special, and I fully intended to take her up on the offer to drop in for a visit one day. "We live right on the main boulevard," she said. They didn't stay long, and using rush hour traffic to explain their early departure, they left. Sitting there it dawned on me that extreme emotions take a physical toll on body as well as on mind. I dozed off.

The next two days were very hectic as I was now a celebrity throughout the building. I found I could no longer journal in the day room; people were always coming up to me wanting to talk. I had to keep the door to my room closed to get anything done. Going to the dining room was a chore I was not willing to give up, so I shrugged and thought, "When will this celebrity thing start to pay dividends?"

Shocking News and Guilt — Chapter Ten

It became clear to me that there may never be any dividends to receive, but there definitely would be a price to pay for celebrity. Network news picked up on my Congressional Medal of Honor nomination, and my phone was ringing constantly. I finally had to unplug it to rest or work. I was not liking this celebrity thing at all.

Late in the second day, after the reading of the citation, I responded to a knock on the door with a call to enter. The nurse handed me a note saying I needed to return an emergency call. I recognized the area code as my home area, but the number was unfamiliar to me. I plugged in the phone, punched in the numbers, and waited for an answer. A very recognizable, eastern North Carolina accent responded, "Thank you for calling Latham and Latham Law Offices, how may I help you?"

"This is Brody Edwards returning your call." She immediately said, "Mr. Latham will be with you in a minute."

A man came on the line and identified himself as Attorney William Latham, stating that his firm had handled my father's business affairs for the last twenty-five years or more.

"Why are you calling me?"

"There was a provision in your father's will that directed me to do so under the appropriate circumstances."

"Wait a minute – my father's will – are you telling me he's deceased?"

"He's been deceased for almost three years. I assumed you knew that."

"I'm stunned. No, wait a minute. Let me try to digest this. How could I have known?"

"We had no idea how to find you. You left suddenly and were estranged from your father. We checked with all your friends. No one knew how to get in touch with you. His will left all assets to a trust which we've managed according to his instructions. Basically, the will prohibited us from searching for you unless you proved yourself to be a successful contributor to society, or you returned voluntarily with a desire to be a contributing member of this community. If those two conditions were not met within five years after probate, all assets would pass to designated charities. The front page of our newspaper carried the story of your nomination for the Congressional Medal of Honor. Based on that, I determined that the provision of his will regarding your being a successful contributor to society had been met. That's why I called. I'm truly sorry to be the one to inform you of your father's death."

"Mr. Latham, I'm so shaken that I just can't communicate coherently. Can I call you back tomorrow?"

"Yes, of course, I understand completely. There's no rush now. I will await your call – at your convenience."

Falling back on the bed, I was overcome with grief. Great sobs racked my body, unlike any I had experienced due to my own traumas. Guilt came down on me like a ton of bricks.

"You left him without even a goodbye. You had two years after you got your act back together to call him and you didn't. Son! You are you not a son; you are an asshole. There is no way to rectify this – you are going to have to deal with it for the rest of your life. You didn't get to tell him about your recovery from alcoholism, not to mention your successful service to your country. How can I deal with this? It's too much!"

"Okay, pity party over. You are no different than thousands before you. Problems happen, they are dealt with, and life goes on. Get off that bed, take a shower and go to sleep. We will face your issues tomorrow, together."

The next morning, I woke up feeling like crap. I forced myself to the cafeteria and back to the room to dress and face my appointment with Shrink. Using crutches had become easier in just the few days I'd had them, and I found myself looking forward to getting rid of them. I wondered how long it would be until I could walk with just the boot. Making a mental note to ask the orthopedist, I turned the knob leading to Shrink's office at exactly 0900 hours. She was standing behind the receptionist's desk and waved me on back, so I didn't even have to sit down.

In her office, she walked to her chair behind the desk, and I sat in my usual chair in front of her desk.

"How are you this morning, Brody?"

"Not too good, Doc. I found out last night that my dad passed away, and it has thrown me for a loop."

"Well, I guess so. Was it a sudden heart attack or an accident?"

"Worse than that. He died three years ago, but I just found out about it last night. I was so shocked that I told his lawyer I would call him back today for more details." Then I told her all the events leading to our estrangement, my arm surgery, the loss of my baseball career, dropping out of school, the year of drunkenness, my recovery, joining the marines, all the guilt and sorrow of the previous night. I just dumped it all out as fast as I could talk.

It must have taken at least fifteen or twenty minutes, and when finished, I sat there in a daze. In the back of my mind I must have expected her to rush around the desk and hold me tight, because when I looked up to see her sitting there with her hands clasped, looking very pensive, I was disappointed.

"Brody, I'm so sorry. It's difficult for me to see you so sad, and I do want to help you deal with this added trauma the best I can. I realize that things seem very dark for you at this time, and I sense you want the kind of comfort I can't give. So, I want you to listen to me very carefully. Our relationship is that of doctor and patient. It cannot and will not go beyond that. If you're fantasizing it being more, you're doing yourself and me a disservice. I admit that because of your special circumstances, I've become friendlier with you than is usual, but that is as far as it goes.

Now! Hopefully these thoughts will be helpful in dealing with your sadness and guilt. I strongly suggest you go immediately to your journal and capture what I'm going to say to you so you can use these thoughts to help whenever you're feeling guilty or sad and/or depressed.

Guilt is a natural and common component of grief. When someone we love dies, it's only human to search for an explanation, to look at what you did or didn't do, to dwell on "what if" and "if only." We agonize and tell ourselves, "If only I had done something differently this would never have happened." The reality is that death would have occurred no matter what. It might have come at a different time or under different circumstances but it still would have happened. In your case – the estrangement issue – I guarantee you, if your father had time to anticipate his death, he would have felt guilty that he had not done more to bridge the gap between you two. It is simply human nature that guilt raises its ugly head at times like these. Here are some helpful tips for you.

"Identify each guilty thought. Journal it. Talk about it. Once in the open, examine it rationally and logically.

"Listen to the messages you give yourself and realize that the past is something you can do absolutely nothing about. It is what it is.

"When guilty thoughts come to mind, disrupt them by telling yourself to stop thinking such thoughts. Don't be afraid to say, "Stop," `out loud if you need to.

"Be your own best friend. What would you have said to one of your best friends if this had happened to them? Say the same thing to yourself.

"Remember the good things you did with your father and all the loving things you did for each other. Focus on the positive things: what you learned from each other, what you did together that brought you joy and laughter. Write those things down, hold on to them, and read them whenever you need to.

"Remember that no one else can absolve your feelings of guilt; only you can do that. So, work out a process whereby you intentionally forgive yourself."

"Doc. You make it sound so easy. Intellectually, I know what you have said is spot on, and I will try to make it work for me."

"Good luck, Brody. I'm going to make your next appointment for one week from today, same time. Is that okay with you?"

"Yes, Ma'am, see you then." I made my way back to the room, surprised to feel encouraged.

Picking up the phone, I dialed the attorney's office and asked to speak with him. His assistant informed me he was in a conference and could not be interrupted, but she felt sure he would call back in about an hour. I dozed off and was awakened by the phone ringing. A quick glance at my watch showed that indeed I had slept about an hour.

"Hello, this is Brody."

"Hey, Brody, Buzz Latham, here."

"Yes, sir, thanks for calling back – but I thought your name was William."

"It is, but everyone has called me Buzz since I was a kid, so you might as well too."

"Okay, I think I can deal with matters a little better than I did last night. Let me start with a question. What happened?"

"Your dad confided in me when we completed his Last Will and Testament that he'd been experiencing 'heart issues.' That was the way he put it. The cardiologist had warned him to lose weight, get more exercise and take better care of himself. Your father expressed regret that he had let you leave with your relationship at stake. He was also talking about getting an investigator to see if you could be tracked down. Evidently, he never got around to doing that because he died two days after he came to the office to sign the will. I'm sorry, but I hope you will be comforted to know that his was one of the largest funerals, in terms of attendance, that I have ever seen."

"Yes, I know he was well liked and respected by many. So, I guess I need to know what was left to me, since I am his only child. In fact, if there's anyone closer than a cousin or two, I'm not aware of it."

"You are the sole beneficiary in the will. The house you were raised in has no mortgage, but it has been closed for the last two years, and I will need direction as to how to proceed with it. He did own one other piece of real estate, but that was deeded to Hannah Johnson just prior to his death. Other than that, there is a small bank account that had about $3,000.00 in it the last time I checked. Lastly, there is a stock portfolio with TD Ameritrade that has a current value of over $300,000.00. All debts, other than what my firm bills to do the final transfer of all assets to you, have been paid."

"Wow! I am shocked. I had no idea he was worth that kind of money."

"Well, son, it isn't a fortune, but it surely will be a nice supplement to your earnings and, if managed properly, should last you a long time. I will say this: the stocks in which he invested are the best companies in America and each produces very safe dividends. You should think twice before you sell any of them. Now let me ask you. What are your future plans?"

"I need to get my arms wrapped around that question. It seems almost certain I'll not be certified to return to active duty, and I definitely won't be allowed to go back into a combat situation. That being the case, it looks like I'm destined to be a civilian again, probably in less than two months. I think I'll come home. I really want to see Aunt Hannah. There are a few classmates with whom I need to renew acquaintances. Then I'll make my decisions from there."

"All right, I know Hannah will be delighted. I'll drop by and let her know what you've just told me – she will be tickled pink." There was a slight pause and then, "Look, I have a sister living in Bethesda, just about a mile from where you are, and she's been bugging me for ages to visit her. So, if you can give me about a week's notice, I'll plan to pay her a visit and swing by on the way back to pick you up. How does that sound, to you?"

"Great! That way I won't have to deal with public transportation, or worry about whether or not I can rent a car using only a military driver's license. By the way, I am really hungering for some North Carolina-style barbeque."

"We can handle that. Ralph's, in Weldon, should be a perfect spot to get that yen taken care of. Call me whenever you're ready. Is there anything else on your mind before we go?"

"Well come to think of it, do you know a Barbara Jean Woolard? She used to be, anyway."

"Oh, yes, and she still is a Woolard – owns and operates Ye Olde Sweet Shoppe, where the Chocowinity Drive-in Grille used to be. In fact, she lives upstairs above her business. I stop in for coffee and doughnuts on occasion. Should I mention that you asked?"

"I think that would be nice."

I hung up and sat there with a big grin on my face.

"Feeling kind of smug, eh, cowboy?"

"Yes ma'am, I guess so."

Don't Apologize — Chapter Eleven

The next few days seemed to fly by, with physical therapy sessions becoming more and more intense. They really pushed me, and I was walking more and more and with less pain. Pain which I associated with the pins in the bone in my leg was almost gone, and the ankle and knee joints were more mobile by significant degrees of movement. "Maybe another week and we will try to get you into your own boot," they told me. "Your records have been sent to the Medical Evaluation Board" was my next bit of news. In anticipation of my question, they said the process usually takes 45 days, "But remember, we sent in the paperwork over a week ago."

I had called Shrink to read her my recollection of the tips she had given me, and she had made sure I had it all down correctly. Now I just had to deal with life – and I began to use those tips on a daily basis. It dawned on me that except for the previous night, it had been several nights since Ali Baba had tried to cut my head off. That really made me feel like things just might return to normal. I spoke too soon.

"Hey, dickhead, you awake?"

"Go away, Rage, I'm trying to sleep."

"Come on, Jarhead, it's 0830."

"I had two nightmares last night and got very little sleep."

"I'm sorry."

"Don't apologize."

"Why not?"

"Because, I would rather stay pissed off at you."

"Heh, heh, heh."

God, I hate that laugh.

Going Home — Chapter Twelve

Two months had flown by, and soon I found myself sitting and waiting for Buzz Latham to pick me up to head for home. The word even sounds strange. Not able to comprehend or at least explain my feelings, I did a quick recap on the major events. The Medical Evaluation Board had certified me as unfit to return to duty. I had declined to appeal their ruling. The Physical Evaluation Board had given me an 80 percent disability rating, placing me on the Temporary Disability Retired List, and awarded me a monthly pension of $1,110.13. The staff had a going away party in my honor – all the goodbyes and thanks were expressed. Some nice firm handshakes and a few hugs were exchanged; a very warm and firm handshake, if I might add, from Shrink. I didn't feel like I was on top of the world, but there was a feeling of hope encouraging me on.

I saw a big Lincoln Navigator pull into visitor parking and watched as a tall man of about 45 to 50 got out and headed toward the front entrance. As I rose to meet and greet him, he spoke first.

"Brody, good to see you at last. By the way, I see your father in you. I think it's the eyes and the jawline. How are you, my boy?"

"Fine, sir. I'm packed, signed out and ready to hit the road."

In the Navigator, he explained that we were just a short distance from the beltway, which we would take around to Interstate 95 and head south, "Unless you would like to go through town to see the monument or other sites."

"No, I'm champing at the bit for the road."

"Let me warn you about the beltway, son. It can get a little scary. The traffic is unbelievably heavy and no one seems to slow down because cars all around them are going 70 and 80 miles per hour."

"I'll close my eyes if it gets to me, but hopefully I'll enjoy the ride."

We were silent pretty much until we got on I- 95 and the traffic thinned out. Then Buzz told me how happy Aunt Hannah had been to learn of my return.

"She'll be waiting for you at the house, I'm sure. She has a key, you know. She looked in on your dad often during his last days."

"She'll be welcome to come and go anytime, as far as I'm concerned."

"I also dropped in to let B.J. know that you had asked about her."

"How did she react to that?"

"I was afraid you would ask. To tell you the truth, I don't know how to answer that question. I thought I saw a flash of anger, an almost-smile and maybe some moisture in her eyes. I think it best to warn you that if you hope to renew a relationship, you've got a lot of work ahead of you. As Grand pappy used to say, 'nuff said.'"

I chuckled. as I could see her in my mind's eye, just as he had described. "It won't be easy, I'm sure," I thought, "Because I was a fool to leave her the way I did. She deserved so much better."

It was 1200 on the button when we pulled into Ralph's parking lot in Weldon, North Carolina. My stomach was rumbling and my nose twitching as I picked up the aroma of barbeque meat as soon as I stepped out of the car. After being seated, I told the waitress, "I don't need to see a menu, I've been waiting for this for three years."

She smiled as she wrote down my order of barbeque platter, fries and Brunswick stew. "With sweet tea, please. The platter does come with hush puppies, right?"

"Absolutely."

Buzz said, "Make that two."

Upon finishing our meal, Buzz insisted on paying for both, and I gave in without too much protest. Noting that he left a generous tip, I felt myself liking him more and more. In the car, I reclined the seat two notches and took a short nap. When I woke up he had the radio on very low, listening to country music. I expressed my surprise at his choice of music. "I thought you UNC grads would be rock and rollers."

"It takes all kinds to make a world, Brody."

"That sounds like something Aunt Hannah might say."

"I don't know where it came from, I just know that I've heard it said by family members many times."

As we neared a community called Old Ford, I pointed out a stand of timber that I had helped my Uncle Bill log the summer of my freshman year of college. Good memories flooded over me as I remember how much I had loved my uncle. I had always been special to him, as he had no children of his own. He, too, had passed away before I left home. The thought came to mind that I had no guilt there. I loved him, and he well knew it.

As we neared the town of Washington, North Carolina, I was glad to see that Smokey's was still in business. Smokey's is a step above a beer joint; it does serve beer, and I've been told you can get something stronger there if you are known and trusted, although I have no personal knowledge as to the truth of that information. I do know that it serves good burgers and fries as well as beer, ale and sodas. There is a small dance floor with room to seat maybe forty people at tables and booths, and standing room at the bar for more. B.J. and I used to go there on Thursday nights for Karaoke. The thought of her beautiful alto voice almost brought me to tears.

Entering the city limits, the thought hit me that most people from North Carolina, when saying Washington, usually are talking about the District of Columbia, and when they want you to know they're talking about this town they say, "Little Washington." The locals did not take kindly to that, and they began to refer to it as "The Original Washington," because it is the first town in America to have been named for George Washington. In fact, this happened before he became President of the United States.

A couple of turns later, on Bridge Street, I noted a sign of importance to these folks. It pointed out the birth place of Henry De Mille, father of Cecil B. De Mille, the famous Hollywood movie Producer and Director.

Crossing the bridge which separates two rivers, the Pamlico to the east and the Tar on the west, we were now three miles from what I kiddingly refer to as the "big town of Chocowinity." I remembered telling my buddies that if you blinked more than three times as you passed through, you'd miss the experience of seeing Chocowinity. At the sight of the sign announcing the entry to Chocowinity, incorporated in 1959, an unexpected feeling of euphoria rose within me, causing me to ask myself, "Why? It isn't anything to brag about. The people, maybe? They are a plain, down to earth, working class people, mostly of a conservative nature. The place, maybe? It's small, just over eight hundred in population. Maybe it's the weather, usually warm, an average temperature of almost seventy degrees to the best of my memory. Maybe it's the fishing. That must have a lot to do with my current feeling. After all, the meaning of the name Chocowinity is "fish of many waters." Seeing the sign to Hardee's, a fast food restaurant that has the best biscuits in the world, just added to my warm feeling and settled the issue in my mind. "It is good to be home!"

As we turned right onto Route 33 west, I expressed my thanks to Buzz for the ride, the meal, for having a cleaning crew prepare my house, and an inspector to come in to make sure the major appliances were operating efficiently.

"You don't have to thank me; it has been my pleasure. And besides, I will be billing you for some of that."

Aunt Hannah — Chapter Thirteen

Pulling into our driveway, I looked to see Aunt Hannah sitting there in that old glider with the green and white leather padded seats just rocking gently back and forth. I thought, "She's asleep, and that leg is just keeping the glider moving out of habit." When I slammed the door closed, she woke up and started beaming at me as if she had just been given the best present ever. I made it to her as quickly as I possibly could. We embraced, and emotions that I was not expecting rushed at me. I began to cry. She held me, as she had so many times, gently swaying from side to side while patting my back. I don't know how long this lasted. I do know that Buzz passed by to put my duffel bag into the living room and passed back by mumbling that he would talk to me in a day or two. When his SUV left the driveway, he must have accelerated to avoid oncoming traffic. It was the squealing of his tires that brought me out of the moment, I think.

Aunt Hannah suggested we go inside for me to reacquaint myself with the house while she fixed us some dinner.

"Is there anything here to fix?"

"Sure. Mr. Latham had some basics put in so you can have breakfast, and I brought some collard greens from my garden. They've been in the pot for the last two hours – you know you can't cook collards too much – not only collards, but I got another surprise for you. You just wait."

I walked around the house, touching things, staring at other things, wondering about some things. "Where did that come from? Why is that here?" crossed my mind a few times. But overall it was a nice experience. I even went into the backyard and reminisced about Dad and me tossing a baseball to one another. I went over to the detached garage and wondered if the keypad codes had been changed. Nope, sure enough, the double door began to rise. The first thing I saw inside was a Cub Cadet riding lawnmower. You, old goat, I thought. "How many times did I complain that our so-called power mower had to be pushed?"

"Hey, when I was a boy we had one of those reel things – now you want to talk about pushing, those things took some pushing."

Did I really hear him say that? Not sure, I continued my examination of the garage, making a mental note to call an exterminator to spray for spiders. I looked over behind the single garage door to see Dad's pride and joy: his vintage 1960 TR 3. Though dusty, you could tell there was a real wax job underneath. He had kept it in perfect shape for years, but I thought I better get someone to look it over before I tried to start it. My ten-speed leaned against the back wall. Both tires were flat, and I thought I should just buy two new ones, as they are probably dry rotted.

Back in the house, I checked to see if the keys were on the pegs by the back door, and they were. Some things change, and some things never change. Picking the lid off the pot of collards, I smiled to see the generous portion of fatback Aunt Hannah always put in when she cooked greens.

"Get out of my kitchen, boy."

"Yes, ma'am. But only if you come with me to the front porch and bring me up to date on the goings-on around this burg."

"I 'spect that'd be a good idea."

We settled in on that old glider, and I could tell by the way she paused to think that there were things on her heart and mind. She wanted to make sure they were presented in a way that showed how deeply she felt about them.

"Brody, things around here are in a mess. My biggest concern today is race relations. It seems like somebody is deliberately trying to stir up trouble. It'd be bad enough if we blamed Satan, but even worse, when I see groups of my own people speaking with such hatred, talking about how bad things are, when they don't know nothing about how hard it was in my day. There is a group calling themselves Black Muslims filling our young people's minds with bad information and spurring them to be violent rather than proactive. I believe Dr. King is rolling over in his grave with the way things are here. We've got some good leadership in the white community, but they are afraid to speak out because it might enflame those who are dissatisfied in the black community. These youngsters complain about every little thing; they don't know nothing about discrimination. Go to the same schools with the whites, eat in any restaurant they want to, go to the same moving picture show – harrumph," she snorted, "I'm showing my age, ain't I?"

"Yes, ma'am, I guess you are. Nowadays we say movies, but you are entitled. What do you think started us on the downhill? Things seemed to be very good before I left."

"I've pondered that a lot. The beginning seems to me to be about the time of the trial. Yeah, that would be the genesis of bad feelings, I think".

"What trial are you speaking about? Remember, I've been gone three years."

"Yeah, I'm well aware of that. This trial got nationwide coverage and I guess I just assumed you would know about it. I'm talking about Lashawn Johnson's – no kin to me – rape and murder trial. He was accused of raping and murdering Wilma Rogers, the wife of Wayne Rogers, a tobacco farmer east of here. The husband claimed he woke up in the middle of the night to find his wife gone from the bed. He said she didn't sleep well and would often heat up a glass of milk and sit on the patio until she thought she could sleep again. The kitchen light was on so he looked out to the patio. Seeing a chair overturned, he ran back to the bedroom to get his pistol and started searching for her. Hearing noise coming from the nearest tobacco barn, he raced down there and saw a black man running away. He shot at him twice, but missed. He went under the barn shelter to find his wife, her night gown bunched up around her neck and a hatchet buried in her head. In his testimony, he stated that he could not be sure, but he thought he recognized Lashawn as the one he shot at. To make a long story short, Lashawn's fingerprints were on the hatchet handle and his DNA was found under her fingernails and in her vagina. He claimed the sex was not only consensual but it had been an ongoing affair which had gone back at least six months. He also said he'd been in her bedroom many times, but the investigators could find no finger prints or other evidence to confirm that. He testified that he'd thrown the hatchet off the tobacco cart to make room for them to lie down."

"Why should that cause unrest? It sounds like an open and shut case to me."

"Well, Lashawn was known to be a hardworking, honest young man, but he did have a reputation for nailing anything that walked. I don't know that for sure, but it didn't look to me like he had to rape anyone to get sex. Women flocked to him like flies to horse droppings."

"Aunt Hannah!"

"I'm just telling it like it is, boy. Anyway, Lashawn had bragged to several of his friends what he was doing with Mrs. Rogers and they testified to that at the trial. The evidence was too strong against him and he was sentenced to death by lethal injection. That sentence has yet to be carried out due to the appeal process, but time is running short for Lashawn. Of course, all the testimony about his wife's sexual appetite infuriated Mr. Rogers, so he spouted off a lot using the N-word every chance he got. The black community called him a bigot and a racist who probably belongs to the Klan."

"I've a great mind to drop in on Mr. Rogers and give him a piece of my mind!"

"If you had a great mind you still wouldn't have a piece you could afford to give him! Heh-heh-heh."

I gave a guttural growl to Rage as I responded, "Well, Aunt Hannah, it looks like we need to show these people it's possible for the two races to love one another."

"Yeah, we can do that. But, I'm not finished. There've been a lot of petty crimes and some not so petty, including armed robbery. Young black men have been accused and some convicted of crimes we can't believe they would do. I'm talking about good boys. A few had alibis that proved them innocent, but something is rotten in Denmark when that many good people are accused of things they didn't do."

"What do you want me to do, join the police force?"

"That might not be a bad idea. You did study criminal justice at Chowan University."

"Umm – I'll have to think about that. But there is enough work around this place to keep me busy for a while."

"Wait – I don't want to leave this subject without telling you about something good that's going on. My pastor, what a sweet man of God he is. He came from

Philadelphia, about the time you left town, to be near his oldest son, who coaches high school baseball and teaches in Washington. I can't wait for you to meet them. Pastor Cooke is six feet, seven inches tall and must weigh over 300 pounds, and when he works up a sweat and grabs that handkerchief out his pocket, he can get a crowd worked up. Woo wee! He meets at least once a month with local law enforcement to discuss issues and ways to improve race relations. I hope to see some easing of tensions as each side begins to show the other more respect."

"That's good," was all I could think to say.

"Oh, my, it's time for dinner and your surprise. On second thought, it might not be a good idea to make it a surprise, because I don't want you to mess up my plan. I've asked B.J. to run to town and get a bucket of chicken, half regular and half crispy just like you like. She will be here any minute, so get cleaned up and be ready to start making things right with that girl."

"Yes, ma'am."

I heard a car pull into the driveway and a loud backfire when the engine was turned off. "What the heck was that?"

"Oh, that's just B.J.'s old Honda. It's got about 300,000 miles on it, and it sure needs some work, but she won't let the local mechanic touch it since he divorced his wife and took up with some young chick."

I saw a cloud of black smoke waft by the window, and Barbara Jean waltzed back into my life. Opening the door without bothering to knock, as she had for years, she tucked that bucket of chicken under her arm and held out her hand for me to shake.

"A handshake for an old friend you haven't seen for years, really? Is that all I get?"

"You're lucky to get that. If Aunt Hannah hadn't worked her magic on me you might have gotten a frying pan to the head. Oh, Brody, look at your head! I am so sorry you got injured."

I could see tears welling up in her eyes, and I decided that I should milk this for all its worth.

"**Asshole!**"

"Keep it quiet in the peanut gallery, please."

"Be careful B.J., a blow to the head with a frying pan would almost certainly kill me. I not only don't want to die at this early stage of life, but it would grieve me to see you charged with murder."

"You big lug, come here."

We hugged, and I felt a jolt of electricity go through me – she felt so good molded to my chest. I don't know what caused her to back away so suddenly. Maybe she felt the same electricity or more likely, I thought, she remembered how I had left her. Either way, she did not look pleased.

"B.J. Edwards, we need to talk, and now is not the appropriate time. So, I'm going to be as pleasant as possible."

"Let's eat!" Aunt Hannah called out from the kitchen.

When we were all seated, Aunt Hannah asked me if I would say the blessing. I declined, and it looked like she expected me to do so, because she quickly added, "Okay then, I will." She reached her left hand out to me and extended her right hand across the table to Barbara Jean. She paused for a few seconds to allow us time to join hands, and when we didn't, she bowed her head and began to pray.

"Lord God Jehovah, I want to thank You from the bottom of my heart for bringing this precious child back home, for using Your mighty power in protecting him from terrorists, for healing his wounds and bringing us back together around a table of plenty. Lord, I pray for Brody, that you might work in the coming days to draw him to Yourself, that you might relieve the stress and turmoil in his mind and heart, and give him peace. I also ask you, Lord, to be with Barbara Jean, to allow her to see the truth of the sermon from this past Sunday, 'Forgiven people forgive people.' Bless this food we are about to partake, that it might enable us all to go out and love others as You have loved us. In Jesus' name, I ask. Amen."

To say that the prayer had a profound effect on the two of us would be an understatement; we both had tears in our eyes by the time we raised our heads, mumbling thanks at the same time.

We didn't talk much during the meal. In my case it was because I was enjoying it so much. It was such a huge improvement over a hospital menu. I suppose B.J. was struggling with the idea of forgiveness, something I hadn't even thought about until now. Aunt Hannah made no effort to carry the conversation, and I can only speculate that she knew both of us were chewing on her prayer as much as we were chewing on the chicken. She always seemed to know when to speak and when not to.

After we finished eating, both women insisted I sit and elevate my foot while they cleared the dishes. I gladly complied, went into the living room and turned on the television. A locally produced educational-type program was ending and as I watched the credits, I noticed that the director's name was James Stewart. I yelled toward the kitchen, "Hey, B.J., is this TV director the same James Stewart we graduated with?"

She hollered back, "Yes, he is. He's done well professionally but his private life is a mess."

I heard B.J. offer to take Aunt Hannah home, and I said, "Thank you for offering – I would if I could."

"Don't you have a car?"

"No, but getting one is on my list of things to do."

Aunt Hannah answered, "I can walk. I take after my granny – now that woman could walk. You know I was named for her – Hannah Cratch was her name. People say I look like her; she was tall like me, and she loved the Lord, too."

Neither of us had the heart to tell her how many times we had heard those lines before.

We did the good night bit – a warm hug between me and Aunt Hannah, and an awkward sort of sideways hug between me and B.J. I settled down on the couch with a paper and pen to begin my things-to-do list:

1. Cell phone
2. Contact Hickman re: TR 3 & mower
3. DMV renew license
4. Yard work
5. Internet

6. See B.J., set up classmate gathering
7. Subscribe to paper
8. Car shop

I sat there listening to an occasional passing car, unable to think or write further. "It would be nice to listen to rain fall on that old tin roof again," I thought. Almost as if I had wished it, the rain began to fall. I headed to the bedroom and was in the sack in no time flat.

"*Feel good to be home?*"

"You bet."

"*She looked good, didn't she?*"

"You bet."

"*Used up your quota of words for the day, huh?*"

"You bet."

"*Good night, Brody.*"

"Good night, Reason."

The next morning, I cleaned up, selected jeans, a light blue and white shirt with button down collar, and an old pair of cowboy boots fished from the back of my closet. Dressed, I rolled up the shirt sleeves once and started walking to the crossroads. Stopping in at Hickman's Garage, I introduced myself and arranged to have someone come by in the afternoon to check on the TR 3 and the Cadet. I explained that they should be prepared to use jumper cables as neither had been started in several years. That out of the way, I headed for my main priority for the day.

Entering Ye Olde Sweet Shoppe at the same time a customer left, I guess B.J. didn't know I was on the premises, because I found her behind the counter looking into a cabinet with her cute little behind almost in my face. I leaned forward and couldn't help but say, "Proverbs 27:20. Death and destruction are never satisfied, neither are the eyes of men."

"Proverbs 27:20," she shot back as I finished the quotation.

Laughing, I said, "Good morning, Miss Woolard."

"Good morning to you, too, Mr. Edwards."

"I'd love a cup of coffee with cream, and two glazed doughnuts, please."

"Coming right up. Just sit wherever you like and I'll bring them right out."

When she brought my order, I invited her to join me, and she did.

"What have you been up to this morning, Brody?"

"Well, I knocked off one item from my things to-do list – I arranged for Charles to come over and get the TR 3 and mower running."

"What else does your plan call for?"

"My number one priority was achieved when I peeked over the counter at your cute self."

"Not funny, Brody."

"Your opinion, not mine. Also, could I talk you into hosting a little gathering of friends and classmates here at the store? It would give me a chance to catch up, and maybe it'll be a boost for your business, too. What do you think?"

"I think it's a great idea. Our classmates are already linked on Facebook, so getting the word out will not be a problem. I think if we give them about a week's notice they will all come. How does Thursday-week sound to you?"

"Let's do it."

I cleared my throat and forced myself to look up from the floor.

"B.J., the real reason I came in this morning is to beg your forgiveness. I was a fool and I know it. I can use lots of excuses – immaturity in dealing with the guilt of what I convinced you to do that night, the fight with my dad, the defeat I felt at seeing my lifelong hope of making it to the big leagues fly out the window, my fall into alcoholism, and even my military service – but those excuses pale in comparison with the shame I feel knowing I have hurt you and allowed that hurt to fester for three years. If you will forgive me, I promise I'll work hard at rebuilding our relationship to the point where you can and will trust me again."

"Oh, Brody, that may be the most beautiful apology I ever read about in a book or saw in a movie, and it's most assuredly the best one I have ever received. It is exactly what I needed to hear from you. I think you know about my coming to know the Lord since you left, and that is an important something we both will have to deal with. I spent a lot of time last night thinking about Aunt Hannah's prayer, and I now know that I can and must forgive you. But trust has to be earned. You say that you will work at building it and I believe you will try, so now we have to see if we both can 'walk the walk' as well as 'talk the talk.' In the meantime, here's how it's going to work. I want you to know that neither you nor any other man is getting intimate with me until I know that his heart belongs to God, he puts a ring on this finger," pointing to her left hand, "and he correctly answers questions put to him by the Reverend David O. Cooke at his church altar. Do you hear me and understand me?"

"Yes, to both questions. But I may be a little confused. I thought Reverend Cooke was Aunt Hannah's pastor."

"He is, and since I've taken her to church every Sunday for the last two-and-a-half years – it's where I was saved, and my membership is there – it will also be where I get married. I may be the only white face there, but it's my church, too."

We both got out of our chairs at the same time to embrace. This time it was so natural, so soothing, so serene, I thought, "I'm home." I smelled her very essence, including baking flour, some coffee, a touch of almond and maybe coconut, I guess from her shampoo. I kissed her on top of her head as we gently rocked each other.

The door chime, warning of incoming traffic, brought us both out of our reverie. I heard a voice say, "Maybe we should come back later."

"You two, get back in here, there's someone special I want you to meet. Joe and Tillie Cooke, this is Brody James Edwards, AKA our local hero."

"Join us," I offered, and they sat down. Tillie looked vaguely familiar so I asked, "Do I know you?"

"Maybe. I was two years behind you in school. I was Tillie Fowler in those days."

"Yep, a cheerleader, too, if my memory serves me right."

"You are right. I remember you pitching some good games for old Chocowinity High. Joe was a baseball pitcher in college. In fact, you two have something in common." With that Joe rolled up his left sleeve to reveal a very familiar scar, so I stuck up my right elbow for comparison purposes.

"Temple University, '06."

"Chowan University, '09."

At that moment, I knew we were to become friends. After placing their order, B.J. left and Joe said, "We've been reading about your exploits ever since the initial story came out about your nomination for the Congressional Medal of Honor."

"You mean there has been more than one?"

"Oh, yeah, in fact we may know more about you than you remember about yourself."

"Damn."

"Shush, Rage."

"So, Joe, I assume you coach the baseball team at Washington High School, right?"

"Guilty."

"I've heard nothing but good things about you, mostly from Aunt Hannah, naturally."

"Bless her heart."

"What are your expectations for your team next year?"

"Pretty good. We have about half of the starting nine returning, and I think my brother will become a mainstay on the pitching staff."

"So, he's good?"

"Well, yeah, but not like you and I were good. He doesn't bring heat like we did, but he's the most accurate with his pitches of any I have ever seen. Really. That's not bragging. But you wait – he's going to make a name for himself in the next few years. His accuracy is phenomenal. He reminds me of that YouTube video of this old fellow from somewhere in western North Carolina who's amazing with a sling shot. He can cut down weeds no bigger than a pencil from 30 to 40 yards away. Well, CJ is like that. I'm telling you, if I took him out to the street there and told him to hit the front door knob, he would hit it 6 out of 10 times, and the four misses would be close."

"When I hear a man with your background say, 'He is the most accurate I have ever seen,' I am amazed! It sounds like he has a future! Maybe I'll find work that will allow me to come to your games next season."

"I hope you do, and I, too, think it incredible and a rather interesting story, if I do say so myself. When I started learning to pitch, my dad's knees would not allow him to stay in a catcher's position for long, so he built a net for me to throw to. He even painted the strike zone on it. We accumulated a five-gallon paint bucket full of baseballs and I practiced for hours on end. When they moved here to be near us, he built a pitching mound in the parsonage yard so that C.J. could use the same net.

"The really interesting thing is that last year, C.J. researched some experiments that he might want to try to duplicate for a science class assignment. He came across an experiment done on a group shooting basketball free throws. They tested the skills of the group at the beginning and then broke them into three groups. Group one practiced shooting 25 free throws every day. Group two was not allowed to practice the entire two-week period. Group three was instructed to visualize the successful completion of 25 free throws every day for two weeks. The testing at the end for groups one and two were only slightly different from their beginning scores. However, group three showed noticeable improvement in their final tests.

"Since reading about that experiment, C.J. developed a routine of practice that includes visualizing making every pitch in his arsenal – the fastball, the curve, the slider and the changeup – going to the exact spot on the edge of the strike zone that he wants it to go. After the visualization exercises, he practices trying to accomplish each pitch as previously visualized. The results have been amazing.

"Now, when he leaves the house, he reaches into the bucket and takes a ball with him, whether it is to the backyard to practice or to go anywhere. He does the visualization exercises at every opportunity."

"I suppose we all know the old adage of 'practice makes perfect' is not really true, but 'perfect practice makes perfect' would be closer to reality."

Tillie interjected, "Hey, you two, enough baseball, okay? Remember why we came?"

"Yes, Dear. B.J., do you want to go to Smokey's with us tonight? It's Thursday, you know."

"Only if you can find me a date."

I jumped up, "I volunteer, I volunteer!"

"I accept."

"Wait – I don't have transportation yet, and I'm not riding in that piece of junk you have parked out back."

"We'll pick you up at seven, okay?"

"Good. I assume we're going to eat there."

"Yep, but we need to scoot. I have a dentist appointment and need to be back at school ASAP."

After they left, I looked at B.J. and said, "A date, wow! Maybe I better pinch myself to make sure I'm awake."

"You better get out of here before I pinch you. I've got work to do."

We were seated in Smokey's by 7:25 that evening. My stomach was growling, having received only two doughnuts for breakfast and a turkey sandwich with a handful of chips for lunch; it was protesting and threatening a riot. I grabbed a menu and told the waitress, "A sweet tea for me, please." Both ladies ordered diet Cokes and Joe said, "Water for me, please." By the time she returned with drinks, I had scanned the menu and knew for sure what I wanted. B.J. got things started by ordering a tuna salad cold plate with chips. Tillie said, "That sounds good. Me, too," and Joe went for a cheeseburger and fries. When the waitress looked at me, I said, "I've only been back in Carolina two days and have yet to get my fill of barbeque, so give me the platter, hold the roll, a side of slaw and add a basket of hush puppies, which I will share with you all if you are good little boys and girls." They chimed in with, "Yes, sir!" in unison. The food was delivered promptly and was obviously quite good as attested by empty plates.

After eating, I did a visual inspection of the place to note very little change since I was last there. There was a chalkboard posting for a band coming that week end: Duke Chandler and Little Creek. I walked over to that old Wurlitzer Jukebox, fed in coins, made my selection and returned to ask B.J. for a dance.

How can I explain my feelings when she stepped into my arms? We glided across that dance floor in perfect timing, our bodies melded together as if they were made to be together. The thought came, "This must be what heaven's like." Why such a thought, I don't know. I remembered Shrink's advice about balancing spiritual and physical things and decided to ponder the matter later. I kissed the top of her head when the music stopped and we made our way back to the table where the two women excused themselves to freshen up.

As soon as I sat down Joe asked, "Brody, if you were to die tonight do you know where you would spend eternity?"

"Where the hell did that come from?"

"Shush."

"To tell the truth, I've not given that much thought. I'm not planning on doing that tonight or any time soon, thank you."

"Well, it's inevitable that you will one day. Maybe you need to think about it."

"Okay. I mean, I've killed people – so they tell me – but really, overall, I've been pretty good."

"Brody, let me assure you, going to heaven has nothing to do with you being good or bad, because all of us are bad and don't deserve to go there. Truthfully, you cannot be good enough to earn your way into heaven, nor can you be bad enough for God to deny you entry, if you have done the one essential thing that He requires; and that, my friend, is to trust Jesus completely."

"That sounds a little too easy to me. But I guess I don't understand what trusting Jesus completely means."

"Everyone wrestles with that. Look at it like this: Before any part of creation happened, there was a conversation in heaven between God the Father, God the Son, and God the Holy Spirit. The conversation went something like this: If we create man and give him free will, he will at some time make a mistake, disobey, or in some way sin and become unholy. When that happens, we will have to separate ourselves from him because we cannot abide with sin. The Holy Spirit pointed out, "A part of our nature is to forgive." The Father admitted to that truth but pointed out, "But another part of our nature is to be just, and wrong must be punished. If man sins, he must pay the penalty for that sin, and only God can forgive sin." It seemed a dilemma until the Son said, "Then there has to be a God-man." And that's what the Bible is all about. From start to finish. It's about the plan for the God-man to redeem us from sin, that we might spend eternity in heaven with Him. So, we see Jesus come as a baby, lead a sinless life to prove Himself to be the Son of God, die on the cross as a substitution for our sins, and rise from the dead to prove He will do the same for us, if we trust Him. If you believe Jesus is the Son of God, He will take your sin unto himself and give you His righteousness. Trusting in that and that alone will get you into heaven."

"That's some heavy stuff, man. I need some time to think about it."

"Absolutely. Just remember, I'm available to discuss it with you anytime you want to."

Acting as if they had not been right around the corner listening and praying, the girls rushed to the table, declaring that it was Karaoke hour. With that announcement, I said, "Barbara Jean please sing 'Crazy' for me. It has been too long since I heard you sing." She hesitated and I quickly threw in, "I'm not above begging if I have to."

"Okay, in honor of your return, I will do it, providing Joe doesn't sing along."

"Hey, I may be the only black man in eastern North Carolina who can't carry a tune in a bucket, but I am still the sensitive sort. You have hurt my feelings, B.J.!"

"You, my dear, are about as sensitive as a rock." We all joined Tillie in laughing at her little joke.

Barbara Jean made her way to the small stage, pausing to tell the DJ what music she needed. The crowd broke out with applause, which told me she had been there recently, they remembered her and were looking forward to a treat. I know I was. The song was one of my favorites, and when she sang the words, "Crazy for loving you," while looking directly into my eyes, my heart did a flip-flop that told me, "You are so hooked."

We thanked Joe and Tillie for a lovely evening, and I walked B.J. to the back stairs to her apartment. Expecting to be invited up, I was already on the first step when she said, "Not tonight, big boy. I'm not ready for that, but I do have a present for you. Consider this a welcome home gift," and she planted one on me. I pulled her tight and felt her begin to tremble almost immediately. Somehow my hands must have automatically slid towards her hip area because she pulled back saying, "You know the rules."

"Yes, ma'am," and I returned the favor by planting one on her with all the heat I could generate. It was a sweet and passionate kiss, and when it was over, I think the tears in my eyes affected her more than the kiss. She placed her hand on my cheek and said, "Oh, Brody, you are so precious, and I am so glad you've come back to me." She rushed up the steps and unlocked the door, then blew me a kiss. I swallowed hard and walked the four blocks home.

Immorality of Liberal Ideology — Chapter Sixteen

The next day, I started ticking off things on my list by getting my license renewed. It took less than an hour, as I only had to take vision and sign recognition tests, and of course, pay my fee of five dollars per year. On to the Verizon store, where a very knowledgeable young man helped me select a bundle of services, including television with the NFL ticket, internet, two cell phone lines that included two Samsung III smart phones. I explained that the phone was surely smarter than I was and how I disliked reading instructions. He volunteered to set both phones up, programming each number into speed dial for the other, and took time to show me several features. I explained that this would certainly be a new experience for Aunt Hannah. After that he slowed down some to make sure I would be able to go over items with her. As he worked, I explained how she liked to read the Bible, but I suspected her eyesight was failing to some degree. He immediately went online and downloaded a Bible app to each phone. He also increased the font size on Aunt Hannah's phone. After thanking him several times, I left there a very happy customer.

As I walked up the front walk, I saw Aunt Hannah sitting on the couch reading her Bible. She looked up and waved me in before I could ring the doorbell. "I've got a present for you," I said.

She looked at the cell phone I was holding out toward her and said, "I don't need that fancy thing. I can walk to anyone I want to talk to." I gave her my prearranged spiel about her getting sick at night and that all she would have to do is punch in one number and I could be there in a jiffy. I could tell that was making sense to her so I went on to show her the Bible app. She became more interested, and when I showed her the large size print, how to skip to any passage she wanted by choosing the book name, and how to use her finger to turn pages, she grabbed that phone out of my hand like it was the widow's lost coin!

"Brody, I thank you for this. I think it will be a real help."

"It will fit nicely in that apron pocket, and who knows? You might be out for a walk and sprain your ankle – you can call me, or just dial 9ll, and help will be right there. By the way, I've decided that the yard is in such a mess, I need to hire help to get it taken care of. Any suggestions?"

"Oh, yes, in fact my neighbor two doors over there has a yard service company. Let me take care of getting him over there."

"Okay. Did you know B.J. and I double dated with Joe and Tillie last night?"

"No, but I'm very pleased to hear it. You can't wish for better friends than those two."

"Unfortunately, I couldn't help but feel the tension as some seemed to be paying us too much attention. I guess it could have to do with my celebrity, but I think it might have had more to do with this race relation thing we talked about the other day. I thought we were past those days."

"Lawdy, child, don't you believe that. The worst is yet to come. This old world is on a downward spiral, heading faster every day toward the end times."

"I don't know anything about the end times, and I'm not sure I want to know."

"Brody, honey, everybody needs to be ready for the Lord's return. His coming back for His people is as sure as the sun rising in the east. The one sure thing in life is that in the end, God wins. The book of Revelation makes that very clear. Old Satan was given freedom to roam this earth and do his work of deception, and he's done his job well; but in the end, his head will be crushed. The woes of this world can be a heavy burden without the Lord. You need to find Him, and you need to do it soon."

"I hear you, Aunt Hannah."

"I'm telling you, son, all these things going on around us will look a heap different when you give God control of your life. You do know that almost every issue we face today is in some way linked to sin. Sometimes it's outright rebellion against the Word of God, sometimes we call it something it's not to mask the fact that it is sin, or we try to cast doubt on people who dare criticize, so they seem guilty of going against common beliefs of society."

"I'm not sure I understand."

"Okay, take the issue of abortion. In an attempt to take the focus off the murder of a child, they call it women's rights. A woman has the right to keep her legs crossed or to spread them, but if she chooses to spread them and she becomes pregnant, she does not have the right to kill the child."

"But, they defend that by saying that life begins at birth."

"That's bull feathers and you know it, Brody. Common sense will tell you that the test for life should be the same as for death. A doctor cannot sign a death certificate as long as there is a heartbeat in that body. The same should be true for life. If a heartbeat is detected, that life should be protected under our system of laws."

"Wow! I guess I never looked at it that way but it does make sense."

"Look at the issue of homosexuality. Now that gay people have come out of the closet and have become aggressive in defending themselves, they say we should be tolerant and accept them as they are. They are perfectly willing to be sociable as long as you don't call their lifestyle sinful, but if you do so, they become as intolerant of you as they accused you of being. They can try all they want to color it or change others' views about it, but it is still a sin in the eyes of God."

"Umm."

"But my biggest concern is the political atmosphere we face today. The hatred I see rising its ugly head, one party against the other. It didn't use to be that way, and

I have to guard against entering into that myself. I left the Democratic Party years ago for three reasons. One, because I was fed up with the way they had captured the black community by doling out freebies for votes. They did the same disservice to us that the company store did after the Civil War. 'More freebies for votes' is the same as more credit than could be repaid to keep people on the plantation. Secondly, there really is immorality involved in much of liberal ideology."

"Whoa, that's going a bit far, isn't it?"

"No, it isn't. If you recall your Social Studies, the government is of the people, for the people and by the people. It has no resources other than those given or taken from the people. So, when any one person says, 'The government should provide me free health care,' or, 'The government should pay off my college debt,' or 'The government should provide my child a free education,' they are really saying that other people should pay for those things, so they can use their own money to do with as they want. To my way of thinking there's little difference in that than going to a local bank or store and robbing them of their money to satisfy your own selfish desires at the expense of others."

"By golly, I can see it when put that way."

"The final straw for me was that party's stance on the abortion issue. How any Christian could remain in a political party with a platform that includes late term abortion is beyond me."

"I am impressed Aunt Hannah; I must have assumed you would be a Democrat, as most of the black community seems to be."

"Well you can't automatically assume that I'm a Republican either. There are a number of things I don't care for there. Nationally, I don't have much choice, but locally I go for the character and ability of the individual and the issues they run on."

"You are an amazing woman, Aunt Hannah."

"Go on boy, flattery will get you no more than a piece of cornbread or a second helping of collards around this house."

"Speaking of cornbread, you got any?"

"Yep, let me get you one for the road."

At home, less than an hour since I had left Aunt Hannah's, I heard noise out in the yard. By the time I reached the front door, I saw a large black man, with four young boys, throwing rakes and hoes out of the pickup truck. They jumped to the task of cleaning up the place as if a contract was agreed too and instructions had been given. "Excuse me," I said, "but don't we need to discuss what needs doing and how much I'm willing to pay before you begin work?"

"Hey, Mr. Edwards, I'm John Harrison. But everybody round here calls me Big John. I'd like you to do the same if you don't mind. Now, as to those two things you mentioned, I can pretty much see what needs doing, as you put it, and the price done been paid. So, can we just get on with the job?"

"Yes, you can, Big John. I will straighten up with Aunt Hannah, later."

"Just so you understand, sir. I could work around your place for a solid month and would still be in Aunt Hannah's debt, so please don't make it a big issue with her. Besides that, let this be a way for me to say thank you for serving our country."

"You are a kind man, Big John; I can only say, humbly, you are welcome. Now let me leave you to your work."

After making myself a small lunch, I took a pitcher of ice water with glasses to the backyard for Big John and the boys. They were so hard at work I had to yell to get their attention that the water was on the patio table. Back in the house, I took my now customary afternoon snooze. Forty-five minutes later I was awakened by the sound of hedge trimmers right outside my window, so I looked to check their progress. As fast as Big John trimmed, the boys would rake and bag the trimmings. It was obvious that all the boys were his sons and were well trained. About an hour later they loaded up all their equipment and my trash in the bed of the truck, waving as they left. I looked over what had been accomplished and was well pleased.

Fishing with Barbara Jean — Chapter Seventeen

I'd been home over two weeks now and had developed a habit of morning coffee and doughnuts with Barbara Jean. That morning I asked her, "Have you been fishing lately?"

"Not since the last time I went with you."

"Well, what do you say to this idea? I will get everything ready and pick you up as soon as you close; we drive down to the bay and catch a few perch and/or bream and take them to my place for a fish fry."

"Yes, yeah, that will be great. Thanks for remembering how excited I get catching fish."

"Yeah, and I also remember how sad-faced you get when you don't catch any."

"Not going to happen today."

"What fixings do you want? I'll stop by Food Lion on my way home."

"We might as well do it up right – cornbread or hush puppies, of course, and maybe some fries and slaw. That should do it, unless you want to include a bottle of white wine."

"Okay, see you at five o'clock sharp."

I wasn't more than ten steps away when she stuck her head out and shouted, "Don't forget a fresh lemon and an onion if you're going to do hush puppies."

I blew her a kiss to add to the real one that was still tingling my lips.

In the Food Lion, I did a mental check of items in the cart before I reached the checkout line. One bottle of Chardonnay, a cluster of scallions, three large Irish potatoes, bag of cornmeal, bud vase with a red rose, one lemon, small container of slaw, jug of cooking oil. Satisfied that I had everything, I headed toward the checkout line.

When I got home, I put things away and got out a dust rag to give the place a going over, ran the vacuum, then headed out to the garage to check the fishing gear. Satisfied that things were looking good, I decided to do some journaling. Before I knew it, the clock showed 3:30, so I shut down and headed to the bathroom.

"*Who ever heard of taking a shower before you go fishing?*"

"I can't take a chance in offending my girl. Besides, I might get lucky."

"*You better wipe that kind of thinking out of your mind. If you mess this up, Rage will join me in assaulting you.*"

"**Damn straight.**"

"*By the way, when was your last nightmare?*"

"Umm, over a week now."

"*Must be the kisses.*"

"Could be. At any rate, I'm going for more of them tonight. I'll tell her she's therapeutic."

"Heh-heh-heh, whatever works for you, big boy."

At 4:30 I did a last-minute check of the house: two pots on stove, cooking oil poured and ready for fish, hushpuppies and fries, Chardonnay and slaw in fridge with the sliced lemon, table set, hush puppy mixed, prepared and in covered bowl, potatoes peeled, sliced and covered in water. Looks good to go. Out to the TR 3, I went through the same process: top up in case it gets cool, back window unzipped, fishing poles stuck through window, stringer, tackle box, bucket, yeah. Now to stop by a mini-mart for night crawlers, and we're ready. I was there at five o'clock sharp.

I pulled up in front and B.J. came out the door and locked up. I admired her outfit of blue Capri pants, red tank top, blue windbreaker, scarf, sunglasses and deck-type tennis shoes. She looked good and I told her so. She gave me a quick peck, and I stood there with eyes closed until she pushed me hard enough in the chest that I had to open them to make sure I didn't fall. "That's all you get for now. Let's go."

We cruised the bay finding several houses that were obviously not occupied, selected one without a "No trespassing" sign on the pier and down we went. Barbara Jean is not the least bit squeamish about worms, and she was baited up and in the water before I finished securing the stringer to the post. By the time I had my baited hook in the water she pulled out her first Bluegill, a keeper.

"Yeah," followed by a fist pump, "Take that big boy."

"You gonna take that, big guy, without a peep?"

"Yep."

"She's gonna kick your ass, you know that, don't you?"

"Usually does – whoa." My pole bent sharply as I muscled a Bass out of the water before he shook the hook out. "He must have been at least three pounds," I yelled.

"Don't cry, baby, I'll catch him for you."

"Don't get obnoxious now."

I pulled in two decent sized Perch in succession and was feeling much better. Then she and I both got another Bluegill each. After that it was as if someone had decreed, "No more fish for you two." Not even a nibble. So, I sidled over while putting one arm around her shoulders and said, "Can't fish, might as well smooch." She looked interested to me so I planted one on her. She evidently liked it because she dropped her pole on the pier and turned her attention to me. It must have gone on for several minutes until we heard a splash and saw her pole drifting out to the middle of the creek. With no way to retrieve it and having enough fish for a good meal, we decided to go home. I filled the bucket about half-full of creek water and placed the stringer of fish in it while she prepared the pole and closed the tackle box.

"That was so much fun. We need to make a habit of this."

"Yes, ma'am, I agree. Now let's get going. I'm hungry."

Back at the house, we worked together in the kitchen. I quickly cleaned the fish, and she began heating the cooking oil and poured the water off the potatoes. I started dipping the fish in batter and before you know it things were sizzling in that old kitchen. I pointed out that the rose was for her and she gave me a kiss on the cheek. Then I asked her, "Would being married to a policeman be something you could live with?"

She turned pale and gulped like something was hard to swallow. "I don't know, I've honestly never thought about that. I suppose it would depend on who the policeman is."

"Me, of course. I know this is kind of sudden, and I don't mean that question to be a proposal; but I do have serious feelings for you and I've always thought I would like law enforcement. Just thought I should know your answer before I talk to the sheriff. If you can't deal with that kind of life, I have to think about doing some other kind of work."

"Well, yeah I think I could, in fact it might mean I would get to see you more. You know all policemen like doughnuts."

"She is so cute and funny."

"Yep."

"Then I think I'll give him a call tomorrow."

"Umm."

We finished dinner. Not much talking went on, but some serious eye contact was made, and I knew we both wanted more than just looking across the table at each other. Together we cleaned up the table; I rinsed the things we had used while she put them in the dishwasher. When the work was done, we went into the living room and turned on the TV. I have no idea if we got a picture or not. I do know there was sound coming from the thing, but she had my undivided attention. It was like old days; as soon as we hit the sofa we were in a passionate embrace. The kisses were so sweet and precious; I was about as happy as I could imagine being. I slid into more of a reclining position and pulled her gently on top of me. We were both breathing so hard and moaning that I thought, "Dad is going to hear us." Then it hit me, we're adults now and he's gone; there is nothing to stop us but our consciences. I broke the kiss and we lay there, forehead to forehead, lower body to lower body, both trembling with excitement. I recalled a promise I had made to myself never to put pressure on her to do something she would regret in the morning, so I said, "Barbara Jean, get up. I need to take you home."

She did, and we made our way to the TR 3 to take her home. Pulling around back of Ye Olde Sweet Shoppe, I asked if she would forgive me for not getting out to see her to the door. She replied, "I understand. Go home. I'll see you tomorrow." After kissing me on the nose she was up the steps and inside in a hurry.

Job Interview — Chapter Eighteen

I awoke to sun shining in my face, and my first conscious thought was, "What a beautiful day the Lord hath made."

"*Was that a biblical quote or an Aunt Hannah truism?*"

"I don't know. I do know it is fall but looks like summer out there and I need to go see my honey." With that, I threw back that sheet and made a beeline for the bathroom. On the short walk to B.J.'s I contemplated whether to call the sheriff's office or just drop in. Arriving, I was glad to see no other customers, which would mean a warm welcome.

Sure enough, Barbara Jean came from behind the counter to give me a brief hug and a nice-but-sweet kiss on the mouth. Not satisfied, I grabbed her into a bear hug and squeezed her to me as tightly as I could. "I don't want to ever let go," I said.

She managed to croak out, "If you don't, you'll be holding a corpse. I can't breathe."

I eased up on my grip but didn't let her go. "I need more than that little peck you gave me," I said, and then kissed her appropriately.

Then the bell tinkled, announcing we had company. I looked over my shoulder to see one of the largest human beings I had ever seen. As I released B.J., I heard him say, "Aha! When the cat's away the mice will play."

"Pastor, no one would ever describe you as a cat – a bull or an elephant, maybe!"

He laughed and gave her a sideways hug and at the same time extended his hand to me. "Pastor Cooke; and I'm pleased to meet you, Brody Edwards."

"The same here. I've been hearing a lot of good things about you from both B.J. and Aunt Hannah." I extended an invitation to join us for coffee, and he accepted.

"I heard that Joe wasted no time in presenting the gospel to you."

"Yeah, caught me off guard, and I couldn't think of a good answer, so I told him I would think about it."

"Well, that's a good start. The proper response to the gospel should be from one's own conviction and not because of pressure. If I might be so bold, a good place to start your search would be in the Gospel of John. I recommend you start your day and end your day with the Word of God. If you truly seek Him, you will find Him, and the best place to do that is in His Word."

"Thank you, sir. I must admit I was a tad leery of meeting you, afraid you might apply the pressure, I guess."

He chuckled. "Actually, you are more likely to get prodded by Joe than by me. I try not to shy away from an opportunity to witness, but I'm influenced by my background. You see, my mother was a Bible thumping, scripture quoting woman who saw her mission in life to be the conversion of everyone she met. Unfortunately, she pushed more people away from God, including me, than she won to the Lord.

That's a long story which will have to come later, as I have to drink this coffee and get to work." He fished in his vest pocket and drew out a business card. "Call me anytime, Brody."

After our warm but brief goodbyes, B.J. came out, pulled her chair up next to mine and placed her head on my shoulder. I basked in that tender moment.

"She is so sweet."

"Yes, ma'am."

"What did you say?"

"Just talking to myself about how great it is to be here with you, my love. I'm trying to make up my mind if it would be better to drop by the sheriff's office to inquire about employment or to call in and ask for an appointment."

"Oh, Brody, I definitely think you should call and ask for an appointment with the sheriff. If you drop in you might get the information you want, but you could easily miss the chance to meet the man who will make the decision to hire you or not."

"Wise, too."

"Amen." I finished and rose to leave. "Wish me luck."

"I'll do better than that. I will pray for you."

Momentarily stunned, I recovered, took her face in both hands and leaned in to kiss her forehead. Seeing her eyes closed, I decided they both needed a kiss, too. When I finally reached her lips, her eyes were staring at me and her countenance was saying, "I love you," even though she did not say the words.

At home, I pulled out my cell phone and found the number I was looking for. While contemplating my approach, B.J.'s words about prayer came to mind.

"Maybe you should try that."

"Lord, I am looking for you, seeking my way in life, really. I know Aunt Hannah says you always hear the prayers of your children, and I realize I do not qualify, but I do need help in finding my way both to You, and in all life matters. Please help me. Amen."

Dialing (252) 946-7111, it rang, and a nice female voice answered, "Beaufort County Sheriff's Office, how may I direct your call?"

"Well, ma'am, my name is Brody Edwards and I was – "

"Oh, my goodness, I don't believe this. The sheriff and I were just talking about you."

"Really?"

"Yes, sir, he is a real baseball fan and followed your career all through high school and college. Wait a minute, he's telling me to put you through to his line."

"Hello, Brody, this is Wes Marslender."

"What a nice surprise to get to talk to you. I was calling to look into the possibility of employment."

"What a coincidence. Ellen and I were just talking about how this department could use someone like you. When can you come in to see me?"

"Anytime your schedule will allow. I could be there in twenty minutes, if I don't have to dress up."

"Come on, I can adjust my schedule for this."

Driving toward Washington, I hit speed dial for Barbara Jean and told her the whole series of events, including my own prayer. She squealed with delight, and I envisioned her jumping up and down.

"Oh, sweetheart, I do believe this is an answer to our prayers. I can definitely see God at work in this. Stay focused and come here as soon as you can."

"I will. Keep praying."

"Okay."

Turning left off Main Street onto Market Street, I looked for the pool hall where I had spent many hours learning the art of billiards. I wondered if it was still owned by the Marslender family and if there was a relationship connected to the sheriff. "I'll have to remember to ask him." Parking behind the building was relatively easy, so I made my way up the steps and into the Beaufort County Sheriff's Office. The receptionist came from behind her desk to greet me.

"Hello, Mr. Edwards, I'm Ellen Buck, AKA Right Arm around here. Let me show you to the Sheriff's office."

Before she could knock, the door opened. The sheriff stepped into the hallway, greeted me with a firm handshake and said, "Come on in, Brody."

Taking a seat at his invitation I looked around the office seeing several pictures of notable sites around the county. There was a picture of him shaking hands with the governor and lots of plaques and trophies on shelves behind the desk. I was impressed.

"So, you're interest in joining us in law enforcement, are you?"

"Yes, sir, that was where I was headed when the train left the track a few years back. I guess I'd better explain that. I had two years of college, majoring in Criminal Justice, when I threw my elbow out and had surgery. Then a disagreement with my dad was my excuse to run off and become a bum and an alcoholic. Fortunately, I got some help that led me to sobriety and into the Marine Corps."

"Okay Brody, this may be the easiest job interview you will ever have, because I'm going to tell you right up front, I want you in my department. I do need to make sure you want to be with us, so I'm going to give you the introductory spiel I give all candidates. So here goes. Our mission statement, which we take very seriously, is to be the best Sheriff's Office in the state. Here is how we will accomplish this mission:

- We will serve all citizens equally and without regard to race, sex, religion or socioeconomic standing.

- We will strive for constant improvement in all areas of operation.
- We will train and prepare to meet any law enforcement need or any other need for service that may arise within our jurisdiction.
- We will be as friendly, helpful, courteous and respectful as possible in dealing with others.
- We will never forget that we derive our strength from those we serve.

I cannot emphasize too highly how important the things are that I've just stated to you. Those are my core beliefs, and I will hold every man and woman employed here accountable to abide by them at all times. So, I have to ask the question, do you think you can support this mission statement and the methods of achieving it, and will you swear to do so at the appropriate time?"

"Yes, sir, I can and I will, if given the opportunity to do so."

"Good, then let me continue. We have almost 50,000 people to protect in our county; we have about 827 square miles of territory to cover, and believe me when I tell you that we have enough problems to keep us busy always. I am convinced, but can't prove yet, that there is some force here that's deliberately trying to stir up racial issues among us. On top of all the normal traffic, criminal activity, family disputes etc., we have had six drug overdose deaths in the past two years. We know that drug trafficking is on the rise but so far have been unable to thwart it, even though we do have NARCs out there to help us. Now let me get to what we can offer in the way of pay and benefits. Our starting pay goes from $32,620 to $45,683, depending upon education and experience. My guess is that you will start at about $40,000, which is in line with the average household income for this area. Of course, we provide uniforms and equipment, health insurance, eleven paid holidays a year, retirement accounts, the average vacation and sick leave package, continuing education help and physical fitness incentives."

"The pay is better than I expected and the benefit package seems good to me. I am definitely interested."

"Now comes the hard part. We must get you qualified to enter the North Carolina Basic Law Enforcement Training Program, usually referred to as BLET. You'll have no problem with three of the four requirements, but there's one that concerns me. The qualifications are for you to maintain a clean criminal record – no problem there – I've checked; to have been awarded a military law enforcement MOS, no problem; to have completed a military law enforcement training program – no problem; to have completed two years of full-time assignment in military law enforcement – not so sure. It's not clear to me whether the last requirement is meant to be in addition to training or to be inclusive of training. So, your job, young man, is to fill out this form F 21 very carefully. Be sure to refer to your training materials and include all the key words like crime scene processing, hostage and/or crisis negotiations, interrogations, evidence holding, those sorts of things. Most importantly make it clear that you are interpreting the requirement to be inclusive of training. You could say 'my Marine Corps Security Forces career began on' the date your training started and continued until discharged date; to the extent possible, don't mention the fact that the last four months were in a hospital. Written properly, I believe I can get it to the right people to have them see it the way both of us want them to."

"How long do you anticipate for the process?"

"They are required to complete the evaluation of your application within thirty days, hopefully sooner. It should only take a couple of days for you to get your enrollment in BLET approved. As soon as those two things are done, I can swear you in. If you're approved for the program, you will receive credit for 142 hours of training; but when you include your two years of criminal justice credits you may already have the required 474 hours of training. It will be interesting to see how it works out. At any rate, we can help you with some office assignments that give you time to do some course work."

"Sheriff, I am so excited! I really want this to work, and I will get this form filled out ASAP and personally put in your hands."

"Great! I, too, am excited, and I believe I can see the Almighty at work here."

"Are you a Christian, sir?"

"Yes, I am a born-again believer."

I popped to attention and thanked him profusely.

On the way out, I gave Ellen a fist bump, a big smile and a silent, "Thank you," as she was on the phone. Then I made it to Chocowinity as fast as speed limits would allow.

Howling at the Moon — Chapter Nineteen

Entering Ye Olde Sweet Shoppe, I found Barbara Jean taking notes for a cake order from a lady I did not recognize. I was so excited I started pacing back and forth like an expectant father, thinking, "If that woman doesn't get out of here soon I'm going to scream." Well, she finally did.

B.J. rushed around the counter and jumped into my arms. "I know it went great, you are absolutely glowing with excitement."

It took me a good ten minutes to relate all that went on at the interview, and by the time I finished she was pacing back and forth. "We are going to wear out this tile if we aren't careful."

"I knew it, I just knew it, this has got to be a God thing. It cannot be a coincidence! You need to go tell Aunt Hannah and get home to get that form completed as soon as you can. You might try getting a nap, too, because we are going to celebrate tonight."

"Really?" I said, while making my eyebrows go up and down, and with a slight sneer on my face.

"Not that much of a celebration, big boy. You are, however, taking me out for a steak or seafood dinner, then I thought we might go down to the KOA Campground and see if we can find a vacant spot on the point. It should be a full moon tonight."

"Hey, I like the way you think. Do you have a chaise lounge chair? I only have one."

"Yes, I have one, so I guess that means we take the Honda."

"Can't get those things in the TR 3. I'll be here by six, okay?"

"I'll be ready."

I speed dialed Aunt Hannah and said, "Are you home?"

"Sure am. You coming to see me?"

"You bet, be right there."

"Don't bother to knock, just come on in."

She stood to greet me, and after a quick hug I said, "I've got good news!" I retold the story I had just related to Barbara Jean. By the time I was finished Aunt Hannah had her hands raised, palms up toward heaven, saying, "Thank you, Jesus." She did that several times as I told her what had happened. That was the exact reaction I had pictured her having as I drove over. I was amazed to find my hands raised and my head nodding in agreement to her response.

"What are you doing, Brody?"

"Exactly what it looks like, Reason, exactly what it looks like."

At home, realizing it was a little late for lunch but afraid I couldn't wait till dinner, I got out the peanut butter and crackers, poured myself a glass of milk and started looking over the F 21 form requirements. As soon as I finished my snack, I tackled the task, thinking how glad I was that I had taken Shrink's advice to journal, as the words began to flow. Later I was startled to find that it was four o'clock already. I decided to get my shower and dress, set the alarm on my cell phone for 5:30 and close my eyes for a short rest before my date with B.J.

I wheeled in behind B.J.'s right on the dot, gave that old Triumph two quick accelerator pats, as was both my and my dad's habits. We both loved the sound of that glass pack muffler. By the time the engine shut off B.J. came hustling down the steps and jumped in.

"You in a hurry?"

"Maybe I'm just hungry."

"Okay, where do you want to go?"

"Why, the best place in town, of course."

I cranked her up again and roared off towards town. Pulling into the waterfront area, I said, "I assume this is what you had in mind."

"Yes, this is still the best in town, not only because of the quality of their food but also because of the variety on the menu." We waltzed into the Waterfront Restaurant with my left arm around her and her head leaning against my shoulder. As we were led to our table, an old fishing buddy, Simon Riemersma, stood up, shook my hand, gave me a shoulder bump, and whispered, "I'll see you Thursday," as he gently pushed me on.

"That was nice that he recognized our need to be alone," she said as she grasped each of my hands in hers.

"I could look into those beautiful eyes of yours all night."

"This is special, but not that special," she reminded me.

Our waiter came, introduced himself as Ben, and asked if he could bring us drinks. B.J. ordered a glass of Chardonnay, stating she was planning on a seafood dinner. "I'll have a glass of something red since I will probably go for a steak. Something on the inexpensive side, please, as I'm not a big wine fan." After the wine came, I noted that we were not given a view of the river, so I scanned around the room, seeing a few familiar faces and hoping none of them would recognize me or at least not come over to interrupt us. Trying to recall my previous experiences of being in this place, I only came up with a time or two that my father and I came, and just one other time, I think prom night, that B.J. and I had come together. My chuckling caused her to say, "What?"

"Just thinking about old times. We couldn't afford this place back in the day."

"Yep. I do want to thank you for this special treat."

"The pleasure is all mine, dear."

We ate slowly and somewhat silently, both obviously going over the day's events. Finished with the meal, I thanked Ben for his service as I returned the signed charge slip to him and put my credit card away. Making sure her sweater was secure on her shoulders, I took her hand in mine and we went out to stand by the river. As we looked up and down the waterfront at the sailboats, yachts and pontoon party boats lining the wharf, I thought, "There is still a lot of old money around this old town."

Back at B.J.'s place, she ran upstairs to get an afghan in case it got any chillier, while I checked the back of her car to make sure the chaise lounge was in place. When she returned, I said "We have to stop by my place to get my chair."

"We don't need but one," was her response. My temperature rose several degrees.

"Down, boy."

"Damn Straight."

"Shush."

She drove us down to the KOA Campground and as we passed the office/mini-mart, she tooted the horn and proceeded down toward the water without stopping. "What was the toot about?"

"Just letting my friend, Emily, know we are on site."

It felt good to know she had gone to the trouble of setting this up, so I asked, "What did you tell her we would be doing?"

"I simply explained that you liked to howl at the moon and we thought this was a good place for that."

I cocked my head, expecting to hear a 'damn straight,' but nothing happened. We drove into a site and set up the chair on the pad meant to be used to house a camper. B.J. adjusted the chair down two notches and said, "Sit down." I eagerly obeyed and she slipped down with her cute little butt between my legs and pulled the wrap over her. The moon was spectacular and she felt so good against me that I was moaning before the action began. Placing her hands on the arms of the chair she pushed her bottom off the chair while using her legs to pull mine together so that she was now on my lap. Then leaning off to the side, she leaned back to lay her head on my left shoulder, and looking deeply into my eyes she said, "I am so proud of you." She followed that with a kiss that brought my moaning almost to the howling stage. We were both really into the passion of the moment when she broke off a kiss, took my hands and placed them on her belt line. "Brody, when I told you that you were not getting any farther than this again until the specified conditions were met, I meant it. Those rules still apply, do you understand?"

I could only gulp and nod.

With that she leaned forward and reached under her blouse to the back and released the clasp on her bra. "You never were very good at that," she said, as she kissed me again.

"This is not right!"

I thought, "Not now, Reason."

"Do what's right!"

So, I said, "Wait, Barbara Jean, don't do that! Let's think about what we're doing here. We both know we're about to run toward temptation rather than doing what is right and running away from it. I want you to know how special I think you are and I do very much appreciate this special setting you've arranged. But I'm also committed to never again place you in a position where you might make a decision you'd later regret."

"Oh, Brody, you are so right! Scripturally speaking, we are doing the exact opposite of what we should be doing. We are playing with fire and hoping not to get burned. My sin nature pulls me to the things I want even though they are forbidden until marriage. What should we do?"

"First, let me say that we are not going to waste this moment. If God ever created a more romantic setting than a full moon shining over an open body of water, I cannot imagine what that would be. Just look! It is magnificent! Secondly, looking ahead; I can see us teaching our kids to skip rocks out there and to catch fish. Man, that will be special!"

"Yes, that sounds so good! I think I would like us to have a small pontoon boat for the kids to use as a diving platform and for all of us to fish from."

"Sweetheart, I want you to know I will work hard to give you the desires of your heart. I like the boat idea; we should be able to do that and even make it fit in the garage too. I also want you to know I've taken Doc's advice and have begun to read my Bible at breakfast and at bedtime. I have even begun to pray, and I think that is something we need to start doing together sometime soon, though I'm not ready for that right now."

"Brody, I am so encouraged! Let's go home and put this special night in dream mode."

I managed a "thank you" before choking up. My emotions got to her, as she again hugged me as tight as she could.

I took the chair and she carried the wrap back to the Honda. Driving out, she honked very lightly as we left. I looked over at her and she had a big grin on her face. Back at her place, we kissed good night and I fired up the Triumph, shouting up to her on the landing, "I'll see you in the morning!" The door closed and off I went, a happy camper indeed.

Wednesday morning, I woke up thinking, "All those doughnuts couldn't be good for me – maybe I should just have a bowl of cereal here." I reached for my phone to call B.J.

"Better think about that some more. What if she thinks you are acting like you did the last time?"

"Thanks, Reason," I said as I put that phone away and headed for my honey.

No one was there, so I took her face in my hands, kissed her and then sang, "You are so beautiful to me."

"Flattery won't get you any farther than you got last night."

"I will be satisfied to get that far anytime."

"Um, I will get your breakfast."

While I ate, several customers came and went. With business going well, I finished up quickly and explained that I was going home to finish the application and get it in the sheriff's hands that afternoon. I also hadn't heard from Buzz, so I needed to check in with him to see if he was ready to finish up the estate matters. I mouthed to B.J., "I'll call you later," over the head of a customer as I left.

Finished by two o'clock, I double checked the package to make sure all the attachments were included, punched in speed dial number four and waited for Ellen to answer. She answered with her usual politeness, and I asked if it would be a good time to bring my stuff by for the sheriff to look over. "Hurry," she replied, "He needs to leave in about forty-five minutes."

"On my way," I said, and grabbed the package and headed out.

When I walked in the door, Ellen caught the phone between her ear and shoulder, kept writing with one hand and pointed with the other for me to go on back. I knocked and heard him call out, "Enter."

He was very pleased with the package, and said, "If this doesn't get the job done I will have to find another way to skin the cat. You finished a full day ahead of my expectations and it is certainly well done. Evidently you got some of your father's writing talent."

"Thanks, Sheriff, such praise means a lot to me."

"Looks like I'll make it to Raleigh a day earlier than expected. Hopefully, Ellen can get the schedule rearranged while I go to my next meeting, and I need to leave now to be on time."

We walked out together and he went straight to Ellen to tell her what needed to be done. I gave her a smile and a little wave as I went out the door.

Next, I called Latham and Latham and listened to the usual spiel. "Brody Edwards calling for Buzz Latham, please."

"Brody, there is no way he can get to you today, but just to let you know, your work is on his desk; he just hasn't had time to double check it and get back with you. I'll try to catch him before I leave and see if Thursday afternoon at three works. Is that good for you?"

"Okay, just let me know."

Stopping at B.J.'s to see if she wanted to do anything tonight, she informed me that tonight was girls' night out. "You are on your own," she said, "And by the way, don't arrive tomorrow until ten minutes after nine. Do you hear me?" She said.

"Yes, dear, but please don't make this into too big a deal."

"I won't, now get out of here. I got things to do." With that she physically turned me toward the door, pushed me in the back and at the same time whispered in my ear, "I love you," swatting me on the behind.

"Wait, you can't possibly expect me to leave with you playing grab-ass and delivering words like that." I grabbed her and lifted her up till her toes just barely touched the floor, and I said, "I love you, too," before I kissed her long and hard. Releasing her slowly, I staggered out the door. Looking across the top of the TR 3, I saw her with her hand over her heart, a big smile and maybe a tear falling from one eye. "How sweet it is."

Private Party with Classmates — Chapter Twenty

Thursday morning, I awoke with a sense of anticipation, jumping out of bed to my habitual routine. Careful with the razor so as not to nick myself, I visualized myself walking into B.J.'s with splotches of toilet paper all over my face to stop the blood flow. That caused me to be even more careful. I spent extra time with the toothbrush, even reached under the sink for the Listerine and gargled. Now for a touch seldom used, I opened the bottle of Aramis, gave it a whiff and poured a smidgen into my hands for application to my face and neck. On to the closet, I inspected again the outfit chosen yesterday evening for my grand entrance. Freshly washed, lightly starched and ironed to perfection, not quite new, boot cut jeans, black nylon tee, just tight enough to have no wrinkles, new, tan ostrich skin cowboy boots, topped by a tan camel hair sports coat. Now fully dressed, I walked to the foyer and stood at the mirror to decide on 'buttoned or unbuttoned.' Decision made, I walked out of the house at nine sharp, knowing that would put me in place at ten minutes after as directed.

"Hey, cool cat."

"Very perceptive, dude."

"Hot to trot."

"Thank you, ma'am."

Reaching for the doorknob I saw a sign taped on the inside that read CLOSED FOR PRIVATE PARTY. The door wasn't locked, and I stepped inside to find the place decorated with our school colors and a crowd of about a dozen people milling around. As soon as they saw me they broke out in song, "For he's a jolly good fellow!"

"Blown away," was all I could think of to say at the moment. Then looking around at the decorations, I said, "Well, it's obvious how girls' night out was spent." Then we all started hugging and exclaiming how well each other looked.

After about ten minutes or so, Barbara Jean turned on the Karaoke system and used the mic to get our attention. "Okay, you all, how about this for a format? Let's give Brody a chance to say a few words; then I will pass the mic around for you to report on classmates who are not here. After that I'll take your orders and serve you. Then Brody can make his way around to each table for a short visit with each of you. I caution you not to dominate his time – even at fifteen minutes per table it will consume an hour's time." She handed me the mic and went to the front door and locked it.

"First, thank you for coming; it is so good to see each of you. How awesome is it to know that everyone still living in the area is here, except Joyce, and we will forgive her, of course, because babies come when babies are ready to come, right?

Next, I don't think I hurt any of you the way I hurt Barbara Jean when I suddenly left town, but I want you to know I've made my apology to her and begged her forgiveness, which she has given; we are reconciled and I am one happy guy. Let me also say that if I have ever done or said anything to offend any of you, please bring it to my attention so that I can try to make amends. I understand that several articles about me have appeared in the Beaufort Observer so I will try to cover just the things they did not or could not have covered.

"Just before I left here, I thought that the loss of a dream of playing in the major leagues was the worst possible thing that could happen. That thinking led me to flee the one place and the people I needed the most; that path also led to despair and ultimately to my becoming a bum, hobo, tramp, whatever you want to call it. I became an alcoholic, often begging for or stealing food or booze. Fortunately, I received a helping hand out of that gutter and ultimately to the Marine Corps to be made into a man again.

"The Marine Corps did its part by giving me dignity and a sense of purpose, and it also proved to me that there are things worse than I had previously experienced. In Afghanistan, these eyes saw things so horrific I do not like to think about them, much less talk about them to anyone. My own close call with death pales in comparison with the disgust I feel at the thought of my killing others." I felt the tears sliding down my cheeks but forced myself to continue. "These experiences resulted in physical and mental injuries. I have recovered nicely from the physical ones, but am still dealing with the mental side of things in the form of post-traumatic stress disorder. PTSD is weird; the symptoms vary from patient to patient. In my case, living the horror again in the form of nightmares is the worst, and that leads to not wanting to sleep. I'm jumpy and easily distracted, and I hear voices talking to me that are so real I often answer them aloud. Actually, that isn't so bad in that those conversations seem to relieve my stress, and I'm sort of enjoying it – almost enjoying it. Finally, I plan on staying here; I've been offered a job with the sheriff's department, if I can meet all the qualification requirements. My application is on the way to Raleigh as we speak, and I would appreciate your thoughts and prayers that everything will go well. Thanks again for coming."

B.J. rushed at me and we embraced, rocking in our accustomed rhythm. She sobbed so silently, I knew it by the shaking of her body rather than by sound. As I looked around, I thought, "There is not a dry eye in the place. I didn't mean for that to happen." I felt her hand slide down my arm, and she took the mic from me and turned to our classmates.

"I think we need to change the order of things slightly so we can all recover from that emotional blockbuster. Brody, maybe you ought to take up public speaking. I'm going to pass an order sheet to each table, and you all put down your names and food order. Brody, you collect them and help me prepare and deliver the food and drinks;

then we can talk about those who are not here. Okay?" Everyone seemed to like that idea and B.J. and I worked as a team to get things rolling.

The rest of the party seemed a blur to me. I guess the emotional blockbuster took its toll. I can only recall a few things that were said. I remember that Curtis Hill had married into money and lived in Greensboro. Esther Lee was teaching school in Bladenboro. Mike Denne had joined the Air Force and was stationed in Japan. Wendell Hatcher was a contractor in Winston Salem. Gary Johnson was an engineer and working in some city way up north somewhere; Larry Schryver, was an assistant golf professional in Williamsburg, Virginia. But there were two events that remained perfectly clear to me.

One, when I sat at the table with my old battery mate, Sam Smith, I kidded him about his lack of the big curl in the front that had given him his nickname, saying, "Well now that you're bald, do they still call you Curly?"

"Oh, yes, at least with you guys. Most of my family call me Sam and some friends call me Smitty, but by and large, I'm still Curly."

"Do you still play any baseball?"

"Kind of hard to play catcher with this." He raised his pant leg and hit my leg with a metal prostheses.

I was totally shocked and said, "I'm sorry, Sam, I had no idea."

"No way for you to know. I've learned to deal with it."

"What happened?"

"Stepped on a land mine in Afghanistan, north of where you were and about a year before your accident."

"Whoa, that is a shocker. But you do seem to handle it well. To tell the truth, I didn't notice a limp or anything."

"I have to admit to a certain pride in not letting it be obvious that I'm handicapped."

"So, what do you do for a living?"

"I am very fortunate. My grandfather, who owned a tire business in Washington, left me an apartment complex that he built and managed in his retirement. It's right across from Beaufort Community College over on Route 264. It keeps me busy, managing it and doing most of the upkeep myself. Drop in and see me when you can."

"I will, Sam, and good luck to you, my friend."

The other standout memorable item was that Johnny McQuaig had gone to some special art school in Los Angeles and had met and married a girl named Carolyn Heisler from there. It seems her family had connections in the film industry, and Johnny had since made a name for himself in Hollywood as a film editor.

The real shocker came when they all left, and before B.J. opened for business. She came to me and said, "Brody it breaks my heart to think that you don't like to sleep because of the nightmares. I want to hold you in my arms, in our bed, so badly, I can hardly stand it."

"I want that, too, but I'm committed to meeting your requirements. Just give me a little more time. I can deal with it. I told her about my three o'clock appointment with Buzz and left for home."

That afternoon I left an hour early and cruised by several used car lots looking at SUVs and minivans. I spied one that caught my interest enough to stop and take a closer look. While walking around it a salesman approached and said, "Hey, you interested in trading that TR 3 in? I could make you a good offer on that baby."

"Ball park the offer if you can. I just might be willing to consider a good offer."

"I think we could easily allow around $35,000 on a trade, maybe more if we get serious, and I have the possibility of moving yours out quickly."

"What about this one? What kind of price do you have on it?"

"Well it's priced at 24K, but I'm not sure it's right for you. It was owned by a salesman here in town, and I know that mechanically it is fine, but the mileage of over 100,000 scares off most people. I think I can find something a bit cheaper and with fewer miles if you give me a chance."

Liking him, I asked for his card, saying, "I have an appointment and will try to get back by later in the day."

At Buzz's office, I was surprised at how many papers I had to sign to get all of Dad's assets changed over to my name. Buzz had an invoice prepared showing his fees for everything – services, filing fees at the courthouse – all laid out for easy comprehension. I signed everything and wrote him a check from my personal account.

When that was taken care of I told him about my conversation at the car lot and how impressed I was that the salesman didn't try to push their vehicle off on me.

"The offer for your Triumph is pretty low in my opinion. I think it should go above $40,000 in the condition it is in. Remember, it is a classic and in certain circumstances could bring even more. To give you an idea of its value, my wife once threatened to run off with your dad just to get to ride in it." We both laughed. "She has a four-year-old, top of the line, Cadillac Escalade that has, last I looked, just over 32,000 miles, probably about 35,000 now. She said to me the other day, 'The kids have flown the coop – what do I need with this big old thing? Why don't you get me a little sporty thing so I can drive around town in the style I deserve?'

"Um, let me see, her birthday is coming up next week, in fact. Brody, I would so much like to surprise her – actually knock her socks off – by giving her the TR 3 she's admired for years. I'm prepared to offer you an even trade. Yes, I will do that, knowing that her car is probably valued at about $5,000 more than yours. You want to think about it?"

"No sir." Pausing for affect, I added, "I want to do it. In fact, I want to knock B.J.'s socks off, too. When she asks, 'What do you want with that big old thing?' I'm going to say, 'To fill it up with our babies.' Man, I like the sound of that."

We talked about making the swap on Wednesday and how he would tell his wife he would take her car that day to get the oil changed. He asked if I knew where the title to the TR 3 was and I assured him I did. In the parking lot, I called Barbara Jean. "Dinner at my house at six – steaks with baked potato and salad – okay?"

"Yes, indeed, that will give me time to clean up and maybe take a twenty-minute nap."

I drove down to Main Street to do my last bit of shopping for the day. About an hour later I made it to Food Lion where I bought butter, sour cream, a nice sirloin weighing l.75 pounds, two very large potatoes, a bag of charcoal, lighter fluid, a box of tinfoil, a bag of salad, and a bottle of red wine.

At home, I washed the potatoes and wrapped them in foil, put items in the refrigerator that needed chilling, but left the steak out to reach room temperature – as Dad had taught me to do – and got down the spice to be used on the meat. Next, I took the charcoal out to the patio and headed to the garage to get Dad's old grill, and pulled it out to the patio. Taking the grill rack inside, I worked on cleaning the gunk and rust off it for about fifteen minutes before giving up and covering it in tinfoil.

At five o'clock I put the potatoes in the oven to begin baking, and started preparing the steak. First, I picked it up and shook it like I had seen my dad do, then felt of it with my fingertips before applying the meat spice. Adding a little salt, I took a regular fork and began puncturing every inch of the meat to work the spice in. Next, I turned on the faucet and used my hands to drip water on the steak to help the spice permeate the meat. I made a mental note of the time to allow thirty minutes before I flipped the steak to prepare the other side. While waiting the required thirty minutes, I used a colander to wash the salad before putting it in a salad bowl, put a fresh stick of butter in the butter dish, sour cream in a small bowl, and set the table. After turning the steak and repeating that very important process, I went out to light the charcoal, now stacked around the grill. Back inside, I checked the pantry to make sure Dad's old apron and chef's hat were handy, then went in and turned on the TV.

Knowing B.J. would be about fifteen minutes late, I watched the first ten minutes of the six o'clock news, then went into the kitchen to check on the potatoes, using an oven mitt to gently squeeze them for firmness. Convinced that they would be just right, I cut off the oven but left them there. Donning my chef's apparel, I grabbed the steak and took it outside to begin cooking. Just as I expected, she came bounding out to the patio at 6:15 and the meat was just about ready to turn.

We kissed and I asked about her day.

"Pretty good. I did have a problem with Mrs. Barnes over the colors on her cake, but other than that it was pretty normal."

"Do you mean my old sixth grade teacher? Is she still alive?"

"Yep, that's her. She was still upset even though I showed her the written order sheet with her initials of approval. If I hadn't started telling her about you, I'm not sure she would have paid me."

"You do not want to cross that woman; she can be tough when she gets riled. Hey, this meat is almost ready. How about you pouring the wine, and I'll be there in a jiffy?"

The meal was great, if I do say so myself. I even enjoyed the cleanup because we worked so well together, and closely, I might add. As we adjourned to the living room, the thought occurred to me that someday my kids might get into my journals. I need to be careful about what I put in here. Umm, better do some editing, too. What a great evening – and I will say that no rules were broken. I drove her home at ten, and after a short and very chaste kiss, watched as she bounded up the steps. On the way home, I thought how difficult it had been to keep from telling her about the car trade I had made. The thought hit me that I couldn't tell her much about the car because I hadn't even seen it.

"What kind of idiot trades for a $40,000 car without even seeing it?"

"He is definitely not as smart as he looks!"

Swapping the Vintage TR 3 for a SUV Chapter Twenty-One

The next morning, I called B.J. to tell her I was doing coffee and toast at home before going to the bank, and to the mall for running shoes. "After that I'm going to look into gym memberships. I really need to work off the effect of all those doughnuts you've been forcing me to eat."

"I hear you. Stop in later if you can."

At the First South Bank, I met the assistant manager who helped me close out Dad's account and transfer the money into my existing account. That didn't take long, so I drove to the mall and caught a sale on a pair of running shoes. The saleslady there advised me to look into Vidant Wellness Center, so I drove over to Cowell Farm Road to check that out. Walking in, I was impressed with the amount of equipment available as well as the cleanliness of the place. Picking up a brochure and noting the operating hours were fifteen hours a day, I told the very physically fit young blonde that I was looking for a 24-hour-a-day operation, as I expected to be working shifts. She advised that I would have to drive to Greenville to find such a place. We went over the costs and I thanked her, saying I might be back.

As an afterthought, I asked, "What about Cypress Landing?"

"Their hours are the same as ours and the prices are much higher."

"Um, well I'll probably be back but need to think about it."

At home, I put on running shorts and my new shoes, topped off with a sleeveless tee shirt, then headed out onto Route 33 and turned west. Deciding to run on the highway rather than go under the bridge and thus have to cross the railroad tracks, I questioned that decision immediately. How can I be gasping for breath after just a few hundred yards, even if going across an overpass? Remembering how long it had been since I did this sort of thing, I took a right onto Cratch Street, named for former mayor, Bill Cratch, who was a good friend of my dad's. Thankfully that street is just a few blocks long, so I made it to the end and turned back for home. Sinking onto that old glider felt so good. I knew at that moment it was necessary for me to get a gym membership immediately and get in some serious work before trying to pass the police physical test. No more searching, I thought; tomorrow morning back to Vidant Wellness Center.

Over the next days I developed a routine of a two-hour workout, including running, weight lifting, sauna and hot tub rotation, and shower. The first week I concentrated on increasing the amount of time I could stay on the machine going at a reasonable trot-like pace, and all weightlifting was restricted to light weights with high count repetitions. The sauna and hot tub got lots of my time. The next week I began to increase my pace and time spent at running, changing the lifting routine to fewer reps with more weight. It was grueling, but later I would find it rewarding.

Wednesday, October third: I called B.J. to tell her I had already had toast and coffee and to give her my schedule for the day, finishing up with, "How about we drive over to Greenville tonight for some barbeque?"

"Sounds good to me."

"Okay, see you at 5:45. Can you be ready by then?"

"Yes, that's fine."

After my workout, I called Latham and Latham to check for a time to make the trade, and was informed that he had me in his appointment book for 3 PM. On to Chocowinity, where I filled the TR 3 with gas and went to Simon's Mini Mart for lunch. He was not there, so I got a Pepsi and an egg salad sandwich with a candy bar and headed toward Blounts Creek. My intent was to air out the TR 3 for the last time and to reminisce. I had finished the sandwich by the time I made my first stop at Cotton Patch Landing. Parking the car, I took the candy bar and can of Pepsi with me and gazed out over the creek, thinking of the many good times I had there. How long that took, I'm not sure, I just realized that I was holding an empty can and wrapper and decided it was time to go.

Putting the empties into a nearby trash can, I checked my watch and knew it was time for my next stop. Back out to Route 33 I turned left to reach our old farm. Driving slowly by the house, it looked as if no one was there, so I pulled into the yard and got out of the car. I leaned against the front fender and looked around, thinking how differently the place looked from my memories. As I gazed out over the field, two memories flashed to mind. One was of this huge albino stag that came out of the woods almost every evening. His routine was so regular that Dad and I would sit on the back steps waiting for him to appear. He seemed as interested in us as we were in him. As long as we could keep the dog quiet he would just stand there gazing at us, and if she started barking, he would saunter into the woods, usually turning just enough to give us a last look. That was a magnificent sight. The second memory was from when I was five or six. I was playing in that very field, watching Sam Nick strategically place fertilizer bags for refilling the distributer, when I looked up to see a black snake about thirty yards away. It was as if we were both puppets – I raised my head to see him, he raised his head to see me. I stood up, he raised up higher. I backed up, he came forward. I backed up faster, he increased his speed. I tried to run but could not. I tried to yell for Sam Nick but nothing came out. Suddenly Sam Nick jumped out of the cart and ran at that snake. The snake rose up even higher and raced away towards the woods. Sam Nick came back and explained that the snake was called a Black Racer and that it was really harmless, just feisty in the springtime. He was special to me before that but I was his shadow for a long time after that. I wondered what ever happened to him.

Heading back to town at a clip well above the speed limit, the thought hit me that it would not look good to have a speeding ticket on file when trying to become a member of the police force. I immediately dropped the speed down to 55, and in less than a mile passed by a deputy aiming a radar gun at me.

"Thank you, Lord!"

"Amen."

Pulling into the parking lot behind Latham and Latham, I saw Buzz heading my way pointing a key remote at two spaces over. I looked to see a white SUV that had obviously been detailed. The tires were shining, and when he opened the doors I saw that it was spotlessly clean. As I rubbed my hands over the tan leather seats, he explained that they were heated as well as air conditioned in the front. He popped the hood and we walked around to the front. I pretended I knew what I was looking at. I did identify the oil stick as well as a few other things, but I'm not mechanically inclined. "It looks brand new," was all I could think to say. He pushed another button and the engine fired up. Slamming the hood, he walked me back to the driver's side and said, "Do you want to take it for a spin?"

I checked the mileage and saw that it registered at 34,875. "No, let's get the deal done."

Buzz said, "Hand me that bow off the other seat," and I did. Tossing it into the TR 3, he pulled out his cell phone, dialed a number and said, "Joe, please send someone over to get the Triumph ready." He listened for a few seconds and then said, "Joe, that car will be ready and I will drive into my driveway by 6 PM with that bow firmly attached to the hood. I don't care how many people you have to use to get the job done. Do you understand?" Evidently satisfied, he hung up and we went inside to complete the deal.

Driving home I determined not to look toward Ye Olde Sweet Shoppe in case B.J. was looking out the window. Pulling in front of my double garage door, I got out and opened the door with the key pad, got the step ladder to reach the appropriate program button and went back to the Cadillac to hold the first button on the mirror so as to record the code sequence into the car. Testing it successfully, I put the car in and noticed that the car and the cub cadet pretty much took up the whole area. Um, I liked the look.

I turned on the TV to watch the first ten minutes or so of the evening news before getting ready. After shaving and showering, I chose black dress pants with a white shirt – no tie – to go with my new boots and tan sport coat. At exactly 5:45 I pulled behind B.J.'s apartment, and she was down the steps by the time I opened the car door.

"What are you doing driving Chris Latham's car?"

"How do you know it's hers?"

"I can see the MADD sticker on the back window and I recognize the license number."

"It will have a different license plate tomorrow, because I just traded the Triumph for this beauty."

"No way!"

"Yes, way!"

I led her around to the front door and held it open as she stepped up to place her knee on the seat and look around. I went back to my side and stuck my head in to better watch her. She was obviously pleased with the car but there was a questioning look on her face. Finally, she said, "What in the world do you want with such a big car?"

"I hope to fill it up with our babies as soon as possible."

She had both knees on the seat, then she settled her butt back on her heels, beginning to pale and get excited, "Brody, are you. . . ?

Reaching into my coat pocket, I pulled out the little black box and flipped it open so she could see the ring. "Yes, I am asking you to marry me."

"Yes, oh, yes. I can't believe it – I have waited so long."

I could see her countenance slowly change and I knew what she was thinking, so I said, "As soon as the first condition is met."

"Oh, Brody!" She reached across that console and started pecking me with kisses all over my face. I didn't object.

"Ready to go?"

"Yes, sir."

As she reached for her seat belt, I said, "Wait, I want to show you something." I started the engine, turned on the AC and hit the button for the front seats. She reacted by raising up off the seat and pulling her dress out from under her, saying, "That feels so good."

"It looks good, too," I said as I gawked at those bikini panties.

She turned a little red but said, "This," showing me the ring, "allows you to look but not touch."

We buckled up and headed for Parker's in Greenville. Every few minutes she would hold up her hand to look at the ring. The second time she uttered, "It is so perfect." The third time she began to cry. By that time, we were in the small community of Grimesland. I found a parking place and took her face in my hands.

"Are you okay?"

"Yes, in fact, never better. These are tears of joy, I assure you."

With that I continued toward Greenville. Pulling into the parking lot, I found it full, as it usually is, and thought it rather amazing that folks around these parts think nothing of driving sixty to ninety miles for a good barbeque meal. During our meal, I couldn't help but notice how it seemed impossible for her to keep her left hand in her lap as she constantly played with the silverware or her hair. Knowing that she was proud of her ring really made me glad I had gone for the larger stone. It was a lovely evening in every way!

Swearing in Ceremony — Chapter Twenty-Two

My phone rang and it was the sheriff. "Good news," I heard him say. "I just got a call from Raleigh telling me that you've been approved, so watch your email and mailbox for the official notification."

"Wow!"

"You bet. I assume you have gone online to view the BLET application process."

"Yes, sir, I have."

"Do you have your college transcript?"

"Yes, sir. Any idea how long that approval process will take?"

"It usually takes just a few days to get acceptance into the program. It may take longer to determine how many credits they will give you based on your previous college work."

The email stating that I had met the state requirements to enter the BLET program came the next day. My acceptance into the program took only three days, and they stated an intent to finish evaluating my transcript within the week. So, I forwarded that email to Sheriff Marslender with the question, "What next, coach?"

Minutes later he replied. "POPAT scheduled 10/22 at 10:00. Written exam 10/26 at 0900, will call you soon. Chaos here."

Taking the physical cannot be classified as a piece of cake, because I remember thinking how glad I was that I had worked out diligently the past month. The same could be said for the written exam which certainly wasn't easy, but any reasonably well-educated person could pass it. I did.

Finally, the long-awaited day arrived. I was sworn in as a Deputy Sheriff of Beaufort County, North Carolina, by the sheriff himself. I was a happy guy. I remember a smattering of applause and the sheriff saying, "Let's get to work. Brody, this is Sergeant Donnie Gurganus. He will be your mentor, and you will become his shadow until further notice." Looking at me intently, he nodded toward Donnie and said, "He's the best I have, so listen to him carefully. Learn to trust him, and earn his trust. Hopefully, I will one day see him in my place and you in his."

After the sheriff went to his office, Sgt. Gurganus took me back to the conference room, explaining that there was very little private office space to be had. "I do have a small office across from the sheriff, but that's being used for a private meeting this morning. One of the first things you'll need to do is check the schedule for use of this room and be prepared to get your materials together and find another spot to work on short notice." He handed me two cards. "These are Miranda Rights cards. There are replacement cards in most rooms if you need them. Let me stress that you must have at least one of these in your possession at all times, so put one in your wallet and have the other laminated and keep it where you can get to it quickly and easily. Shortly, I'll take you around to show the entire operation and introduce you to fellow workers. That may well take most of the day, but I want you to direct your attention to those two notebooks on the table. They're to be your focus until further notice. It is essential that you absorb the materials in those. You will not go out on patrol until I'm convinced you know what is in those manuals; that is, other than as a ride along, which I will see that you get as part of your training. Law enforcement has a jargon of its own just as you had in the military. Ours is primarily expressed in numbers rather than words. For instance, if I come on your radio with, 'Edwards, what's your 10-20?' or sometimes we simply say, 'what's your 20,' that means I need to know your location, and I don't have time for you to look up the code or question me as to what I mean. Now, you will see that I've taken the time to highlight the more frequently used codes. You'll be quizzed on those as we go. It will probably take a month or more to get you into your own cruiser. Any questions?" I shook my head to say no. "Then let's go meet your support."

Looking back at my journals months later, I remember thinking how little I had written about this period, but then I also remembered the long hours at the Police Academy, the hours of commuting and the study time devoted to the learning process, and how tired I was when I got home. I had, however, recorded my first pull-over. I was pulling a night shift and saw a vehicle with only one working tail light, so I made the stop. Calling in the license number, I approached the car, knowing who would be the likely driver. Sure, enough there were two black teenagers in the car, and the passenger was acting very nervous, so I asked, "Why are you so nervous? Have you done something wrong?" The driver answered for him, "No, sir, he's been with me all evening. He's just acting the fool, been listening to those stories going around about police killing unarmed black men."

"Guys, you have nothing to fear from me, in fact, I'm not even going to issue a warning ticket because I know I can depend on C.J. to get that tail light fixed tomorrow."

"Yes, sir. You can bet I'll be at Auto Zone when they open. But how do you know me?"

"Your brother, Joe, and I are friends, and he's been bragging on you, C.J. I look forward to seeing you pitch this next season."

"Thank you, sir."

I started to leave but felt a strong urge to say more about the issue that was obviously bothering them, so I leaned down for a direct and personal look at them both and said, "I know the issue of police being accused of killing unarmed blacks is a hot issue right now, and believe me it has my attention. I also want to make sure you know that I am concerned enough to have thoroughly researched the issue. Last night as I went from site to site on the internet, I found this statement, 'A police officer is 18.5 times more likely to be killed by a black person than an unarmed black person is to be killed by a policeman.' So, I guess each of us have reasons to be nervous, depending upon our focus." I remember patting the top of the car and wishing them a pleasant evening.

Months later, I placed a handwritten note in the journal saying, "Wish I had been saved at the time and had the forethought to tell them, we should all exercise our faith and trust God to do what He said He would do, in Romans 8:28. "Work all things together for good for those who love Him and serve Him."

Brody's First Time in Church — Chapter Twenty-Three

December 15, 2012, I worked evenings, but as usual, I texted B.J. when I was on the way home. "You awake?"

"Yep, just waiting for you to check in," she replied.

"Can I stop by for a goodnight kiss?"

"You bet."

As soon as I stopped the cruiser at her back steps, she came flying down to jump into my arms. Even in that big old bathrobe, flannel pajamas and bunny slippers, she looked good to me. After the sweetest of kisses, I said, "Holding you like this takes away the stress of the day. I love you so much."

"I love you, too, Brody, even with that old Kevlar vest between us."

"It's cold out here and you need to get up to bed, but I need to know if you think it okay for me to wear my uniform to church tomorrow, as I have to report in by two."

"Why of course, that's acceptable. Where are you planning on going?"

"With you and Aunt Hannah, of course. What time should we leave?"

"Service starts at 10:45, but Aunt Hannah likes to be there by no later than 10:30, so I usually arrive at her house by 10:00."

"Okay, I'll pick her up then come get you on the way."

"Sounds good," she said, and ran up the steps. After she was inside I thought I heard something like a, "Whoopee!" come wafting down toward me.

The next morning, I picked up Aunt Hannah right on time. When she showed no surprise at seeing me, I knew the two of them had been on the phone all morning. By now the Pastor, Joe and Tillie, and maybe half the elders and deacons would know I was coming. Barbara Jean was waiting as we pulled up, and I was barely stopped before she was in the front seat and leaning in for her kiss. Walking into the church at 10:25, guess who just happened to be standing in the foyer to greet us. Joe and Tillie gave us a quick hug and warm handshake, respectively. I whispered to B.J., "Where do you want to sit?"

"Aunt Hannah always sits on the front pew; the roof might cave in if she doesn't, so she claims. You will, of course, sit between us."

"Yes, ma'am."

At exactly 10:45 the worship leader began the service with a solo of "Amazing Grace," and on the second verse, the singer motioned us to stand and join in. I looked around the church to find the place packed, and saw that most people had at least one hand raised; heads were tilted toward heaven and bodies were swaying in rhythm with the music. The sound was awesome, and somewhere not far behind me was a bass voice that belonged on Broadway. The music was designed to segue from song to song so that the instruments never ceased playing. I was enraptured.

At exactly eleven o'clock the music stopped and the Reverend David O. Cooke took his place at the podium. Dressed in a black suit, a medium blue shirt, a yellow and black necktie with matching hankie in the front coat pocket, to say he was an impressive figure would be an understatement.

"Good Morning, saints and sinners," he said loudly as he positioned his Bible on the pulpit. A chorus of 'good mornings' rebounded from the audience. As his eyes scanned the audience, he evidently saw something in the balcony he didn't like because he said, "Young people, I can see those cell phone lights, so turn them off now. If I have to come up there I will squash you like a bug." Next, he looked directly at me and said, "Well I see we're making progress around here; two white faces rather than the usual one. Brody, don't be embarrassed, please stand up so the people can see you better. Folks, I am pleased to introduce Deputy Sheriff Brody Edwards. Not only is he our local hero, having been nominated for the Congressional Medal of Honor, he's also recently betrothed to our very own angel, Miss Barbara Jean Woolard."

I took my seat, basking in the warm applause they gave. Aunt Hannah rose to her feet, and the pastor asked if she had something she would like to say.

"Yes, Pastor, I do." Grabbing my arm to make me stand with her, she turned us to face the audience. "See this man? This is my boy. I know he doesn't look like me, he doesn't even have the same color skin, but this is my boy," patting my chest. "I'm the closest thing he has ever known as a momma, and he's the closest thing I have ever known as a son. Now what I want you all to know is, if anybody hurts my boy," she shook her head and her finger back and forth, "If anybody hurts this boy, well let me put it like this: I might not be able to squash you like a bug, and I might not be able to chase you, but I can still shoot!"

The church broke out in laughter and applause along with a chorus of comments. "Tell it Aunt Hannah, I hear you, yes ma'am, go on now, ain't nobody gonna mess with you Brody, uh-uh, no way."

The pastor finally had to raise his hands and motion the flock into silence. "We are living in perilous times today. I'm so concerned for our community. There are influences out there who are trying to stir up trouble among us, and some are using hate and lies to try to keep us from doing the very things that Jesus directed us to do: to love one another. We need wisdom to help us find our way. That's why I've chosen to let most of my message today be the very Word of God. I will, of course, try to expound upon it to some degree. What preacher could resist? So today for the first time, I will be using one of the newer translations called The Message."

He began reading Proverbs, Chapter One.

"These are the wise sayings of Solomon, David's son, Israel's King –

"Written down so we'll know how to live well and right, to understand what life means and where it's going; a manual for living, for learning what's right and just and fair; to teach the inexperienced the ropes and give our young people a grasp on reality.

"There's something here also for seasoned men and women, still a thing or two for the experienced to learn—

"Fresh wisdom to probe and penetrate the rhymes and reasons of wise men and women.

"Start with God—the first step in learning is bowing down to God; only fools thumb their noses at such wisdom and learning.

"Pay close attention, friend, to what your father tells you; never forget what you learned at your mother's knee.

"Wear their counsel like flowers in your hair, like rings on your fingers.

"Dear friend, if bad companions tempt you, don't go along with them.

"If they say, 'Let's go out and raise some hell. Let's beat up some old man, mug some old woman. Let's pick them clean and get them ready for their funerals.

'We'll load up on top-quality loot. We'll haul it home by the truckload.

'Join us for the time of your life! With us, it's share and share alike!'

"Oh, friend, don't give them a second look; don't listen to them for a minute.

"They're racing to a very bad end, hurrying to ruin everything they lay their hands on. Nobody robs a bank with everyone watching. Yet that's what these people are doing—they're doing themselves in.

"When you grab all you can get, that's what happens; the more you get, the less you are.

"Lady Wisdom goes out in the street and shouts. At the town center, she makes her speech. In the middle of the traffic she takes her stand. At the busiest corner, she calls out: Simpletons! How long will you wallow in ignorance? Cynics! How long will you feed your cynicism? Idiots! How long will you refuse to learn? About face! I can revise your life. Look, I'm ready to tell you all I know. As it is, I've called, but you've turned a deaf ear; I've reached out to you, but you've ignored me.

"Since you laugh at my counsel and make a joke of my advice. How can I take you seriously? I'll turn the tables and joke about your troubles!

"What if the roof falls in, and your whole life goes to pieces?

"What if catastrophe strikes and there's nothing to show for your life but rubble and ashes? You'll need me then. You'll call on me, but don't expect an answer. No matter how hard you look, you won't find me.

"Because you hated knowledge and had nothing to do with the Fear of God. Because you wouldn't take my advice and brushed aside all my efforts to train you. Well, you've made your bed—now lie in it; you wanted your own way—now, how do you like it?

"Don't you see what happens, you simpletons, you idiots? Carelessness kills, complacency is murder.

"First, pay attention to me, and then relax. Now you can take it easy—you're in good hands."

Then he began his sermon: "If you think you're in good hands with Allstate Insurance, wait until you're securely in the hands of God!" If he had notes, it was not obvious. He spoke with authority, constantly looking from one side of the auditorium to the other. It was as if we were mesmerized; he had our complete attention.

His major points were:

- The first thing I want you to see is that God tells us in Proverbs that this book was written so that we can attain wisdom, discipline, understanding and insight. This is not ordinary wisdom; it is the wisdom of God Himself.
- Next, we see that the wisdom of God is attainable, all we have to do is read His Word to find it or to pray to Him and ask for it. This simple yet powerful truth means that God is not some distant god who wants us to fear him without knowledge or expects us to stumble through life without a clue. No, God is a loving, caring, sharing Father who has given us guidance and wisdom to live a full life.
- The Bible is not a textbook to study; it is a life book to live! In it we have access to His Word and to the author Himself. Each of us needs to be in the Word every day, not just on Sunday, but every day.
- Thy Word is a lamp unto my feet, a light unto my path. Psalm 119:105. We need wisdom folks, not emotional feelings but a wisdom that is sanctified common sense. Listen to God, not to those out there who want you to hate and do evil things that will lead to imprisonment and maybe even to death.
- The most important task we face in this life is to find, follow and claim His plan of redemption as our own.

"May God, bless you and keep you until you have done so. Amen."

Solving my First Big Case — Chapter Twenty-Four

I must admit that my first six weeks on the job were much more exciting, rewarding and yes, more tiring than I had expected. The hours of poring through the manuals, answering the sergeant's constant queries and trying to pick the brains of everyone I came in contact with seemed to spur me on rather than to drag me down. I suppose the fact that both the sheriff and the sergeant were generous with their praise had a great deal to do with my enthusiasm and thus my progress. I must give B.J. credit as well – she was totally understanding of the extra time I wanted to spend in learning and doing research. It didn't take long for me to realize what a valuable resource we had in Ellen Buck; she was the most knowledgeable resource on the computer and filing systems. I learned so much from her and will always be grateful for her patience and willingness to share her knowledge.

I suppose it's natural for anyone to remember the first time they experience bloody activity, danger and death on the job; in my case, it's nice to be adding editorial comments like, it was not my blood, danger or death that I'm reporting to you.

I was in the office turning in some written reports when I heard dispatch take a call from a lady who identified herself as Wanda Alligood. "Someone has broken into my house," she said.

That got my attention and I strolled back toward the communications center to get a better feel for what was going on.

The dispatcher said, "You are about two miles north of Old Ford on the right, is that correct?"

"Yes, sir."

"Okay, ma'am, stay in the car, lock your doors or go to a neighbor's house until I can get a unit out there."

He called for a 20 on Unit 37. Calvin Thompson responded, "Cruising north on 17 coming into Old Ford." He was given the address and, then dispatch called Mrs. Alligood back to advise an ETA of three minutes or less.

Calvin arrived at 10:26 and checked the house to make sure the intruder was not present. He then called the owner in to assess the situation. She immediately noted that some jewelry was missing and she thought that some of her husband's clothing was missing from his closet. At that point Calvin remembered that as he was coming to the scene he had passed a man carrying a large plastic bag. Asking her to stay outside and wait for the evidence collecting team to arrive, he called in that he was cruising back toward town to try and find the man he had seen earlier. At that point, I finished my work as soon as I could and decided to ride out that way.

At 11:02, Unit 37 reported the suspect in sight, walking south on US 17. Calvin pulled the cruiser over in front of the man and got out with his hand on his pistol. The man put the bag down, raised his hands and said, "I'm not armed."

Calvin asked, "What is in the bag?"

"Just some clothes I'm taking to the laundromat to wash."

Calvin had the man come to the trunk of the cruiser and take a stance for a pat down.

After a thorough check satisfied him that the man was not armed, Calvin went back to the bag and opened it to find a man's suit on top. "This needs to be dry-cleaned not washed," he remarked.

He asked the man for some identification and was told he had left his wallet at home. "Okay, just give me your name and address."

The man refused to do so. With that, Calvin took him to the front of the car so the camera could pick up the arrest and the reading of Miranda Rights.

At 11:18, Unit 37 reported that he was transporting to the jail an unidentified black male, estimated to be about forty years old, 6' 3", and about 175 pounds. Calvin made two critical mistakes in that he handcuffed the man with his hands in front of his body rather than behind him, and he placed him in the front seat of the cruiser rather than the rear.

As they approached the city limits, the suspect grabbed the steering wheel and pulled the car into the ditch. Calvin slammed on the brakes but could not avoid the crash. The suspect grabbed Calvin's pistol, and they began a wrestling match for control of the weapon. Merle Morris, the owner of the restaurant across the street heard the crash and came outside to investigate, and he heard Calvin yell for help. Rushing to the car, Merle opened the door, leaned across Calvin and began choking the suspect. Calvin reported later that the suspect's eyes rolled back into his head and only the whites of his eyes were visible; Calvin felt sure the yet-to-be identified man would pass out momentarily. But, with an amazing last-minute surge of strength, the suspect wrenched the weapon from Calvin's hand and shot Merle in the chest. The restaurant owner backed out of the car and started walking back to his place of business while Calvin and the suspect rolled out of the car on opposite sides.

I pulled into the restaurant parking lot to see Merle walking toward his wife with blood spurting about two feet in front of him with every heartbeat. I yelled into my mic, "Get an ambulance out here now!" I ran to grab the towel from his wife and began applying pressure to the wound. Dispatch must have already sent the ambulance because one arrived in just a minute or two.

Meanwhile the suspect, having shot at Calvin twice, decided to run for it as the highway was now jammed with cars. An off-duty ABC officer opened his trunk and threw a 30-30 rifle to Calvin, who shot the running suspect when he failed to obey his command to stop. The bullet hit the man's spine and some other vital organs, and he was pronounced dead on the scene.

Three weeks later I was delighted to report that Merle Morris survived and was pictured in the local paper leaving the hospital. The doctor reported that he believed Mr. Morris survived because he had an expensive fountain pen in his front shirt pocket. That pen had an aluminum casing to hold the ink bladder, and it must have put just enough spin on the bullet to cause it to miss the heart and only cut an artery before passing out his back. The Fraternal Order of Police later awarded Merle Morris the state's highest award for his action in assisting us.

In my second month, I began to use extra hours, unpaid I might add, to go through robbery cases over the past two years. I took extensive notes from each case and used those notes to create a matrix in which to classify all aspects of each case. The largest category of physical sites included small businesses like 7-Eleven, mini-marts and mom and pop groceries. As anyone would expect, cash was the number one target; it was involved in every case.

I was, however, surprised to find that in most of the cases there were large quantities of cigarettes taken. I kept digging and found that in every case where the robbery was not captured on surveillance cameras, an anonymous tip was given to the same deputy in our department. The tips all pointed to young black men, most of whom were ultimately convicted, largely on circumstantial evidence. The puzzling thing to me was that the deputy was also black. I remembered Aunt Hannah had said on several occasions, "If you can't believe or prove what is being said about somebody, look closely at the finger pointer." I determined then and there to do that.

Looking into anyone's personnel file is not an easy matter, so I'll not go into how I obtained the information; but I did find that Calvin Thompson had been on the force for four years and had one letter of commendation for having identified a number of suspects which led to their convictions. There was also one letter of reprimand for sleeping in his cruiser while on duty. I made a mental note to get Aunt Hannah's take on him.

The more I pored over my notes and pondered the data, the more important the cigarettes seemed to be. Checking statistics online, I found the percentages of young people who smoke were declining year to year even in tobacco-producing states like North Carolina. The speculation for the decline involved a better-informed populace on health issues, cancer etc., and the increase of e-cigarette usage. I concluded that cigarettes were being used as cash equivalents to buy drugs, which meant the cigarettes had to be shipped north where they would bring a much higher price than they would in North Carolina. A plan slowly evolved.

I called Joe Cooke and told him what I'd been doing, explaining that I believed cigarettes were being fenced for cash, and the cash was probably being used to buy drugs.

"Makes sense to me. Now what are you going to do?"

"No, now what are we going to do?"

"We?"

"Yes, we. I think you can help by putting the word out around school that I need the name of the fence who's paying cash for cigarettes. Make sure they understand there will be no retribution. It can't be traced back to them because you will not reveal your source to me."

"Okay, I'll get right on it. By the way, Tillie wants to have you two over for dinner soon, so talk to B.J. and get back to us with a good night for you."

"Okay, Joe, and thanks for your willingness to help."

Three days later, Joe called me to say, "I think the man you want is named Clarence Mills, but everybody calls him Squirrely."

"Wow! That was quicker than I expected. Any other info or description?"

"Yes. Here's the way he was described to me. 'Find a white dude who dresses and acts like he's black, and you'll have Squirrely.' He even lives in the hood, I was told."

"Thanks, Joe, this is huge. I'll keep you posted."

Of course, Squirrely had a record, having done time for breaking and entering. He got lucky and was released with only half the time served, due to crowded conditions and good behavior. The file contained mug shots and other photos that confirmed the description Joe had given me: Baseball cap with flat brim worn tilted up and cocked sideways; baggy pants that looked ready to fall off his butt at any minute; long wallet chained to his belt loop; tattooed fingers and arms.

I found the closest truck rental agencies to his residence and went through their records, finding that he had rented working vans on four occasions during the past six months. In every instance, the van was rented around mid-month and returned with just over eleven hundred miles of usage. The mileage checked with my suspicion of New York being the destination for the contraband.

Convinced I had the right man and that he'd be making another trip soon, I went to the sheriff. He was impressed with my methods, especially my matrix, and was very complimentary of the quantity and quality of my work. "This is your baby," he said, and placed me on special assignment to follow up on this case exclusively. Picking up the phone, he called the Washington Chief of Police and requested surveillance on Squirrely's residence for the next few mornings, giving instructions to call my cell number if a van or truck was on the scene. Based on my suspicion that a member of our department might be involved, we agreed that only Sgt. Gurganus would be advised of the plan and my special assignment.

Two days later, as I was having my breakfast at B.J.'s, my phone rang. It was from Officer Bill Dean, who was the surveillance man on Squirrely.

"We have a white Ford van being loaded from a shed in back as we speak."

"Are you getting it on video?"

"Yes, I have good footage of him putting boxes into the rear of the van."

"What about the license plate on the van?"

"No, it's parked side view now but I'll get it as he drives out of the driveway."

"Any sign of assistance in loading, or has he had any visitors?"

"No sir, but I'll keep watch and call you as soon as he leaves the property."

"Good job. I should be in place within ten minutes."

I had just turned off the engine on the cruiser when he called me back. "Okay, he's pulling out of the driveway now, and I have a good shot of the license plate and of him driving the van. Wait a minute, he's parking the van on the street and getting out. Um, checking his watch – he's obviously expecting someone to meet him. Oh, boy, I'm not sure if you're going to like this, but one of your cruisers just pulled up."

"Is it Calvin Thompson?"

"It's him. Is that the visitor you expected?"

"Yep! Make sure you get a good shot of anything he adds to the load."

"Okay, he's getting a box off the back seat, handing it to Squirrely . . . now another box . . . closing the cruiser door . . . taking the box to the van, and he's putting this one in himself. Got it all on record." A pause, then, "Thompson is leaving, and Squirrely is rolling your way."

"Good work, Dean. Now if you get that footage downloaded to the sheriff ASAP, I'll make sure he gets a letter of appreciation to the chief in the next few days."

Within minutes I saw the van pass, and I allowed several cars to go by before I pulled out. Thinking he might still have another stop or rendezvous to make, I visualized the best place between there and the Martin County Line to make the stop. In the next few miles it was obvious he was going to obey the speed limit, and I thought, "Maybe he is smarter than he looks." Reaching the community of Old Ford, I hit my lights and siren, and Squirrely pulled into the church parking lot, just as I had hoped he would.

At the van, I saw he'd rolled down the window, so I asked him to step out of the vehicle. He did, and when he saw my right hand on my pistol, he quickly added, "I'm not armed."

"Good, but I have to make sure." I took him to the front of the van, had him do a spread with hands on the hood while I patted him down. "Keep that stance," I told him, "while I look inside the van."

I found an open box on the passenger seat with snacks, a couple of Mountain Dews, a couple of wrapped sandwiches and I could see several cartons of cigarettes on the bottom of the box. Knowing I had enough to make an arrest, I called Sheriff Marslender. He advised that I make sure the dash cam on the cruiser captures both the arrest and my reading him his rights.

He also said, "I have a tow truck dispatched. You get Squirrely in here as soon as the tow truck gets there."

Under interrogation and when informed that we had an iron-clad case against him, he was still somewhat cocky until we revealed the sentencing guidelines for his charges. The fine of $5,000.00 didn't have much impact, but when he heard the five-year imprisonment part he immediately started pleading for a deal.

"What do you have to offer?"

"I can give you the sources where I got the stuff."

"Not good enough. Most of them are petty crooks that we'll get eventually anyway."

"What about if one of them works for you?"

"We already have him on camera delivering goods to you. He's going to get his due justice no matter what happens to you."

It became obvious that Squirrely was wrestling within himself as to what to do next. It must be big, I thought. We remained silent to let him stew on it. Finally, he said, "What if I could give you the biggest drug dealer in the area?"

The sheriff said, "Now you have my full attention! But you need to understand this: I would not let you off scot-free even if I could. You're going to do time for this; the only question is how much time. The one thing I feel confident I can deliver on is making sure Judge Martin Luther Crabtree is not assigned to your trial. You know he is extremely tough on cases like yours, and I'm confident you would receive the maximum sentence if he presides. As for the other judges, I may not be able to get the exact one most likely to be lenient, but I know I can help you there. I'll meet with the DA and get him to intercede for leniency, and even testify for that in court if necessary. My best guess is we can save you two years, maybe even three years of prison time."

He looked at the back of his hands and exclaimed, "For two or three years of freedom, I'm willing to make the deal. Is this being recorded?"

"Yes, of course."

"Will you agree to give my lawyer a copy of the recording?"

"Yes, I will."

"Okay, then, as soon as I'm given the lesser sentence, I'll give you the information."

"No deal. It must be like this: I give your lawyer the tape of our deal, and as soon as he reviews it, you give me the information; if it checks out you get my part of the deal. No compromise. Take it or leave it."

I am totally impressed with the sheriff; he is one shrewd dude.

POTUS Disapproves CMOH — Chapter Twenty-Five

Several days later Right Arm called to advise that a Sgt. Major Owens from Marine Corps Headquarters was on the line. "Do you want me to transfer the call to your cell?"

"Yes, please do."

I answered the phone to hear, "Hello Brody, this is Sergeant Major Charlie Owens. I doubt you remember me, but I was at the hospital for the reading of your citation several months back."

"I do remember you. In fact, I did a little day dreaming about one day being your replacement up on the hill."

"I'm flattered, but I might as well get on with the reason for my call. It is my unfortunate duty to advise you that the President has declined to sign off on your Congressional Medal of Honor award. He sent word in this morning stating that he had information that the kill count was not confirmable and the photo showed no evidence of gunshot wounds. The individuals could have been killed by lightning for all he knows. Therefore, he concluded that a lesser award was in order. This information will be released on the evening news. Just wanted to give you a heads-up and advise you personally that the General has said that the Navy Cross is a cinch."

I thanked him and said I was not at all disappointed. "In fact, it may be a relief to be out of public attention."

"I doubt that, son, but good luck."

After we hung up, I called Barbara Jean to give her the news and asked her to call Aunt Hannah, because I needed to get on the road. She said, "You better let the sheriff know, because that place may be crawling with reporters soon!"

"Good idea, Sweetie. See you tonight."

When I advised Right Arm of what had happened, she said, "I better put you through to Sheriff Marslender. He will definitely have some questions."

I did my best to relate the information as I had received it. His response was, "How are you taking it, son?"

"I'm not at all bitter or even disappointed," I said. "In fact, maybe even relieved to have it behind me. The only thing that bothers me about it is where did he get his information?"

"You mean, did he get input from Afghanistan?"

"Yes. That bugs me a little."

"Be careful with that, Brody."

"Yes, sir, I will. You might warn everyone that we may be in the news for a few days."

"Brody, I want you to go home to B.J. and Aunt Hannah and lay low for the rest of the day."

"Thank you, sir. I think that's a good idea."

I headed for my house with the intention of getting out of uniform in order to better feel my honey's presence in my arms, and was surprised to find Aunt Hannah sitting on the glider, doing her usual swing AKA nap. I was tempted to hit the siren but resisted. I got out as quietly as possible, and I almost made it to the porch before she opened her eyes and said, "Come here, my boy." I did so gladly and sat down with my arm around her shoulder. She patted my knee and picked up the pace of the glider. "How you feel about all this, Brody?"

"I'm at peace with it. I never thought I deserved such a high honor anyway. In fact, I'm sort of pleased that he turned down the award. This celebrity status is not all folks make it out to be. I hate it when people stare at me or come up to me as if I were their own personal hero. Don't you worry about me, okay?"

"All right, I'll amble on home to finish my nap. I assume you'll be heading to B.J.'s."

"Yes, ma'am, as soon as I change out of this uniform."

At Ye Olde Sweet Shoppe, I marveled once again how much better everything seemed when B.J. and I were holding fast to one another. When I had accepted the sheriff's offer of time off, I thought disappointment might arise, but I was wrong. Holding her, sensing her love for me, taking in her smell, her touch, made me feel more important than any medal ever could. I don't know how long the magic moment lasted but I do remember being thankful that no customers arrived for a long time.

Finally, she said, "I have some work to get done. Why don't you go upstairs and take a nap? I'll order dinner in and we can watch the news here – in case some reporter has been given an early scoop and is hanging out at your house."

"Um, sounds good to me."

"Chinese or pizza?"

"Either, your choice. Surprise me."

She led me over to the inside steps up to her apartment. "The couch is very comfortable. Use it. Stay out of my bedroom and no looking in my underwear drawer."

"Yes, ma'am."

I awoke at 5:15 according to the clock on the wall, and smelled pizza. I looked over my shoulder and saw B.J. pouring Pepsi from a two-liter bottle. The woman knows me. I have to have Pepsi with pizza, milk with peanut butter and jelly sandwiches, and iced tea with BLT's. When I got up, she said, "Let's eat, then catch the six o'clock news." That's the way we did it.

As expected, all the major news services reported that POTUS had turned down the award. None of them made a big deal out of it but one reporter did mention the fact that I was on medical disability retirement from the Marine Corps; his contact in the Marine Corps Headquarters had indicated that I would likely be granted the Navy Cross, the next highest award. Someone called B.J. to tell her that the channel they watched reported that I was now employed as a deputy sheriff in Beaufort County, North Carolina.

The ten o'clock news brought more coverage, and of course, several anchors filled airtime speculating the reasons for the turndown. Hannity gave it more attention than any other channel or network and challenged reporters to do their job and ask for more answers.

"Uh oh, the doo-doo done hit the fan!"

"Rage, you need to clean up your act if you're going to hang around here."

I walked home around 11:30, cut into my neighbor's drive and walked down his hedgerow to cross into my back yard. I entered through the rear door and did not turn on any lights – simply checked to make sure everything was secure before hitting the bathroom light to do the necessary things one does before bed time.

The next morning as I dressed for work, the sheriff called to advise me that there was a crew truck from the local TV station out front and what looked to be at least a half-dozen reporters he didn't recognize.

"What do you want me to do?"

"My experience says to face the issue head on and get it out of the way so we can get on with our work. How about this as a plan? You have your usual breakfast with B.J. and arrive here at a few minutes after nine. I'll have the media people gathered in the conference room by nine o'clock. I'll introduce you and give you the opportunity to make an opening statement; then we let them ask as many questions as they want to. When it's time, I'll ask them to leave us alone, as we have some important work to do."

"That sounds fine to me."

"By the way, that question that's bugging you – forget about it. I think it'll be covered nicely in the next White House briefing."

"How's that?"

"I had a talk, off the record, with a source on the Washington Observer, and they have just the right person to send to ask our question. My source says this reporter will likely drop a few fire ants in POTUS' knickers.

I walked into the conference room at exactly ten after nine, followed by Donnie, Ellen Buck and some others. The sheriff motioned me to come up front with him.

Even before he began, it was obvious that everything was being captured by all forms of media apparatus. "Ladies and gentlemen, I realize Deputy Edwards needs no introduction, as I'm sure you have all done your homework. You know him for his past deeds, which were significant, and in my humble opinion, worthy of the Congressional Medal of Honor. However, you don't know that in the coming days he will be recognized as a hero for his work as a deputy sheriff here in Beaufort County. I wish I could tell you more but I cannot. The timing is too sensitive and there are still arrests to be made. You will be back here before too long to interview him again, I am sure of it. Deputy Edwards, the floor is yours."

"Ladies and gentlemen, I had not planned on making a statement, but as I stood here looking around this room I feel the need to express some of my feelings. You are looking at one happy and very fortunate man. Just a few months ago I was unsure that I would live, and came close to questioning whether I wanted to or not. Not knowing who you are is a harrowing experience, but to suddenly remember you've seen a monster holding your friend's head aloft and crying out 'glory to god' is one that will rock anyone to their very core. I was rocked but I have not been defeated. I am home. Let me say that again. I am home. I have put a ring on the finger of the only girl I've ever loved. I have been trained by a fine law enforcement professional in Sgt. Donnie Gurganus standing over there. I've had tremendous help from colleagues, and let me take this opportunity to recognize the special help Ellen Buck has been. You folks ever want to do a special interest item, you should look into her work here. I will not say she runs the place because I don't want to offend the boss. Let me just say she keeps all our clocks wound!" Everyone from our department clapped for her and she turned beet red. I went on, "I want to thank Sheriff Marslender for his faith in me, for his support, for giving me the opportunity to rebuild my life and to work toward making life here better for all our people. Now, I will try to answer your questions."

The questions came so fast I could not possibly remember them all. Finally, I said, "It's obvious that you're in search of a story, and I've tried to convince you I'm not bitter about the President's decision to turn down my nomination for the award, so, let's have a compromise. I'm not a fan of the president's politics. In fact, I seldom agree with anything he says. This decision is, in my opinion, one of the few good ones he has made since his election."

The sheriff rose and closed the conference with the words that we needed to get to work, and he looked forward to seeing many of them back here in the not-too-distant future.

Two days later at the White House news briefing, a reporter from the Washington Observer was recognized by the press secretary. He made this statement. "A few days ago, the President advised Marine Corps Headquarters that he was not going to approve the award of the Congressional Medal of Honor for Lance Corporal Brody Edwards. He gave this as explanation, and I quote, 'I had information that the kill count was not confirmable, and the photo showed no evidence of gunshot wounds.

The individuals could have been killed by lightning for all I know.' So, my question is, "Where did the President get his information, and exactly what is the information?"

"Well, I assume he got his information from either Marine HQ or the Pentagon," was the press secretary's answer.

The reporter did not sit down but said, "No sir, that does not satisfy me or the people of North Carolina. I spent all day yesterday at Marine Headquarters and I've been assured by people at the very top that no such information could have originated from either of those places. We want an answer from the president. What information does he have and where did it come from?"

The Press Secretary said, "I will see what I can get on that."

"I will be waiting."

That night, all major networks picked up on what had happened in the morning White House briefing. It was a major news item on Al Jazeera which means it would be covered in all Middle Eastern countries including Afghanistan. All of Fox News programs, O'Reilly, Kelly, Huckabee, and Van Susteren gave it mention, with Hannity hitting it hardest. He made the statement, "No matter how bad it might look for the President, every time I think he has fallen into the crapper, he comes out smelling like a rose."

The next day the Press Secretary reported that the President received his information from a classified intelligence report from Afghanistan sources, and he could not or would not reveal the information or the source. End of story.

Two Missing Teenage Girls — Chapter Twenty-Six

At 12:36 AM Saturday morning a call came in to 911. The man was frantic. "I need help! My daughter is not home yet, and she never misses curfew! I can't reach her on her cell! I know something's wrong!"

"Calm down, sir, I need to get some information."

"She left a party at around 10:30 with her girlfriend, Cheryl Hayes, in a red Honda Prelude. Have you received any calls for roadside assistance or something like that?"

"No, sir, not in the last two hours. I've been right here."

"Your name, please."

"Okay, start writing. I will give you pertinent data. If I leave anything out, you can ask later. This is Dave Dixon, my wife is Joan Dixon, our missing daughter is Karen Dixon. She's seventeen years old and will be eighteen on the 26th of January. Weight, 110-115 pounds, 5'5", black hair, very curly, hazel eyes, almost like a cat, very tan and healthy looking. She has a mole on her right cheek, just above her mouth. Wait, my wife's phone is ringing. Oh, no, it's not Karen. It's Judy Hayes. Cheryl has not come home and they can't get her on her cell, either."

"Mr. Dixon, have your wife tell the Hayes to call 911 immediately. I need their description and personal data on Cheryl. I will get an APB out ASAP. I'll call you back as soon as I can.

911 dispatcher, how can I help?"

"This is Ben Hayes. My daughter, Cheryl, has not come home from a Friday night party and I'm worried that something is wrong."

"I understand that she and Karen Dixon were together – I just got off the phone with Mr. Dixon. Is that, right?"

"Yes, I think so. They usually hang out together."

"Give me a brief description of your daughter and the car. I'll get an APB on the wire immediately, and if we don't get a quick fix, I'll dispatch an officer to your residence, ASAP. Okay?"

"Let me put her mother on, she's better at that sort of thing."

"Judy Hayes here. Cheryl is eighteen, blonde, wears it parted in the middle, usually in a ponytail, 5' 7," about 135 pounds, blue eyes, very pretty, and her right front tooth has a small chip from a fall."

"Where was the party and when was she last seen?"

"The party was out on River Road. I called her boyfriend, Kenny Stone; he said they had a little disagreement and she and Karen left together at about 10:30."

"Did he say where they were going?"

"He didn't know."

"Okay, let me get to work. We'll let you know something as soon as we have anything to report."

Attention all units: Be on the lookout for a red 2010 Honda Prelude, license number HAYES 4. Two teenage girls reported as missing; both last seen around 10:30 last night, leaving a party on River Road in the Honda. Any positive sightings, report immediately."

Waiting two minutes without a reply, the dispatcher sent another "attention all units" directing them to converge on a five-mile radius around Washington city limits. "Cover all roads and territory, report in every hour, copy?"

Next the dispatcher called both sets of parents; he gave them the information that no sightings of the car or girls had been made, all units had been directed to converge on the area around Washington, and to call in hourly reports. He asked each family for permission to dispatch units to their respective residents to obtain a recent photograph and description of clothes the girls were wearing when they left home.

"Unit 61 checking in."

"Brody, what are you doing out there? You were supposed to clock out at midnight."

"You know me, I usually give it an extra hour or two. I was just about to call in my checkout time when you put out the APB. Since then I've covered every street off River Road toward town – nothing to report. I volunteer to stop by the Dixon residence before I call it a night. That way the other guys can stay on patrol."

"Thanks. I'll take you up on that offer."

He gave me the address and said he would call ahead so the Dixons would be expecting me. I pulled into their driveway at 2:33 and saw that all the downstairs lights were on. "No sleeping in this house tonight," I thought.

The Dixons were younger than I expected, in their mid-forties, attractive, even though bleary eyed from crying and too much coffee. They recognized me and started to express sympathy for my recent bad news, but I cut them off, assuring them I was fine and was here to take care of more important issues. They handed me a recent headshot of Karen. She looked a lot like her mother, and I told them so. They took it as a compliment as I had intended. I asked several questions about the boyfriends of both girls, getting Jimmy Kane's address along with a complete description of the clothes Karen was wearing when she left the house.

At the station, I made a copy of my notes and gave the copy, along with the photo, to dispatch. Clocked out at 3:15.

Home at 3:38, I decided I could function on five hours' sleep, texted B.J. that I would pick her up for church, and hit the sack.

Brody Gets Saved **Chapter Twenty-Seven**

On the way to church the next morning I went over the happenings of the last evening with Aunt Hannah and Barbara Jean, telling them everything I could remember. They were shocked to tears, both expressing solace for the parents, and I could see in the mirror that they were lifting up prayers for the girls and their families. Aunt Hannah asked me to please share this with the pastor before he preached. "I just know he'll want the whole church to pray for those people." I waited in line to get to speak with him and was able to impart the story just in time before the music started.

Reverend Cooke stepped to the pulpit with his usual, "Good morning saints and sinners. Before I begin my message today there is news that needs to be shared so we can all join in prayer for the good of our fellow citizens. Deputy Edwards has informed me that two Washington High School seniors did not come home last evening from a party. Both are white girls; one is Karen Dixon, the other Cheryl Hayes, and neither has been located as of about twenty minutes ago. Please join me in prayer."

I was astonished to see that about half the congregation went all the way to their knees, many turning around to place elbows on pews. His prayer was heartfelt, as you could tell his emotions were straining to be released in tears. He begged for heavenly intervention, for peace and comfort for the families, for an outcome that would show the community that, "You are a good, good Father." At the end, he added, "And all the church said?"

A mighty chorus of "Amen" arose. His sermon was taken from the Gospel of John, chapter 3, and verse 16. It was powerful enough to grab my total attention. I wish I had the ability to relate it word for word, but I cannot. The more salient points were:

- The great initiator: God does not wait on us to love him. No, He loves us first; even before we were born He loved us. He is the reason we exist; in Him we have our being.
- The greatest act: A love so deep and so pure, and it was most costly to Him. He did it anyway.
- With great compassion: His love for us does not depend upon us being good or earning His love. No, His love reaches out to us when our most sinful and obnoxious behavior is at play. You cannot be good enough to earn His love, and you cannot be bad enough that His love will be withdrawn. His great love and compassion has already been expressed on the cross.
- The greatest number: God loved not a few, not some, but all creation. He loved the whole world. God does not love just good people; he loves us all. Remember

great men of God: Moses was a murderer, David an adulterer and murderer, yet he was described as a man after God's own heart.

- The greatest gift: God's one and only Son. Can you fathom a love so sincere that you could allow your child to be the sacrifice so that someone else's child could live?
- The greatest invitation: Sent to whosoever, or to all who will accept His gift.
- The greatest simplicity: The only thing required of you is to believe. It can't possibly be any simpler than that. Don't try to make your eternal salvation more difficult than it is. Believe in His Son!
- The greatest deliverance: Those who believe will be transported from the very gate of Hell into the very presence of God.

When he finished preaching he issued an altar call to any who would like to accept God's gift. I was the first to reach him with a firm statement that I believe Jesus is the Son of God. We embraced, and Barbara Jean and Aunt Hannah rushed to make it a group hug. He asked if I wanted to be baptized and I replied, "Yes, and membership in this church, too, please."

Wedding and Honeymoon Chapter Twenty-Eight

On the way home, we stopped by KFC for a bucket of chicken to add to Aunt Hannah's greens and cornbread. It doesn't get much better than that! As we ate, Aunt Hannah said, "Brody, you have made me a happy woman today. I'm going to ask the Lord for enough days to rock some of your babies, *then* I'll be ready for the Pearly Gates."

"I hope He will grant you many more days with us, and I, too, want to see you rock my babies."

Barbara Jean piped in with, "You have made it a happy day for me, too. In fact, maybe even happier than the day I got saved. I don't understand how that could be true, but I almost peed my pants when you went forward." We all laughed. We finished eating and B.J. and I left Aunt Hannah for her nap.

At my house, B.J. jumped into my arms and gave me a kiss that had my head spinning. She pulled me down on the sofa and we did some serious smooching. Finally, she said, "The Apostle Paul said, 'It is better to marry than to burn.' I want you to know that I'm burning for you Brody. I can't wait much longer. Let's get this thing done."

"Okay, tomorrow morning we'll go to the courthouse as soon as it opens and apply for the marriage license. Do you want to close the shop or have Emily come in for you?"

"I'll get Emily. And after we get the license we can stop by the parsonage or church and see how soon Doc can do the job for us."

"The only people whose schedules have to be considered are Joe, Tillie, Sheriff Marslender, Donnie and Right Arm. Aunt Hannah can make it anytime we can."

With that she jumped up and started bouncing up and down. "I feel like a freshman in high school who has just been asked to the Junior-Senior Prom by the star quarterback!" Suddenly she rushed to the bathroom. Coming out she asked to be taken home. "I just did what I said I almost did in church." In the car, she said, "Don't worry about your seats, it's not that bad. Go home and watch the game. The Redskins play at four and Denver and San Francisco have the late game. I'll see you at breakfast."

Back home, I felt a need for prayer. I thanked God for drawing me to Himself, for saving me and giving me peace about my future. I asked for wisdom to know how to be a good husband to B.J., for protection as I try to be the best deputy sheriff I could be, and I asked for an ability to understand His Word and His right to direct my life. The first thing I noticed was that the body tension I'm sure was a result of the lust of the flesh was gone; I was at peace, and I had a desire for more of God. I do remember that the Redskins won, which made me happy; and I think I left the

TV on for the other game, but I have no idea of the outcome of that game. At some point during the later game, I started rummaging through Dad's desk drawers. Surprisingly, I found a small Gideon New Testament with Psalms and Proverbs. I opened it to the back cover and found that Dad had written his name in as being a believer. The date he had entered was just weeks after I had left home. "How sweet it is."

At breakfast the next morning I showed Barbara Jean the testament, and we rejoiced together. "I don't ever remember him going to church, but it's great to know he had trusted Christ."

As we entered the courthouse, I kiddingly said, "Oh shucks, they've been open for a whole fifteen minutes." We were greeted with a, "Good morning Miss Woolard and Deputy Edwards, what can I do for you?"

"Are you telepathic or something?"

"Oh, no. I just read the local paper and you have been featured there enough for most of us to know who you are. I also know where to get my sweet tooth taken care of, therefore your names pop out of my brilliant mind. I bet you two are here to apply for a marriage license, right?"

"Yes, ma'am. What do we have to do?"

Reaching under the counter, she handed us a form and said, "Fill that out. Both of you sign it, pay me sixty dollars, and you're good to go."

"No blood test or waiting period?"

"That's right, just get the dirty deed done."

We were in and out in less than twenty minutes.

Stopping at the church next, we found Pastor Cooke in and willing to meet with us. We explained that we wanted to get married as quickly as possible and since neither of us had any close relatives, we just needed to see when Joe and Tillie could stand up with us as witnesses. He looked at his calendar and said, "I can do it tomorrow night or Thursday night." Barbara Jean squealed and grabbed her phone to speed dial Tillie. They talked for less than a minute and B.J. said, "Tomorrow night." The time was set for 7 PM.

We were back at Ye Olde Sweet Shoppe by eleven o'clock, wondering how we got it all arranged so fast. Emily agreed to stay for the rest of the day, so we went upstairs to make a lunch of BLT's – with iced tea of course. B.J. called Aunt Hannah to advise her of how fast things were moving, and I called the station. I talked to Ellen to express how much I would like for her to be there, and she assured me she would be. "Good. Can you contact Sgt. Gurganus and extend our invitation to him while I talk to the sheriff?" Phone calls made, we decided to head to the mall to shop for new outfits for each of us.

On the way, B.J. informed me, "Emily has said on several occasions that if I ever want to sell the business she would like to have first crack at it. What would you say if I sold out and we started work on filling up that back seat with babies?"

"I think that would be great." We both had silly grins on our faces as we entered the mall.

Two hours later we were both pleased with our purchases. She had an off-white suit, a medium blue blouse with ruffled sleeves and front, matching blue spiked heels and elegant accessories. I had a dark blue three-piece suit, white shirt, a red, white and blue striped tie and black winged tip shoes. Now to see if I could get the pants cuffed in time without having to burden Aunt Hannah with the task. The local dry cleaners close to B.J.'s shop promised to have the pants cuffed by two o'clock the next day!

While Barbara Jean discussed the possible sale of the business, I went online and made reservations for Wednesday and Thursday nights at Atlantic Beach. I was able to secure an oceanfront condo at A Place at the Beach III. I felt good knowing that even though the weather would be cold, it would be nice watching the waves roll in. Reminding myself to pack the binoculars, I went to tell B.J. the plan.

That night, working my last evening shift, I reviewed the day's events and realized how blessed we were to have everything work out so well. Just catching my shift change so that I had three days off was most fortunate. Best of all would be having Barbara Jean as my life mate. The night's work was thankfully uneventful.

The next day, our wedding day (whoopee!), we discussed over breakfast whether we should be concerned with tradition or not. Barbara Jean pointed out that we'd already broken tradition by having breakfast together. "You may as well drive me to the church."

"Should I make a stop at the drug store?"

"No way. You do know how to make babies, don't you Brody?"

"I think so."

"The correct answer is practice, practice, practice."

As I got up to leave, she reminded me to pick up my pants by two o'clock and take a nap. "You are going to need it, because you won't be sleeping much tonight!" She gave me a quick kiss, turned me toward the door and patted me on the tush as I left.

The three of us arrived at the church at 6:30. I gave the license to the pastor, and we talked through the process. He suggested we take a five-minute break before proceeding.

Returning from the bathroom, I watched Barbara Jean come toward me and thought this was as good as her coming down the aisle. Joe and Tillie stood slightly behind us as Doc began the ceremony. I listened carefully and answered all his questions with a firm, "I do." Barbara Jean did likewise, showing little if any nervousness. His, "I now pronounce you man and wife," was music to my ears. His, "You may now kiss your bride," was obeyed promptly and with enthusiasm.

Unknown to me, Tillie and Aunt Hannah had prepared refreshments, so we were invited to the basement for a reception. We cut the wedding cake and fed each other nicely. Joe gave me a big hug and told me how happy he was at my trusting Christ and showing wisdom enough to marry Barbara Jean. In return, I thanked him for pointing me toward Christ, and for his friendship. It was nice, but I confess to wondering how soon we could get out of there.

We took Aunt Hannah to her house, and we both walked her to the front door. After giving us both a kiss on the cheek, she said, "Now go home and make me some babies to hold!" We all giggled.

I parked behind the store to retrieve my small overnight bag from the rear of the SUV and headed up the back stairs. "I am really going to get to spend the night!" Inside B.J. instructed me where to put my bag and yelled over her shoulder, "Dibs on the bathroom!" I had just removed my coat, vest and tie when she came back into the bedroom. She had removed everything except her heels and matching underwear. I know I have called her beautiful many times before, but this time I was totally blown away. "Beautiful" came from my mouth followed by the thought, "That's an understatement." I've always had this fantasy of stiletto heels and lacy underwear; the real thing almost did me in, if you know what I mean. She obviously enjoyed my gawking, as she shifted her weight from one leg to the other, one knee tilting toward the other with her hips going in the opposite direction. My next thought was that it was not the fancy underwear, which left nothing to the imagination; it was her. You could see all of Barbara Jean Edwards. "Wife, come here!" I love the sound of that.

The next morning Barbara Jean used the inside stairs to check in with Emily, to go over lastminute instructions and to review orders that were due while we would be away. I used the back stairs to put our bags in the Escalade. On the road, we passed through New Bern, a very nice town laid out between two rivers, and I told her one of my family stories:

My grandfather, whom I never saw, was very proud of the fact that he had seen President Harry Truman pass through town in a small motorcade. He had a very good view and never forgot how enthusiastically the President waved to them as he passed by. I think the year was 1948 or 1949.

Passing through Morehead City, I started thinking about the many good seafood restaurants in and about, and my stomach started rumbling. Crossing the bridge to the Outer Banks, B.J. suggested we stop at a mini-mart to grab something for lunch that day and breakfast the next. We did that and then made our way down toward APAB III. Checking in, I was assured that we had the top floor unit which put us almost on the dunes and had a great view up and down the banks. A Place at the Beach encompasses several buildings, and we had to go almost a mile further to get to our unit. Pulling into the parking lot gave me a surprise. I think I was expecting a brick and block high rise sort of place; this was entirely different. I thought, "How clever." At the beach front, there were two wings that tapered back to become narrower in the middle and then spread back out as you went to the rear. I suppose it would look like a huge X from the air. The neat thing was that this gave all the units a view of the ocean from their balconies. I later discovered there were two duplicate buildings with shared swimming pool, water slide and playground between them. Of course, it was too cold to do those things, but I got a vision of us bringing our children there.

Making our way up to unit number 302, I thought it would be nice to have an elevator, but none was available. Our unit was small: two bedrooms, two baths, kitchen, living room and balcony. I suggested we change into our beach wear, including hoodies, and use the binoculars to check out the place before we ate lunch. We started changing clothes.

Later, on the balcony, I used the binoculars to find the Cape Lookout Lighthouse on Harker's Island, then handed them to her. I felt her intake of breath as she took in the beauty of the sight. She finally decided to survey the panorama before us and began swinging the glasses out toward the ocean, on past our condo and up toward the main pier in downtown Atlantic Beach. Before I saw what was happening I realized her excitement as she began bouncing up and down. "Look! Dolphins!" For the next five-minutes we watched a pod of eight to ten dolphins lazily make their way from our right to our left. They were only about thirty yards out from the shoreline. "I hope you know, I ordered that just for you."

"Thanks, my love."

A light snack for lunch and out to stroll the beach. Over the dunes, we turned left toward Fort Macon State Park. The sun was nice and bright, the wind was up to about twenty miles per hour, thus a pretty good surf. Enough of a roar that hearing was difficult, we mostly just enjoyed holding hands and dragging our toes in the wet sand. Just before we reached park land, Barbara Jean found a sand dollar, something I'd never achieved on the ocean side of the banks. She was thrilled. We turned around and made our way past the condo and went on up to the pier and back, putting in maybe three miles before we finished. This time we took a nap.

The first evening, we went back to the mainland and cruised Morehead City to pick a place for the evening meal. We selected the Red Fish Grill, new to me. I think the deciding factor was the sign claiming to have the best scallops on the coast. Nothing on the menu proved more interesting, so I went with the scallops, a baked potato, a side salad with both French and blue cheese dressing, and sweet tea. Barbara Jean chose to have crab-stuffed flounder, with the same sides I had. The sign outside proved to be correct as far as I was concerned. Thankfully, B.J. left some of her flounder and I was more than glad to finish it off for her. Back at the condo, we selected a DVD movie and settled on the couch to watch. Whether it was the inferiority of the movie or the peacefulness of having my wife in my arms, I cannot judge; I know we both fell asleep only to awaken in the middle of the night. I shooed her to the bathroom while I put the disc away and cut off the TV and lights. Hearing her come out of the bathroom, I took my turn at getting ready for bed. Crawling into bed I welcomed her as she came over to snuggle. "You don't have on any clothes!"

"No, I don't!"

The next day started with a brisk walk on the beach. Then we drove down to tour the Old Civil War Fort Macon followed by a short drive to the town of Beaufort, where we toured the historic houses there; a stop by the Chocolate Factory to satisfy our cravings, and back to the condo for a rest. An afternoon walk on the beach included a serious discussion about where to eat the evening meal. We finally decided on Spooner's Creek Marina. Viewing the menu, I thought the steaks looked good, but common sense prevailed and I ordered the Mariner's Platter. I told myself, you can get a good steak anywhere; you can't always find quality seafood. B.J. went for the crab meat salad.

The last night of our honeymoon, do I dare ask for a repeat of the stiletto and lingerie performance of two nights ago? "You have not because you ask not."

Superman? Chapter Twenty-Nine

We checked out early the next morning and headed home. On the way, I was thinking how good it felt to be married. I must have been grinning, because my wife asked, "What's that grin about?"

"I'm thinking about how nice it is that you are my wife."

"No way."

"Yes, way. "I feel like I'm Superman."

"I thought I took all the S out of Superman last night."

"Well, maybe you did, but then I can be Rocky Balboa, running up those steps to the Philadelphia Art Museum, raising my hands above my head and shouting, "Barbara Jean is mine!" Or maybe I'm Sam Baldwin pointing that spotlight on the Empire State Building to show the huge red heart with your name spelled out for all to see. Or maybe I'm Rafiki, standing on that hilltop holding you up in your wedding suit, presenting you as my Queen for all the jungle to see – except when he brings you down it's me holding you and you only have your stiletto heels and blue lacy things on."

"Stop. Stop talking and pull this car over."

I did and she planted one on me. "Brody, you take my breath away."

We arrived just about nine o'clock. I fixed myself a cup of coffee while she and Emily went over business matters. I called in to check on things, and Right Arm said, "Hey! Glad you called! The sheriff has been wanting to call you, but hesitated to do so on your honeymoon. I'll put you through."

"Hey, Brody, good news! Squirrely's lawyer has reviewed the video of the deal and has agreed to a guilty plea. As soon as the system assigns the acceptable judge to the case, Squirrely will reveal what he knows about drug operations in our county."

"That is good news!"

"And tomorrow's news will cover the arrest and your part in breaking the case. Be prepared for more notoriety."

I thanked him for the heads up and returned to B.J.'s to help her start moving her things to my house. We talked about my working shifts, the duty hours of each shift and when I needed to sleep. She found it confusing and asked that I write it down for her. I made her this note to put on the refrigerator.

SHIFT	WORK HOURS	SLEEP HOURS
DAYS	8 AM to 5 PM	11PM (or 12 AM) to 7 AM
SWINGS	4 PM to 1 AM	7 AM to 3 PM
MIDS	12 AM to 9 AM	3 PM to 11 PM

Looking it over, she concluded that since I would be asleep when she got home and she would be at work when I got off, there would be no time for practice.

"Look, honey, there are nine hours of work scheduled, and we only need seven hours of sleep. That leaves eight hours to work out practice time. We will learn to deal with it!"

My first night was basically uneventful, so after signing out, I stopped by the mini-mart and bought a newspaper. The banner headline on the front page read:

SHERIFF ANNOUNCES MAJOR BREAK IN ROBBERY CASES.

The article read:

The Beaufort County Sheriff's Department has arrested two people who have been connected with several past robberies in Beaufort County and in the City of Washington. Clarence Mills, AKA Squirrely, was arrested while driving a rental van containing stolen goods worth thousands of dollars. His arrest came as a result of hundreds of hours of off duty investigation by rookie Deputy Sheriff Brody Edwards. In his research of all robberies over the past two years Deputy Edwards developed a matrix that brought out the fact that cigarettes were the second largest items stolen, next to cash. He then theorized that the cigarettes had to be fenced and transported to a place like New York City where they would be priced at a much higher value than here. Due to Deputy Edwards' close working relationships within the community, he sought and received a tip that Clarence Mills might be a possible fence; then he researched rental companies to find that indeed Mr. Mills had a history of renting vans almost monthly and returning them with mileage comparable with a trip to and from New York City. With that information, surveillance was authorized on Mr. Mill's activities. That surveillance led to the arrest of a second individual, Deputy Sheriff Calvin Thompson, who was caught on surveillance taking stolen items from his cruiser and placing them in the van driven by Mr. Mills. Thompson is accused of possessing stolen goods and has been terminated from his position as deputy sheriff.

On page two of local news I found an article that caught my attention. The heading of that article read:

APPELLATE JUDGE FAYAZ AMMAR DENIES PETITION OF LASHAWN JOHNSON FOR A MISTRIAL - ORDERS EXECUTION AS SOON AS POSSIBLE.

Judge Ammar wrote:

For those who study the law and are interested in justice, indeed, to all who read this decision, I will remind you that the petitioner, Lashawn Johnson, has received, as all who are sentenced to execution do, an automatic appeal. The appellate court has looked at every aspect of his trial and sentencing and found no evidence to support a retrial. It is now my duty to address his latest petition for mistrial based on his claim of judicial prejudice. It should be noted that both the petitioner and the judge are African Americans.
In order to dig deeper into the case than was possible in the simple reading of his charges, I went to the state penitentiary and met for over an hour with Mr. Johnson. In all my years as a lawyer and a judge, I have never met a man more convinced that he is not guilty, nor have I ever met a man more convincing in his presentation of his innocence. Unfortunately for Mr. Johnson, I'm not allowed to make that judgment. If I were, I either would have to declare him innocent or nominate him for the Academy Award for Best Actor. In this case I had to address the issue of whether Judge Martin Luther Crabtree allowed prejudice to enter in his decision to mete out appropriate punishment. In that endeavor, I thoroughly reviewed all five of the cases involving an execution decision made by Judge Crabtree. Since lethal injection is the only form of execution used in this state and since there are no degrees of death, I was left with the question: Did Judge Crabtree treat the petitioner differently than others in similar situations? In all the cases, Judge Crabtree followed guidelines set forth by the State of North Carolina, and in every case the decision he made was one that any reasonable judge, including myself, would have made. I therefore had no choice but to deny Mr. Johnson's petition for mistrial.

"Wow . . . wonder if this is going to cause trouble for us over the next few days."

Finding the Body — Chapter Thirty

My week of midnights passed without any items worthy of recording and I soon faced my first day shift with a sense of anticipation that things were about to get exciting here in Beaufort County. Maybe my feelings resulted from the fact that B.J. and I would be on the same schedules, but it seemed to be more than that. When I clocked in, the dispatcher stated that I should probably cruise down to Aurora to make our presence known; we hadn't been down that way in the past two days. I made two stops in Chocowinity asking business owners how things were going, then headed down that way. I also stopped at the Blounts Creek crossroads to look in on activities there. One of the owners I talked to said, "Watch out for glass on the road when you pass the Bloody Bucket, I hear they knocked out some windows last night."

"I'm glad I wasn't on duty then."

Back out on Route 33 East, I noticed that the Bloody Bucket did have sheets of plywood in two windows. Just after passing there, I remembered that my Uncle Bill had logged a large tract of land a few miles farther. I slowed down to see if I could still identify the spot. Yes, just up on the right. Man, how I had sweated to put in a culvert to allow us to cross the ditch onto the property. In passing, I noticed that although it was overgrown, some traffic had obviously been on the property recently. Having already passed the entrance, I started to accelerate, when a strange feeling came over me, something almost like a voice telling me to go back. The feeling was strong enough for me to call out to Rage and Reason, "Are you trying to tell me something?"

No answer.

I made a decision, did a quick U turn, then made a left turn into the property, stopping the cruiser well off the highway. I opened the trunk, and changed from dress shoes into rubber boots, tucking my pants legs inside. "Probably just a teenage make-out spot," I thought; but by the time I passed into the trees I was beginning to sense that something was not right. I reached down to unfasten the safety strap on my pistol. Twenty yards in, the smell confirmed my suspicion. I paused, calling on all my senses. It was warm, but not enough to make the air seem to waver as it does in the deep woods when extremely hot. The sound, that's it. Weird how the sound of flies' travels in the woods – more than a soft drone, like an energy unto itself – the buzzing came at me, pushing me to an even greater alertness. I pulled my pistol out and moved forward like a deer hunter. Another thirty yards in and I rounded a slight bend to see a red Honda, Hayes 4 license plates, both doors open. I called in to make my report but kept surveying the area. The only thing in the car was one women's shoe on the passenger side. On the ground in front of the car was a pair of silver sandals and track marks suggesting something had been dragged over into the brush. I followed the tracks and found a human skeleton, picked completely clean by predators. There was enough yellow hair remaining for me to be reasonably sure I was looking at the remains of Cheryl Hayes.

As I talked to the communications center, I suggested we get crime scene guys and equipment onsite ASAP and that the sheriff be contacted.

"Done," was his answer.

While waiting for assets to arrive, I walked further on and saw no evidence of any other vehicle or human traffic. I did a visual search on both sides of the path but found nothing. I checked the path back toward my cruiser for tracks other than the Honda's but found none. I backed my car out and parked it to the east side of the entrance and awaited the crime lab team.

Once they arrived and completely dusted the car for fingerprints, we were able to release the trunk lid and found nothing of import. I was concerned that Karen Dixon's body would be in there. Other members of the team had begun to expand the search around the vehicle but found nothing. I suggested we call in a bloodhound to see if a scent from the shoe in the car, which matched the description we had of Karen Dixon's, might lead us somewhere. "Good idea," Donnie said, and in about an hour the handler and dog arrived.

The handler let the dog smell the shoe and then led him all around the car. The dog finished the lap and sat as if to say, "What else do you want me to do?" So, the handler gave him another sniff of the shoe and took him on a wider 360 degrees around the car. Nothing. We sent them home, concluding that Karen must not have been in the vehicle when it was driven in here. Later, around three o'clock, Sheriff Marslender called me aside and asked me to go to the Dixon residence and advise them of what we had found. He took the unpleasant task of going to the Hayes with the bad news.

As I made the right turn off Route 33 East onto Route 17 North, I felt the need to stop at B.J.'s, so I went in. Thankfully, there were no customers, so I told her what I had been doing all day and about the task ahead of me. Cautioning her not to speak about it to anyone, I asked her to pray with me for wisdom about what and what not to say to the Dixons. We also asked God to protect Karen and to help us find her soon.

I called the Dixon residence to ask if I could stop by for a few minutes to discuss aspects of the case. Joan immediately went into high gear.

"Have you found her? What's going on? Come on, Brody, please tell me you've found her and that she's alive!"

"I wish I could do that, but this is not the time for that. Is Dave home?"

"Yes, he just walked in the door."

"Okay, I'll be there in fifteen minutes."

Before I could knock, they opened the door and almost pulled me into the house.

"What is going on? I know you wouldn't come by if you didn't have some news about the case," Dave asked.

"Look, I don't have any bad news for you about Karen, nor do I have any good news. Let's sit down and I'll tell you what happened today.

"Unfortunately, the news for the Hayes family is bad. This morning, I found Cheryl's car up an old logging road off Route 33 down past Blounts Creek. We found what I suspect, but officially cannot confirm, her body. The body had been dragged away from the front of the car into the bush, and we found only skeletal remains. The clothing scattered about matched the description her parents gave us, and there was some blond hair remaining which will give us DNA to make an official identification.

"There is some news I think you can interpret as positive. We brought in a bloodhound and let him get the scent of one of Karen's shoes found in the car, then we led him around the area, doing a 360 around the car twice. He could not pick up her scent. We think that means she was not in the car when it was driven into the woods. Personally, I am encouraged that she may still be alive, and I hope you are."

Joan fell to her knees off the couch and cried out, "Dear Jesus, please let it be so! Bring our baby home to us safely!" Dave and I joined her on the floor, all of us crying out to God.

Dave asked God to comfort Ben and Judy Hayes.

Before leaving, I told them my church was praying continuously for both families.

It had been several months since the arrest of Calvin Thompson, and I hadn't even thought about him for days on end, when suddenly it seemed that everyone I talked to had some news. Looking back, I find that weird, but that was the way it happened.

I ran into Buzz Latham as he walked past the station, and he mentioned that a colleague of his had taken Calvin's case as pro bono service; that he'd convinced Calvin there was no way for him to beat the grand larceny charge; there was simply too much evidence against him, and that the best thing was to try to get the District Attorney to drop all other charges in return for a guilty plea. He thought the county might go for a deal to avoid the time and expense of a trial. The other charges, having to do with covering up for guilty parties and being culpable for the conviction of innocent parties, though not as certain for conviction, could add years to his sentence if proven. Thompson agreed to the plea bargain.

Donnie had more info: the sheriff had told the DA he was against the deal, but if the DA went for it, he wanted to make sure Judge Crabtree was assigned the case. He told the DA he wanted the book thrown at him.

So, I was not at all surprised when Ellen Buck called that day to pass a message from the sheriff that the plea bargain had been accepted by the DA, and Judge Crabtree had set a sentencing hearing for the next week.

"That should be interesting," I thought. "I'll definitely post that information as soon as it's available."

Nine days later I wrote this post script:

Judge Martin Luther Crabtree read the riot act to Calvin Thompson, calling his attention to the fact that although he swore to uphold the law, in fact, he'd not only broken it, but he'd also dragged the reputation of law enforcement through the mud by his actions. He pointed out that Calvin had disgraced himself, his family and his race by his greed and eagerness to enhance his own financial wellbeing at the expense of others. "You have given fuel to the fire of those eager to criticize law enforcement," was the one quote I remembered. He also told Calvin that he was lucky North Carolina law only allowed him to be tried as a single case of grand larceny, even though he'd been involved in accepting goods from multiple robberies.

He ended his admonishment with, "I hereby sentence you to eighty-four months in the North Carolina State Penitentiary, without parole."

Tip Leads to Drug Bust — Chapter Thirty-Two

My cell phone rang. It was 08:30.

"Hello."

"Sheriff Marslender here. Brody, I'm calling for several reasons. I want to say again what a My great job you did yesterday. Your perception that even an unlikely spot could be the place to look, the way you took care not to contaminate the crime scene, and your idea to call in the dog team were all the markings of a true law enforcement veteran. I'm amazed you've accomplished so much in such little time. Keep it up, and you will move up fast in this department."

"Thank you, sir, that's quite a compliment, and coming from you makes it even more special."

"The other reason for my call is that the schedule for upcoming cases has been posted, and Squirrely's lawyer is satisfied that we got the best judge possible for them. He's agreed to us meeting with Squirrely tomorrow at 9 AM. Since you were responsible for getting us this far, I thought it only right that you be in on this all the way, until we find out where it leads."

"Thank you, sir, I'll be on duty tomorrow. I assume the meeting will be in the conference room."

"That's right. See you there."

The next day at the meeting, Sheriff Marslender kicked things off by announcing, "There will be no recording made, audio or video, of this meeting. I also assure you there are no bugs in the room. We are doing that knowing you would not want to be tied to the drug issue in any way. We will, of course, take notes and ask questions as we go. I don't foresee any circumstance in which we would need your further testimony. It's only fair that I remind you, Squirrely, that if you give us bum information and we waste a ton of resources, without positive results, I can have your case transferred to another judge. Understood?"

Both, Squirrely and his lawyer replied, "Yes."

Squirrely began, "I don't do drugs, I don't sell drugs. One of the names I'll give you used to peddle pills, uppers, whatever, and I've heard he's moved up to the hard stuff. My girlfriend's grandfather, Mr. Leroy Davis, hand grapples for catfish, mostly in Chocowinity Creek – you may have seen his picture in the paper last summer. He does it at night – catches them by feeling around for a hole with his bare feet. Then he sticks his hand in the hole and into the fish's mouth, grabs 'em by the gills and pulls 'em out. We were sitting on the front porch drinking beer when he tells me this story. He was sitting in the water taking a rest when he saw a pontoon boat – no lights – coming toward him. It was rigged with two electric motors, and didn't make a sound. As they passed, he saw a man with an AK-47 rifle on board.

He could hear them and he knew they'd landed just a couple hundred yards up the creek. So, he climbed out and made his way to a tree line; he saw boxes being offloaded from the boat and placed into a pickup truck. Dwight Andrews, a guy we both know, took possession of the boxes. The boat crew left out of there immediately, and the pickup truck headed to the nearest tobacco barn to unload. Leroy saw that the door to the barn was locked with a large padlock. He saw this happen three times, and each time it happened on a night with a full moon. He figured it was to enable the boat crew to maneuver the creek without lights. Oh –one other thing – after the boxes were in the barn, Andrews took one box to the back door of the house and gave Rogers the box and the key to the lock on the barn door."

Donnie asked, "Did he see any exchange being made, like a bag or box going back on the boat?"

"No. In fact, Leroy said he thought that was weird."

"An electronic transfer of funds was probably accomplished before the goods were delivered," offered the sheriff.

I asked Squirrely, "Did Mr. Davis mention a particular time of month the exchange occurred?"

"Yes, I'm pretty sure he said that each time it was toward the end of the month."

Sheriff Marslender stood and said, "I believe that should wrap things up here. I'm encouraged that we just might make a raid on that farm on the next full moon. Squirrely, your story makes sense, and I promise you, if we get these scumbags, I'll help you in every way I can, including employment when you get out."

Donnie stuck his head out and yelled to Right Arm, "Go online to see when the next full moon is, please." The sheriff and I looked at each other and smiled.

Moments later, she yelled back, "On the 25th."

"Thanks."

"Okay, that gives us three days to get ready."

I asked, "Which judge will you use to get a warrant?"

"Gentlemen, this is too sensitive for that. With the kind of money drugs command, I don't trust anyone. If we catch them red-handed, we won't need a warrant. We can bust down doors and search all we want. No one outside this room, except the state DEA folks, will know about this."

"Brody, I want you to get in time on the rifle range. We'll probably need your marksmanship before this is over. Donnie, I want you to get the boat crew ready to roll, put a spotter on shore to alert us of their arrival in the creek and inform us where the pontoon boat goes after delivering the goods. My guess is they'll rendezvous with a speed boat or yacht anchored nearby. The boat crew is to know only that they'll have authority to search and seize, once the pontoon is attached to the boat. Hopefully, we can find drugs on that boat and can eventually put that baby on the auction block. I'll get with DEA today to lay out a plan and brief you when we're set. Let's roll."

That night I took my wife – I love saying that rather than her name – and Aunt Hannah to Ayden for barbeque. It was the first time I'd been there in about five years, and the food was as good as I remembered. On the way home, I casually mentioned to Aunt Hannah, "Didn't you tell me you once worked for a Mr. Rogers, a tobacco farmer just outside Chocowinity?"

"Yes, I think I talked to you about that. What in the world made you think of that?"

"Ah, I guess it was thinking about how soon the execution of Lashawn must be."

"I hate to even think about that. It just brings up bad memories. Rogers' father was a mean man, and the bad apple don't fall far from the tree, if you ask me. I still think there was something fishy about that whole trial. Brody James, are you telling me you know something about that man you can't tell me?"

"All I can say is, your perception is very keen. What I need from you is anything you can tell me about the house or the man."

"Now, that's more like it. Let me see, now – I thought I already told you this, but maybe not. There's something about the library that just ain't right. I remember on at least two occasions; the man went in there and when I checked on him he wasn't there. When I checked back later, he was there, and I know he didn't go out the door and come back in. So there has to be a trap door or something back by the bookshelves that hides a secret compartment."

"That just might be the most valuable piece of information this police department could get in the next few days. Keep it quiet, please."

Astonishing Results Chapter Thirty-Three

Two days later, in the conference room, six of us were introduced. There were three from DEA and three from our department. The DEA leader started off.

"Let's make this as easy as possible and hopefully no one will get hurt. The main thing is to get this whole transaction on camera. These two gentlemen are the best we have, and they'll have the best infrared technology available to get the job done. I want us to all go together to your communications commander and have him integrate our equipment so we can communicate on a secure line. We've been going over satellite views of the property, and my men have been briefed as to location and timing of entry onto the property. Once Andrews delivers the package to the house, we can make the arrest. Sheriff, what do you have to say?"

"We've kept this as secretive as possible. Even the spotter at the bay or the boat crew who will hopefully stop the escape at the appropriate time, don't know what we'll be doing. The three of us will be in Brody's cruiser, known as Unit 61. We'll drop off Sgt. Gurganus at the western-most loop of the road in front of the Rogers farm. Donnie, you will have a hike of about a mile to get in position by the barn where Mrs. Rogers was killed. Brody and I will proceed down Route 33 to the eastern loop and await the signal to move in. DEA, as soon as they begin unloading the boat, call Unit 61 into position. We'll come in quietly and without lights, to block the driveway. There are only three ways to get off this property. DEA, you'll be responsible for the water exit. Donnie, you'll have the barn line back to the road, and Brody and I will have the driveway. Let's use simple codes and communicate as little as possible. How about D1, D2, D3 for you guys, we'll use B1, B2, B3, and the spotter will be Baywatch. The last thing is this: D1, I want you to have a constant bead on the guy with the AK-47; if he even looks like he's going to use that thing, take him out. I don't want one shot coming out of that thing much less twenty or thirty. Any questions?"

There were none, so we all headed back toward the communications center.

The next night at 11:00, I was fully dressed for work and watching my wife get ready for bed. She sensed something was unusual and came over to give me a good hug. "Something big is going to happen, isn't it?"

"Yes, at least we think so."

"Dangerous?"

"Possibly more so than normal, but I'm not concerned, so don't you be."

"No time for practice, before you go?"

"No. See you in the morning."

At the station, I went through my mental check list of items I'd need; satisfied that everything was in order, I began to change into the necessary gear. I even blackened my face before I put on my helmet with night goggles strapped on. Then the three of us met at armory to get our weapons for the night. I loaded my rifle clip with six armor piercers and six regular M-16 shells. We pulled out at 12:15, a little earlier than necessary, but I think we were just anxious to get things underway. When we dropped Donnie off, I wished him luck and safety, thinking I had an extra fifteen minutes of cold time because of our nervousness. As we headed east toward where we had planned to stop, the sheriff suggested we cruise down to Cotton Patch Landing to make sure the teenagers weren't up to something. "If they come in early, we can get back in time from there," he said. Nothing amiss at the landing so we headed back and took our position at 1:15.

While we were waiting, he asked, "How's married life?"

"Couldn't be better," was my reply. I told him what happened on the way home from Atlantic Beach. He got a big kick out of Barbara Jean saying, "I thought I got the S out of Superman last night." He grinned at the Rocky Balboa line, then asked, "Who the heck is Sam Baldwin?"

"Didn't you see Sleepless in Seattle?"

"Oh, yeah. So Rafiki is the baboon who held up Simba, right?"

"Right!"

At 2:35 AM we heard, "B2, pickup truck arriving."

2:38 - D1, "Truck in position at creek. Two males, no sign of arms."

3:03: "Baywatch Alert."

3:13 - D1, "Bird has landed. Roll B3."

We pulled out on to Route 33 West for one mile, then a right turn onto the loop road, where I cut the lights and slowed the pace. I pulled the cruiser up the slope and turned it across the driveway. We got out, closing the doors as softly as possible; I put the mic to the loud speaker through the open window for the sheriff to use as he saw fit, and set my tripod on the trunk deck for maximum stability. I thought it may be a bit brazen but it needed saying, so I cautioned the sheriff not to use his night goggles until I had time to take out the truck lights.

3:29 - D1, "Alert Baywatch."

3:38 - D1, "Barn locked."

3:39 - D1, "D2 & 3, this is critical."

3:43 - D2, "I got a great shot."

3:44 - D3, "Me too." D1, "Truck headed your way. Hit those battery pack spots, now."

The house and yard lit up like it was Christmas. The truck came to a screeching halt and the sheriff used the loudspeaker. You are surrounded. Get out of the truck with your hands in the air. I saw Anderson start to spin the steering wheel, and I took out the headlights with two shots. Pointing the rifle in the air, I squeezed off the rounds of light ammo and then put all six armor piercers into the block of that engine. The truck went just a few more yards before the engine seized up and the two men jumped out, running toward Donnie's position. I heard Donnie's warning to stop or he would shoot. At least one of them must not have stopped because I heard just one more rifle shot.

Running toward Donnie, I arrived on the scene just a few seconds before the sheriff. The one man, whom I did not know, was already on his knees with his hands on his head. I patted him down, cuffed him, and then turned my attention to Dwight Andrews. I heard Donnie say, "I'm sorry man, I tried to get you in the leg, but it cut your artery. You're bleeding out, and I can't stop it or get an ambulance here fast enough. So, if you have any last words, I'll try to get them to whoever you say."

Andrews said, "I knew I shouldn't have done it. I knew God would get me for that. I mean rape is one thing but I choked her to death, too."

"Who are you talking about?"

"The Hayes girl." Those were his last words.

The sheriff said, "I think we can consider that a death bed confession."

The sheriff fired up his lapel mic. "Okay, guys, no need for secrecy any more. Has anyone spotted Rogers?"

"No sign, I can see both doors and he hasn't come out."

"Okay, DEA, stay covered and we'll get a cruiser in place and see if we can get a rise out of him."

It didn't work. We told him we knew he was in there and we could burn him out if necessary. Still nothing. We decided to call in the coroner and another unit to transport Andrew's body and our captive, and to await daybreak for further action on the house. The sheriff asked for a report from the boat crew and found that they had taken possession of a yacht worth millions of dollars.

"The owner and his mistress are being booked, along with the three members of the pontoon boat crew. We haven't yet found drugs on the yacht but I believe we will. The yacht has a crew of four that claim to be contracted for a two-week period and don't even know the owner."

"If their story checks out, release them; if you find they are full-time employees, book them too."

At 6:00, the sheriff called in to say, "Get me a vending truck out here with coffee and breakfast food." He added, "STAT" with a big grin on his face. My admiration for the sheriff increases day by day. "Man, I could eat a cow!" Well, not all a cow or even a pig, but those three country ham biscuits with two coffees did taste good, and filled the need, too.

By 8 AM the place was teeming with backup, crime scene people and DEA agents who were anxious to take control of the stuff in the barn. The sheriff put teams to work searching all out buildings, starting with those farthest from the house.

I caught Sheriff Marslender by himself and told him of Aunt Hannah's suspicion that there was a secret room under the library, and asked permission to let me have a shot at finding it. He agreed. I got the RAM from my cruiser and we burst in the front door. He dispatched three men upstairs to do a search. One of the men pointed to the steps and said, "We have to check it out, but I can guarantee no one is up there; look at all the dust on these steps." They gave an all clear sign in no time flat. Then they took a quick turn thru the first floor with the same report.

The sheriff and I entered the library, first moving all rugs, a sofa, two chairs and a desk aside, and found no trap door under them. I went to the bookshelves and began to move books, expecting to find a switch of some sort that might make the shelves move. No luck. I stood there staring at those bookshelves for a long time, and then I saw that there was something different about the carving of the flower in one corner from the other. I went to the right corner first and found a daisy-like design which looked perfectly normal. When I approached the one on the left, I found that the flower was not all one piece; indeed, the center was cut into a complete circle, separate from the rest of the flower. I reached up and pressed the center part, and it moved. Immediately I heard a motor, and the shelf began to move toward me. Grabbing my pistol and staying out of line of fire from the steps, I shouted, "Okay, Rogers, you can come out now! There is no way for you to escape! Don't make this more difficult than necessary. We can send down tear gas if you force us to."

Seconds went by, then pop, pop, pop; followed by a shotgun blast, followed by more pops so fast I could not count them. We looked at each other in puzzlement, and then a female voice yelled, "He's dead! Help!"

I tore down those steps as fast as I could and hit the light switch on the left wall. To my utter astonishment I saw Karen Dixon with one hand cuffed to the iron bedpost and the other holding a smoking pistol. When I took the pistol out of her hand, she grabbed on to me like she would never let go; totally oblivious to her nakedness.

I held her, but asked the sheriff to find the keys to the cuffs so we could free her. She pointed to the desk drawer. Once freed, she stopped shaking as badly as before and began rubbing her wrist. I wrapped her in the comforter from the bed and she said, "I thought sure he was going to kill me every day. He raped me whenever he wanted to – there was nothing I could do. He kept me so doped up I'm sure there are things he did that I don't even remember."

"How did you get the pistol?"

"When the motor started opening the entrance, he jumped up from the desk to grab the shot gun, and it fell out of his back pocket. I don't think he knew he had dropped it. I was barely able to reach it. Then I got on my knees and with both hands on it, I used the bedside table as a brace. I was so afraid I would miss, I just kept pulling the trigger until it stopped shooting."

"Oh, honey, I'm so sorry you had to go through this, but your mom and dad are going to be so glad! I was at your house and prayed with them just a few days ago. We need to get an ambulance to get you to emergency medical care right away."

"Wait, there is something important you need to know about this man. He is evil personified. That black man who was convicted of raping and killing Mrs. Rogers, did not do it. There is a disc in that laptop that shows them having sex and she was enjoying it. When the black man left, she bragged to that monster, pointing to Rogers's body, how good it was to have someone who could last more than a few seconds. He hit her with his fist and she fell on the same tobacco cart she had just had sex on, and began to cry. The sound of her crying seemed to drive him crazy, as he looked around frantically. Seeing the hatchet, he grabbed it by the blade with both hands and drove it into her skull. It was the most sickening thing I have ever seen; but it really turned him on. He had to watch it before he could do anything to me."

When the ambulance arrived, we told them she needed the best care possible for both drug addiction and sexual abuse. They believed she should go to Greenville Hospital. Once they left, I asked the sheriff how much time he had to stop Lashawn's execution.

"It is set for tomorrow, I think, but I'm about to call the Governor to have that stopped."

"Can I have the pleasure of notifying the Dixons and taking them to the hospital?"

"Of course, they have called several times to thank me for the way you have met their needs."

On the way, the idea hit me to get Barbara Jean to help us. Calling her, I said, "We found her, she is alive."

"Oh, thank you, Lord. What?"

"Stop, put a "Closed for Emergency" sign on the door and be ready to ride in five minutes. We are going to give them the good news together. I'll need you to drive their car to the hospital in Greenville. There's no way we can allow them to drive in the state of excitement they'll be in."

"Yes, sir."

When we pulled into their driveway I turned on the flashing lights and hit the siren two little beeps, which I knew would get their attention. Barbara Jean and I were running up the driveway, and when they opened the door, I shouted, "We found her!"

We both shouted, "She is alive!" The four of us were hugging, jumping around in circles, screaming and shouting so loudly the whole neighborhood was soon joining in. The Dixons went from neighbor to neighbor hugging them and thanking them for their prayers and support. We finally got them inside where I explained to them, and to B.J., what had happened. I started off with, "She has been through hell, over a month of sexual abuse, fed drugs to the point of addiction. Because of her special needs, she's been transported to the Greenville Hospital.

"We're going to take you to her as soon as you can pack a bag with things you will need over the next couple of days. I am sure once you see her you will not want to let her out of your sight for a while. Barbara Jean will drive your car and I'll continue to fill you in as we drive over there."

While they were packing, I gave Barbara Jean some of the details as to how the drug bust had gone, the fact that both the number 1 and 2 guys were dead, and an innocent man would be free soon. "What a red-letter day for justice!"

On the way to the hospital, they both sat in the back to be near each other, and we could see each other in the rear-view mirror. I gave them the particulars as to the names of the men involved and the fact that she had been forced to watch the video of Wayne Rogers murdering his wife. When I explained that Karen had been the one to kill Rogers, Joan cried out, "Oh, my poor baby!"

Arriving at the hospital and seeing that Barbara Jean was behind us in their car, I proceeded to the emergency entrance. "You two go on in, and as soon as we get parked we'll come in to give you the keys and see if there's anything else we can do for you before we leave."

They jumped out and literally ran into the ER. By the time we got inside, a nurse was leading them back into the treatment area. Joan looked back and called out, "Can you wait a little while?"

We gave her a positive nod of heads and watched her smile as if this was the best day of her life. As we sat in the waiting area, we talked about how they must have surely thought over these past few weeks that their daughter was dead. Now to find her alive, there couldn't possibly be any better day than this. We put our heads together and thanked God.

About thirty minutes later, the Dixons came out to explain that the doctors had sedated Karen because of withdrawal reactions and she would be out for some time. I suggested we call Sheriff Marslender to discuss timing and content of a press release. The gist of the three-way conversation was, we were too tired and the Dixons were too excited to deal with it today; therefore, it was set for tomorrow at 9 AM in our conference room. Barbara Jean handed them their car keys, and Joan said, "Brody, I think both you and Barbara Jean are going to have to learn to deal with a case of teenager hero worship, as she is raving about how Brody Edwards saved her!"

We'll each have to cope with this situation in different ways – it's good to know that all of us have the very best supporter. Thank you, Lord.

Press Briefing **Chapter Thirty-Four**

Early the next morning, I received a call advising me that due to public interest and the large number expected to attend, the press conference had been rescheduled for 10 AM at the Army National Guard Gymnasium. When I arrived, the parking lot was almost full, trucks from television stations from all over the eastern part of the state were visible. Inside, a stage had been set up with a podium that had six microphones attached. The sheriff motioned me to join him on the stage, showing me a seat next to Donnie. He came over and explained that earlier he had conversed with Squirrely's lawyer, and since the major parties in the drug case were deceased, he saw no danger for his client, should the cases be linked. "I will not be giving him any credit or airtime, but the DA's office will be able to put two and two together and maybe go a little softer on him."

At exactly 10 AM the sheriff stepped to the microphones and gave this statement. "Ladies and Gentlemen, I am extremely happy and pleased to announce that we have four major news items to release to you today. Each one of these items, could easily lay claim to be story of the year in our little county. It is amazing that all four of these stories became so entangled as to be resolved simultaneously. I will cover them chronologically and allow sufficient time for you to question and interview individuals as you see fit.

"Two nights ago, the two deputy sheriffs you see on the stage behind me, Sgt. Donnie Gurganus, Deputy Brody Edwards and I, along with the support of three State Drug Enforcement Agency employees, began a surveillance operation of the property of Wayne Rogers, whose farm backs up to Chocowinity Creek. He is the same Wayne Rogers whose wife was murdered on that same farm about three years ago. That trial received nationwide news coverage and resulted in the conviction, for both rape and murder, of Mr. Lashawn Johnson. At about 3:15 that morning we digitally recorded the transfer of drugs from a pontoon boat to the truck of Mr. Dwight Andrews, the subsequent transfer of those same drugs to a tobacco barn on the property, and the deliverance of a small package from Mr. Andrews' hands into the hands of Wayne Rogers. At that time, we turned on our flood lights and called for their surrender. Mr. Andrews chose to flee but was blocked from leaving via the front entrance by Deputy Edwards. When Andrews again refused to obey the command to halt, Deputy Edwards disabled the engine of the truck with armor-piercing ammunition. Mr. Andrews then chose to run toward another exit which was covered by Sgt. Gurganus, who shot Mr. Andrews in the right leg. Unfortunately, that bullet hit an artery and Mr. Andrews died before medical attention arrived. At that point, I made the decision to await daylight before trying to capture Mr. Rogers.

We had a constant watch on the house and knew he had to be inside, but he would not respond. We had to use force to enter the house, and a thorough search could not find him. Based on information given Deputy Edwards by Ms. Hannah Johnson, who worked at the house years ago and who had suspected a secret room beneath the library, Deputy Edwards was able to find a secret switch which caused a book shelf to move to reveal steps down to that hidden room. When Deputy Edwards called for Rogers to surrender, we heard three pistol shots and a shotgun blast, followed by a series of pistol shots. The net result of that exchange was the death of Wayne Rogers.

Now let me recap briefly the first case:

1. The death of two individuals who we believe to be the head of drug operations in Beaufort County and maybe an even larger area
2. The seizure of drugs, yet to be valued, but in my opinion, will exceed two million dollars
3. The arrest of one yet-to-be-named individual on the Rogers farm, who helped store the drugs
4. The arrest of the three individuals who delivered the drugs on the pontoon boat
5. The arrest of two individuals on a luxury yacht anchored on the Pamlico River, where the pontoon boat returned
6. The capture of more drugs, yet to be valued, onboard that yacht
7. The seizure of that luxury yacht which will most likely be sold at auction for millions of dollars

That wraps up case number one.

"You will undoubtedly be glad to know that the second case will go much faster. Mr. Dwight Andrews made what is considered to be a deathbed confession to having killed Miss Cheryl Hayes. We now consider that a solved case, and we can only add our heartfelt condolences to the Hayes family. That wraps up case number two.

"I am overjoyed to announce that we have rescued Miss Karen Dixon. She had been kidnapped by Mr. Rogers, who forced her to take drugs and kept her in the aforementioned secret room for the entire time since her disappearance. In his hurry to reach for a shotgun, Mr. Rogers dropped his pistol. Karen shot him with his own pistol as he prepared to ambush any who descended the steps. Her parents, Dave and Joan, have asked that you honor their request for privacy as they try to deal with the trauma of these horrific experiences. That wraps up case number three.

"Based on information provided by Miss Dixon, we found video recordings in the room that showed Mrs. Rogers having consensual sex with Lashawn Johnson; that same recording showed Mr. Rogers arriving after Mr. Johnson left. It also showed him hitting Mrs. Rogers and murdering her by picking up the hatchet by the blade and slamming it into her skull. Yesterday evening I contacted the governor and he halted the execution of Mr. Johnson. This morning Judge Crabtree issued an order vacating Mr. Johnson's sentence of rape and murder. I've been advised that Mr. Johnson left prison a free man about two hours ago and is being transported here; his arrival is anticipated momentarily. That wraps up case number four.

"Let me finish by saying that I have to be the most blessed law man on the face of this earth. To have four major cases solved in one fell swoop is colossal, and I don't know if that has ever happened before. I do know that it makes me proud to serve this county and these people. I am so proud of all the people in my department, especially these two fine officers behind me. They will be receiving special recognition as soon as I can find time to write them up."

The questions came fast and furious and the session had lasted for almost an hour when Lashawn Johnson showed up. The attention shifted immediately to him, and the sheriff asked if he would like to make a statement.

"Yes, I would like to say a few words." Taking the microphone, he said, "I have experienced living hell for over three years. I suppose that facing death from a disease is tough to deal with, but to face death imposed upon you when you know you are innocent is a burden no one should have to bear. It can and did produce tremendous malice and hate within me. Fortunately, some Gideon paid for a soft covered Bible to be placed in our prison library, and that Bible became mine. In it I found the Lord, and He gradually helped me overcome the hatred and malice. I am not the same man I was when I left. Though scarred, I am not defeated. I return with the intention of being a productive member of this community. I hope you will allow me to be. Gentlemen here on the stage, my deepest appreciation for the work you did in bringing about my freedom. May God bless all of you!"

"Wow!" Totally blown away, I rushed forward to shake his hand. I think we both saw the love for the Lord in each other's eyes, and we embraced.

A few minutes later, a reporter posed this question, "Deputy Edwards, you seem to be making a career of this hero thing from your nomination for the Congressional Medal of Honor to being prominently involved in the solving of at least five major cases in your first year on the force. Do you have the proverbial horseshoe hidden somewhere?"

"No, I assure you there is no hidden horseshoe. I will tell you, as I told my classmates at a get-together a few months back. I, like Lashawn, have faced death, and for a while I didn't care whether I died or not. Since then I have found the love of my life, who is now my wife; I have found the Lord, who is now my Savior. I am blessed by Him every day, and He has given me the desire to be the best law enforcement officer I can be. That's the only explanation I can offer you."

I finished off my shift without any further excitement, taking time to call my wife to ask her to invite Aunt Hannah for dinner. "Tell her the six o'clock news is going to be a blockbuster. I will get a bucket of chicken."

"Okay, but I want to invite Joe and Tillie too, so get enough for them. Knowing Aunt Hannah, she will want to start cooking greens at our place by early afternoon."

"Sounds good to me. I'll pick you up at about 5:15. Love ya."

Sure enough, when I pulled into the driveway, there was Aunt Hannah gently swinging in that old glider. I tried to coast past her but that big old Escalade made too much noise; by the time we got in the back door, Aunt Hannah was lifting the lid to check on her greens.

Barbara Jean took command – after all it was her house now – directing me to go clean up. "Lie down for a few minutes, if you like." She told Aunt Hannah, "Joe and Tillie will arrive at about 5:45, then we'll all watch the six o'clock news; it will be something you don't want to miss. You just need to time when you want to put your cornbread in the oven. Now you sit and rest while I set the table and get things a little neater around here".

Our guests arrived on schedule, we all took our seats in the living room and I turned on the news; we watched the local channel cover the entire news conference. After I answered the one question directed to me, Barbara Jean came over and jumped into my lap, throwing her legs across the arms of the recliner. With her arms around my neck and her lips against my ear, she said, "Brody, you say the sweetest things. I love you so much."

When it was over, Joe said, "Wow! Was that God-honoring or what? Just think, those testimonies are going into homes all over our state, and maybe farther."

"I just hope I didn't come on too strong and cause a backlash."

Aunt Hannah said, "Don't you worry about it; you were simply doing what the Lord told us all to do. Brody, I believe you have been given a platform that most Christians never will have. Just use it wisely. If you make Him the focus, and guard against self-aggrandizement, everything will be fine."

"Woman, you amaze me, aggrandizement is not in the vocabulary of most college graduates, and I have to admit, you caught me by surprise with that one."

"Brody James Edwards, I know sometimes I let an 'ain't' creep in, and sometimes I fall back into old habits like dropping the 'ex' off of 'expect;' but I will tell you just like my Granny Hannah used to say, 'I ain't no dummy.'"

We all laughed, and you could hear several of us saying, "That's for sure!"

Joining the Work of the Gideon's — Chapter Thirty-Five

Three days after the news conference, on my first day off, I called Right Arm to get a home address for Lashawn Johnson. Arriving at his mother's house, I found him sitting in the front porch swing reading his Gideon Bible. He was glad to see me and invited me to sit.

I said, as I joined him in the swing, "Just thought I'd drop by to see how you're coping."

"That's mighty nice of you Brody, and I'm glad to report that I'm on cloud nine at the moment! You're not going to believe this – well, maybe you will, because you know the sheriff better than I do – he came by day before yesterday to let me know he had arranged a job interview with the manager of Chick-fil-A. I interviewed yesterday and it went well. They hired me on the spot. I start in their manager training program next week, and if successful, I'll be the assistant manager when I finish the training." (My esteem for Sheriff Marslender went to an even higher level.)

"Yes, he is really a nice man, and I just keep finding more to like about him. Lashawn, to be honest, there is another reason for my being here. I wanted to invite you to our church. I'm sure you will like it, as Reverend Cooke is a dynamic preacher."

"Thanks, Brody, I may come for a visit but I, too, have to be honest. My heart is really with the Gideon Ministry. As you know, it was due to them that this Bible was placed in my hands and allowed me to find the Lord. I have already researched the local Gideon Camp and found that several of their leaders here in the county go to the local Bible church. I promised them I would visit there this week."

"I understand completely and I wish you well. The invitation to visit us is open, just come any time."

"Brody, have you ever heard any testimonies of how people get saved by reading the Bible in a hotel or motel room that was placed there by a Gideon?"

"No, I have to admit I know very little about that organization."

He responded immediately with, "They are an international organization that has members in or has distributed Bibles in 197 of the 211 or 212 recognized countries or territories in the world. In fact, they have distributed over 1 billion and a half Bibles since their beginning back in the early nineteen hundreds. They train their men to speak in churches everywhere to partner with them in raising funds to support the ministry. All funds donated by church congregations go directly to producing and transporting scriptures around the world, whereas individual Gideon's contribute to cover the expenses of the organization. They are also big supporters of the jail ministries through their camps and their churches. If it were not for this organization I would still be a bitter, unsaved man, doomed to a Christ-less eternity."

"Wow! I see why you are so turned on to the ministry! It sounds like something I need to investigate further. Nice to see you so turned on, and I wish you well."

"Brody, I'm going to join the organization and attend their weekly prayer breakfast this coming Saturday morning. How about I call you as soon as I get my feet on the ground and then I'll arrange for you to be a guest at the next prayer meeting – is that okay?"

"Sure, I would like to do that. Just let me know when and where. Well, I better get rolling, see you soon, I hope."

Driving away, I called the sheriff to thank him for helping Lashawn.

"How did you find out about that?"

"From the man, himself. I stopped by to invite him to our church and he told me all about it; he was very pleased that you helped. You did know he got the job?"

"Yes, I know. Brody, while you are on the line let me make you aware that I've nominated you for our Policeman of the Year Award, and I believe you will be a shoo-in to win it. The board will not make the decision until late November, but I'll keep you posted."

"That was totally unexpected! I thank you very much!"

The final item on my mental list of things to do that day was to talk to Doc about my concern to improve relationships between the churches of our community. At the church office, before I could explain why I was there, I heard him call out, "Come in here, Brody!" Coming around the desk, he greeted me with his usual bear hug. "What can I do for you, son? Sit down, please."

I explained that in my morning devotion I had read Psalm 133 about how pleased God is when there is unity in the body of believers, and how I thought we should make some special effort to increase the unity not only in our church but in churches throughout the community.

"That certainly is a worthy goal! Do you have anything specific about how that might be accomplished?"

"Yes, sir, I have a few ideas. First, the monthly pastor's luncheon and prayer time could be used to broach the subject and to seek input from all churches. That would give us a feel for how far the various pastors think their congregations will go to improve things. I have two ideas I would like to see considered.

"You select a pastor of a predominately white church and try to arrange a joint service one Sunday night a month. We rotate the services each month. Even if this only lasts a few months, I can see friendships and relationships coming about.

"This idea comes from a man I met in the hospital at Walter Reed. He told me how his church back home had an annual shrimp boil dinner that everyone loved. They had four propane burners with huge pots to boil the water in; they cooked the shrimp, sweet corn on the cob, carrots, whole onions, red potatoes and polish sausage all together in the same pot. When fully cooked, they drained off the water and dumped the whole meal on a table covered with plastic and newspapers. Rolls with lots of butter finished off the feast. I thought if that is successful in the springtime, we might also consider an oyster roast in the fall."

"Well, both ideas have merit. I like them, but I better run them by the elders before we get too excited. I think we should charge a break-even fee to cover costs, don't you?"

"Yes, sir, I would think so. We certainly can't afford a freebie!"

"Okay, I know the two men I believe will work with us on this. I'll talk with Mark Carey and John Fletcher. You, young man, should be prepared to take a lead in the planning process as soon as I can get leadership approval."

The next day I related details of my visit with Lashawn to B.J., and told her that the Gideon ministry sounded like something we might be interested in doing together. She told me she had been thinking along the lines of our being involved in some sort of outreach together. "This may be the thing for us," she said.

When I told her about the invitation to come to the Saturday morning prayer breakfast, she said, "Do it and find out how wives can participate, too." I had just given her my assurance to do so when my phone notified me that Lashawn was calling.

I answered, "Must be evidence that great minds work together! We were just talking about you!"

"I don't know who would agree with that 'great minds working together remark,' but thanks anyway."

"Nor do I know of any who would agree – it was something that just popped into my head – I guess I remember hearing my dad say that. It certainly doesn't apply to me. How are you doing, Lashawn?"

"Very well, thanks for asking. I was just calling to give you the time and place for our Saturday morning prayer breakfast, if you can come."

"Yes, I would like to do that. Barbara Jean wants me to find out more about the ministry, as she thinks it's something we could do together in reaching out to the community."

"That's great! We meet at 7:30 at the Golden Corral restaurant on Carolina Avenue. There's a private meeting room in the back that they reserve for us every Saturday morning. Go there first, and I can introduce you to the guys. We'll have a blessing and then get our food. The prayer session is immediately following breakfast. Oh, be aware, we get on our knees to pray, so dress accordingly."

"Thanks, I look forward to seeing you at 7:30 Saturday morning."

Saturday morning at the Golden Corral restaurant, I found ten men in the meeting room. Lashawn introduced me around and I recognized one of the men as an acquaintance of my dad. After we returned to the meeting room with our food, I wound up sitting next to Dr. Bob Meadows, the president of the camp. As we ate, he gave me the "skinny," as he called it, on the work the Gideon's do here in the county. Obviously, Lashawn had briefed him on Barbara Jean's interest, because he covered the wives' participation, via the auxiliary, in detail. He went on to say, "I received Lashawn's application for membership and was very impressed with Pastor Carey's recommendation. It was very positive, considering the short period of time he's known Lashawn. I'm confident he'll be approved for membership at our next business session."

"I was not aware you had to have the recommendation of a pastor to join the Gideon's. Maybe you should go over the qualifications for membership before I get too excited."

"Sure, I'll be glad to. First and foremost, our organization is a group of business and professional men, excepting the clergy, who believe in the Bible as the inspired Word of God, believe in the Lord Jesus Christ as the eternal Son of God, have received Him as our personal Savior, endeavor to follow Him in our daily lives, and who are members in good standing of an evangelical or Protestant church."

"Did I understand that preachers and pastors are excluded for membership? If so, I'm not sure I will be interested in becoming a member."

"First let me say I like your response. I remember feeling the same way. We do exclude them from membership because we believe they have a much higher calling, and we don't want to detract from that work in any way. They have a tremendous responsibility in taking care of the spiritual needs of their flock. We try to be supportive of their work, and in fact, every camp puts on a Pastors Appreciation Banquet every year to treat them and their wives to a feast and to honor their work."

"Okay, I can understand that, but I'm not sure I can qualify as a professional businessman."

"Don't be concerned. Although you've not yet achieved a managerial position in your profession, you are the joint owner of a business here in the county, and you will be qualified on that basis. I also understand that Coach Cooke has expressed an interest, so be sure and let him know he qualifies as a college graduate and as a teacher in our educational system."

Before leaving, I went over and renewed my acquaintance with Reed Smith, the local cattleman who I knew had been friends with dad.

Two days later I got a call from Bob Meadows. "Brody, I'm calling to invite you and Barbara Jean to our next monthly dinner meeting. The emphasis this month is on new members, so we're trying to get as many who have expressed interest in the work to come. Do you think the two of you can make it?"

"If I am not working I'll be there." When he explained that they always meet on the third Wednesday night of the month, I checked my calendar. Seeing that I was off, I gave him our confirmation of attendance. “Have you invited Joe and Tillie Cooke?” I asked.

“They are next on my list to call. I do hope all of you will come, as we have one of the most sought-after speakers in the state coming to address us. Elliott Ossowit, a pastor from Jefferson, North Carolina, was saved by reading the Bible in a motel room where he had intended to commit suicide. He was an unsaved Jewish young man, now a grandfather, who has been a pastor for many years. You do not want to miss his testimony.”

“Yes, sir, we will definitely be there!”

Operation Hookup — Chapter Thirty-Six

That night, when I told Barbara Jean about making arrangements to attend the prayer breakfast on Saturday morning, she said, "Do you know if Lashawn has a love interest in his life?"

Having no clue, I sort of shrugged my shoulders and said, "I don't know if he does now, but I suspect you and Tillie have some suggestions to make about that."

"Are you implying that we meddle in other people's business?"

"No, but I do know you two like to help solve every problem you think exists."

"Brody Edwards, I'll have you know, Tillie and I are smart enough to know that a man without a wife is not necessarily a problem, we just think that having a helpmate will make some things easier for him. So, yes, we have discussed some possible ways to help in that area."

"And just who do you two think might just fit the bill as a perfect life mate for him?"

"We think he and Laverna Miller would make a very cute couple."

"Wow! I will say this: From a looks point of view you could not have made a better choice! She is certainly beautiful, but if memory serves me, she has a two-year-old son. Having a readymade family might not set well with Lashawn."

"We don't believe that will be a problem. That little boy is so cute and sweet, he'll capture the heart of any man his mother lets him near. I'm more concerned about Laverna and whether she will even agree to get to know him. It's been over two years since her husband was killed, and she really needs to get on with life. That little boy needs a daddy."

"Hey, you girls may have your hands full trying to work this one out. I think I remember Joe telling me after I was first introduced to her that she is bitter because her husband took that trucking job against her will. Not only was he gone too much, the job led to that horrible accident up on Interstate 95."

"That's true, but the realities of life change us all. In her case, she sees the need for a male role model for her son, plus she recently expressed her concern that her mother may not be able to continue providing child care due to her deteriorating health."

"Sounds like the timing is right. I'll talk to Lashawn to see if he's interested in meeting her. If so, I would suggest a triple date on a Karaoke Night at Smokey's. What do you think?"

"I like the idea for a triple date. Let me talk to Tillie tomorrow and we will work out a plan to put Operation Hookup into action."

Shaking my head and wondering what I'd gotten myself mixed up in, I went into the bathroom to prepare for bed. By the time I got to bed, Barbara Jean was already asleep, so I settled into my nightly prayer routine. I remember asking the Lord to recall the unfairness Lashawn had already experienced and asking Him for the very best for the three of them. I think my last words were, "Bless them, Lord, and please don't let Operation Hookup be a meddling mistake."

Awakening, I reached over hoping to find something warm and soft with which to cuddle, only to find cold sheets. Realizing that Barbara Jean had been at work for several hours already, I hurried to do my get-ready-for-work routine and meet her for breakfast.

Entering Ye Olde Sweet Shoppe, I found her on the phone with Tillie. Obviously, she liked what she was hearing, as she occasionally bounced up and down and gave a fist pump. A customer came in and she pointed to me and motioned for me to take care of her. I hurriedly washed my hands at the work sink, went to the counter, put on my best smile and said, "And how may I help you ma'am?" I filled her order of six glazed doughnuts, rang up the order, gave her the change and issued my standard, "Thank you, and have a nice day."

"Nice job, businessman!"

"Thank you, Reason, it's nice of you to say so."

When Barbara Jean hung up, she gave me a big hug and exclaimed, "Laverna is willing to do the triple date thing, if he is willing. Tillie didn't want to handle this over the phone so she dropped by the Baymont Inn to talk to her face to face. You do know that Laverna is the head housekeeper there, don't you?"

"I knew she worked there but I didn't know she oversaw housekeeping."

Barbara Jean said, "Wait until you hear this! Laverna was not interested at first, although she admitted she'd seen him on TV and being impressed with his looks and the way he handled himself.

"According to Tillie, that all changed when she mentioned the fact that Lashawn had joined the Gideon's. She said, 'It was like I had flipped a light switch on when I mentioned him being a Gideon.'

"Laverna told her, 'You will not believe the number of notes and even money people leave to show their appreciation for the Bible being in the room. I give strict instructions to my staff to turn those in so I can present them to the Gideon's when they come to service their Bibles.'

"Then she told Tillie, 'I think I would like to meet a man who thinks so highly of that ministry.'"

After taking my two sweet pills (glazed doughnuts) and finishing my coffee, I kissed my wife goodbye. Heading toward the door, I threw this remark over my shoulder, "Well, it looks like the next part of Operation Hookup is up to me!"

Opening the door to the car, I hit Lashawn's number on speed dial and waited for him to answer, as I knew he didn't work until the evening shift. When he answered, I said, "Are you ready to get married?"

"What? What. . . ." he stammered.

"Oh, I forgot that you didn't know about it yet. But don't let that bother you, just be aware – Barbara Jean and Tillie have picked out a woman they think will be a great wife for you. And by the way, she already has a two-year-old son, so you'll not have to go to all the trouble of having sex to have progeny."

"Why, that is so magnanimous of all of you, I can hardly wait! When do I get to meet my new family?"

"How about this Thursday evening? We thought we would start you out with a triple date, dinner at Smokey's, then karaoke. We did agree to let you set the wedding date, as we didn't want to seem too intrusive."

"You guys are so considerate, I hardly know how to thank you. But I have to warn you, if she shows up wearing a burka, the deal is off."

"Sounds reasonable to me. Can you do this coming Thursday?"

"Sure, anything for you guys."

"All kidding aside, pal, this girl is drop-dead gorgeous, and, by the way, Aunt Hannah has blessed the match. You are going to be so happy!"

We both broke into laughter and then I went on to give him her background information and make the arrangements for the date. When I told him of her initial reluctance until she found out he was a Gideon, I heard him gasp, and immediately asked, "What's wrong?"

"Brody, this is so cool! I've been avoiding my old crowd, as many of them would love to lead me back into the old ways. Actually, I have recently been praying that God would bring someone into my life who would feel as I do about the work of the Gideon's."

"Let's hope this will prove to be an answer to that prayer."

Thursday arrived, and Joe and Tillie picked up Lashawn and then Laverna, the women having decided that this was best, since Laverna might want Lashawn to meet her mother and little Ricky. We met them at Smokey's at seven sharp and immediately realized things were proceeding nicely, as they were both grinning like kids in a candy store.

The dinner portion of the evening progressed nicely, all of us enjoying the food and the conversation. I did overhear Lashawn telling her how cute he thought Ricky was. I thought, "That's a plus."

It was the karaoke portion of the evening that was so impressive as to be memorable, not only to the six of us, but to the whole crowd. It didn't take long for all within hearing range to realize we had two very accomplished musicians on hand. Not only did they have beautiful sounding voices, but they were both well trained and had the ability to change parts to create the best harmony. After two or three numbers, we found ourselves listening to them rather than singing ourselves. I watched in amazement as he gave hand signals when he wanted them to switch parts. Soon, everyone was asking them to go on stage and do a duet.

They had a short conference, he grabbed her hand, and they glided toward the stage, stopping to request music for "Happy" by Pharrell Williams. As soon as the music started, I knew they had both watched Pharrell's video many times, as they clapped in perfect timing to the music. Lashawn sang the first verse as a solo in his first tenor range:

"It might seem crazy what I'm about to say
Sunshine she's here, you can take a break
I'm a hot air balloon that could go to space
With the air like I don't care, baby, by the way
Uh"

Laverna joined in singing alto on the chorus.

"Because I'm happy
Clap along if you feel like a room without a roof
Because I'm happy
Clap along if you feel like happiness is the truth
Because I'm happy
Clap along if you know what happiness is to you
Because I'm happy
Clap along if you feel like that's what you wanna do"

She switched to soprano to sing the second verse as a solo.

"Here come bad news talking this and that, yeah,
Well, give me all you got, and don't hold it back, yeah,
Well, I should probably warn you I'll be just fine, yeah,
No offense to you, don't waste your time
Here's why"

They did the second chorus together, Lashawn singing tenor and Laverna on the melody. Then on the bridge she switched to soprano and he took the baritone part, singing,

"Bring me down
Can't nothing bring me down
My level's too high
Bring me down

Can't nothing bring me down
I said let me tell you now
Bring me down
Can't nothing bring me down
My level's too high
Bring me down
Can't nothing bring me down
I said"

When they started the final chorus, they had to encourage us to join them in singing as we were all mesmerized by their talent. Some did join in but most of us continued to gape in amazement. I thought, "That looked as if it had been choreographed and practiced for weeks."

The place went wild. Everyone was standing, clapping and hooting, and calls of "Encore!" were heard from every direction. Looking again at them, I saw that it indeed was a magic moment for them. He kissed her, and it was not a little peck. He did it firmly yet gently. I could see him talking to her and saw her react in amazement, but could not hear what was being said. I knew it was significant and made a mental note to ask him later.

In the parking lot as we all expressed what a fun time it had been, I gave him the universal signal to call me later. He nodded that he understood and we left for home.

At home, just as we started upstairs for bed, the phone rang. I punched the speaker button and said, "How did it go?"

"Great! I want to thank you both for getting us together. I'm sure God has a plan for us as a couple."

"Wow! I knew it went well but I did not expect to hear you say that!"

"Well, you probably didn't expect to hear me say that I asked her to marry me on the first date either, but I did!"

"No way! I have heard of quick romances, but asking someone to marry on the first date is unheard of!"

"Well, you have heard of it now! We're not officially engaged even though I'm fully committed. She is willing to see where God leads. I believe she will see God at work in this relationship very quickly."

We said our goodbyes and Barbara Jean and I remarked at the same time, "It looks like Operation Hookup was a huge success!"

Baseball Chapter Thirty-Seven

Springtime in Coastal Carolina is special; my favorite time of the year, in fact. It's warm enough to wear short sleeves most days, the flowers are blooming, and the colors of azaleas generously paint the landscape. Fishing is good.

We found out there were two babies in the oven, and for the first time in years my fancy turned to baseball! I started dropping by the high schools watching practice for a few minutes when the opportunity was available. I have to admit to some bias toward Joe's team in Washington, probably due to the desire to see C.J. develop as Joe hoped he would.

On one of our frequent double dates, Joe suggested that I not miss their home opener with Kinston, which went undefeated last year. He planned on giving C.J. the starting assignment as his number one pitcher. Kinston had a first baseman, a senior, who was expected to sign a major league contract as soon as eligible to do so. This guy had hit .498 the previous year as a junior, and over .500 in the summer county league play. No doubt there would be scouts at every game he played in this year.

So, there I sat, watching the teams warm up, growing more impressed with the first baseman from Kinston. He was big for a high schooler, more like a man than the others. His smooth athleticism on defense reminded me of a ballet dancer. With proven hitting skills and that kind of athleticism, he looked like a can't-miss candidate for the big show. I checked the program: number 3, Charlie Shackelford, 6' 3", 198 lbs., senior. Impressive, indeed! This should prove to be a real battle!

In the first inning C.J. gets the first two batters to tap out to shortstop and second base respectively. "Now batting third for Kinston, the first baseman, Charlie Shackelford," is announced over the loud speaker. The first pitch is a called strike on the inside corner of the plate – strike two on another fastball on the outside corner. I'm thinking, "C.J. will probably waste a pitch or two trying to get him to go for a bad pitch." No, a sweeping curve ball catches him looking and unable to pull the trigger. Strike 3. C.J. strikes Shackelford out again in the third inning in a similar fashion, the difference being the third pitch is a tremendous change-up rather than a curve ball.

Fifth inning: Shackelford takes a mighty swing and tops a ball down the third base line, which he barely beats out for a hit. We score a run in the bottom of the fifth inning, and now it's one to nothing. C. J. strikes him out in the 7th inning on 3 curve balls, each progressively slower than the other.

By the top of the 9th inning, the tension is evident to all. C.J. is fuming because he's already issued one walk in the 6th, 7th, and 8th innings, all due to miscalls in his opinion, by the umpire. Shackelford is equally steamed at having struck out 3 times. A classic finish seems almost inevitable as the lead-off hitter is the first up, executing a perfect drag bunt for a hit. Now with the tying run on first, C.J. strikes out the next batter on 3 pitches. He's obviously anxious to get to the big guy.

Shackelford steps into the box, pounds the plate with his bat and digs in. Everyone knows he's thinking a home run will put them up 2 to 1. Strike one comes on a swinging miss of a curve ball. A sneaky fast ball, probably C.J.'s fastest so far, caught the batter off guard for a called strike two. Now the batter is clearly trying to squeeze the sawdust out of the bat, wagging the bat across the plate again and again.

C.J. shakes off the catchers call with 3 straight shakes of his head, finally calling a time out for consultation. The catcher approaches the mound, they put their heads together and C.J. tells him what the pitch will be. Play resumes with a pitch that at first looks like a change-up, but it's a knuckle ball, the first such pitch of the day. It's so slow it probably looks as big as a softball to Shackelford, and it doesn't flutter until just before it reaches the plate. With that little flutter, Shackelford swings as hard as he can, missing the ball by at least a foot.

The cleanup hitter, probably thinking, "It's hero time," swings on the first pitch, hitting a pop-up to the infield for the final out. I check my score card and see a one-to-nothing win, 6 hits allowed, 5 errors, 13 strikeouts and 3 walks: A very impressive pitching performance. But Joe is going to be very upset with that many errors.

As I prepared to leave the stadium, I looked over to see Joe scanning the scorekeeper's book, and he did not look happy. The kids were jumping up and down with excitement as he slapped that book against his leg; I thought, "Wait till he gets you in that locker room."

He told me later that he read them the riot act and told them they would all be doing some extra laps next week. He is obviously a man of his word, because when I stopped by on Tuesday for practice, the boys were sweating from extra exertion. Joe had the infield huddled together and he was yelling, "Back to the basics, guys! Do not look at the runner – I don't care if you throw him out by one foot or by twenty – what I want you to do is charge the ball, set yourself for balance to make a good throw and then cut it loose. Jimmy, don't let the ball play you. You have to play it. Judge your speed to catch the ball coming down from a bounce, not up from one. Get that left leg out front with your right leg turned, so if you do miss the ball it will hit the fleshy part of your leg, not the bone. With proper foot and leg placement the arms will be in between to make the play, and you won't have to worry about the family jewels. Now, get out there and show me you know how to play this game!"

To his outfielders, Joe barked, "If I see you throwing to the wrong base or making stupid throws behind the runner, you are going to be warming the bench, do you understand me?"

I don't know how the rest of the week went, as I was unable to make it to practice, but the next game there was marked improvement in all categories of play.

As the season wore on, college scouts began to show interest in several players, especially C.J. By mid-season, he had six wins, zero defeats and an average of only one walk per game. One night I talked to Joe, and he told me that the scout for Vanderbilt University had said they were definitely interested in recruiting C.J. "He is so excited, he said, 'Joe that means I might get to go to Omaha and play in a College World Series!'"

What a fantastic year it was for Washington High School baseball: A record of 23 wins and only 2 losses! Joe Cooke was named High School Coach of the year and C.J. got a full ride to Vanderbilt University!

Johnson/Miller Wedding — Chapter Thirty-Eight

Two weeks following our first triple date, Barbara Jean informed me that we were to do a repeat performance the following Thursday night. Same place, same time, the difference being we would all meet there. When we pulled into the parking lot it was full, and I thought, "Uh-oh, maybe they know Lashawn, Laverna and Barbara Jean are coming." Luckily, we only had to wait about fifteen minutes to get a table for six.

While we waited, I observed Lashawn and Laverna, and thought, "They look so natural together, obviously in love – he never let's go of her hand." Occasionally they would lean toward each other, bump shoulders and smile as if to say, "Hey baby!" There was such a calm assurance between them that an observer would assume they'd known each other for years rather than two weeks.

In the waiting area Lashawn told us, "We are officially engaged and planning our wedding for two weeks from tonight. Your attendance is mandatory!"

Laverna quickly interjected, "If for some reason one of you can't make it, we will consider another date. It's just that we'd love to tell our grandchildren we married one month after meeting each other."

The women began hugging and squealing, we men shook hands, and congratulations were offered, not only from us, but from those standing near enough to overhear our conversation.

I thought, "This is weird! So soon, yet their confidence in their love for one another and their faith that God was bringing them together compels my support." We all assured them we would not miss the event.

During the karaoke time, we were in for another surprise. I think we were all stunned when we saw Joe and Tillie heading for the stage. I was thinking, "What are they doing? He can't carry a tune in a bucket!" I soon realized they had made some pre-arrangements with the deejay when they simply nodded at him and turned toward the dance floor rather than the stage.

The volume on the sound system was up a notch or two when "Rock around the Clock Tonight" boomed out at us. Joe and Tillie started to jitterbug, and in no time flat the entire crowd left tables and formed a ring around the dance floor. They were fantastic. He slid her under and between his knees, flipped her over his back, and they twirled away from each other and back together. I wondered, "Where did they learn a dance like that?" Maybe their fathers made them watch reruns of the Dick Clark show, as mine had. If that was the case, they must have enjoyed it, because the performance tonight would equal that of any of the 1950's crowd. In fact, it was so good the crowd demanded an encore.

When we returned to the table, they were breathing hard and Tillie exclaimed, "I'm going to be sore tomorrow." We all expressed our pleasure at seeing their performance, and just as we quieted down, I heard a comment from a nearby table. "He may not be able to sing, but the man can dance!"

Our conversation returned to wedding plans. Lashawn and Laverna explained that they had chosen to have the wedding at six in the evening and not to make it a more formal event to make it easier for all of us to attend. Suits and dresses would do. Lashawn added that his boss, the manager at Chick-fil-A, was giving them the gift of a catered meal for the twenty-some people who would be there. I thought, "How generous!" Later I learned that the manager was also the owner of the franchise but he didn't make that public knowledge. The bride and groom asked the four of us to stand up with them as witnesses and attendants. We agreed without hesitation. Laverna pumped her fists up and down, stamped her feet and squealed, "I'm so happy!"

Barbara Jean smiled at me and whispered, "Me, too."

The night of the wedding turned out to be a typical eastern Carolina stormy night. That did nothing to dampen the happiness we all felt as we gathered in the basement of our church. As we milled around, I started counting heads, and came up with 22: Pastor Cooke, his wife, C.J., the Six Amigos, as we had begun to call ourselves, mothers of the bride and groom, little Ricky, Bob Meadows, President of the Gideon Camp, and his wife, and others from the couple's workplaces. B.J. and I made our way over to Bob to meet his wife. He introduced her as Connie, and I thought, "What a beautiful smile she has."

As Connie and Barbara Jean started talking about the Gideon Auxiliary, I checked out the entire basement: Tables were arranged at the end near the kitchen for the buffet and for guests to sit. The other end of the room had a small, one-level riser, platform stage, set up with one chair and two microphones on stands. There were two rows of chairs facing the platform, making a total of sixteen seats, arranged out front without an aisle to distinguish between sides. At first the number concerned me, until I realized that seven of us would be standing during the wedding. I directed my attention back to the ladies just in time to hear Connie exclaim, "We are so happy that the four of you have decided to join our work. The Lord knows we can use all the help we can get."

Before I could respond to that, Lashawn grasped our elbows and led us to a gathering of the Six Amigos to go over the plan. He explained that we were to make sure everyone was seated by 5:55 and then to stand off to the side, the women on the left and the men on the right. The couple had remarks to make to begin the program, and we were to come forward when the pastor stood to begin the ceremony. "Heavy responsibilities, but even an ex-jarhead should be able to handle them," I thought. And we did it excellently, I might add.

We were in our places just before six o'clock. Lashawn and Laverna walked to the front, hand in hand, at six sharp. They each took a microphone and faced their guests. Lashawn began. "We welcome you and we thank you for coming to be with us on this special occasion. I want to express a very special "thank you" to my boss, Larry Mizell, not only for my job, but for his generosity in providing a buffet meal for all of us to enjoy at the end of the ceremony.

"It is our desire to testify to our confidence in God, that He is the One who has brought us to this place and time, that we might be the answer to each other's prayers. We also want to use the God given talents He's blessed us with to make this a memorable event for all of us. We've chosen to begin the ceremony with solos to each other, and to end it with a duet."

With that said, he stepped back and lowered his microphone.

Laverna stepped slightly forward, raised her microphone and said, "All of you know it's not easy raising a child as a single parent. Actually, you can't really know just how difficult it is unless you've experienced it. For three months before Ricky's birth and through the first year of his life I was a bitter woman. Not bitter toward God – some women would have blamed Him for taking away their man and the father of their child – but I was bitter at men in general. It seemed they either died or ran off with another woman to abuse. Then right after Ricky's first birthday, I began to pray for someone to come and help me raise this wonderful little boy. I prayed every day and every night, and the only requirement I requested of God was that the man He would send would love Him first, so that he would be able to love Ricky and me better.

"So, when Tillie and Barbara Jean told me they had found the perfect man for us," she pointed to Ricky and then to herself, "I was skeptical. When Tillie said, 'And he is a Gideon,' I agreed to go on a triple date with them. That night I prayed, Lord if he is the one let me know quickly.

"On the evening of our first date I was watching out of the front window when they drove up. Watching Lashawn come up the walkway, I thought, he is one fine looking man, Lord! At the door, we introduced ourselves and I asked him in to meet my family. I held up two fingers to Joe and Tillie to indicate we would be out shortly and turned to introduce Lashawn to my mother. While they were shaking hands, Ricky, who is usually shy around men, came forward and tugged on Lashawn's pant leg. Lashawn dropped to one knee, and said, 'Hey little man!' Ricky held up both arms and Lashawn picked him up. They embraced as if it were the most natural thing in the world. I learned several days later that Ricky had whispered a one word question in Lashawn's ear, 'Daddy?'

"We went to Smokey's for dinner and karaoke, and when I hear the man sing, I was blown away. After the first few songs people began to beg us to do a duet. As we made our way to the stage, I added a requirement: Please, Lord, let my man be able to sing like this man can.

"At the end of our song the man had the audacity to kiss me right there in front of everybody – I enjoyed it, too! He was even bolder, asking me on our first date to marry him. I wanted to say yes, but convention or reason would not allow me to, so I told him I'd think about it.

"On our second date, I invited him to dinner at my house because I wanted to prove I could cook. The meal was a success, thanks to my mother. Afterwards Lashawn took Ricky to the living room while we did a quick cleanup. I know it didn't take more than fifteen minutes, but when I got to the living room I found Lashawn reared back in the recliner with Ricky on his chest, both sound asleep. I stood there thinking, please ask me again, please – He didn't!

"On our third date, Ricky saw Lashawn drive up, and he ran to me saying, "Daddy come! Daddy come!" I responded with a silent prayer, please ask me again. He did!

"So, after a whirlwind courtship and a year of serious prayer," – the music background track began to play – "I can sing,"

She did a wonderful job of Etta James' version of "At Last."

At last my love has come along
My lonely days are over, and life is like a song
Oh yeah yeah at last the skies above are blue
My heart was wrapped up in clover, the night I looked at you

Lashawn went to her, placed both hands on her cheeks and gave her a very sweet kiss. Turning to the audience, he wiped tears from his cheeks and said, "You all know my story: imprisoned, wrongly accused, facing death. I found the Lord by reading His Word, which had been placed there by the Gideon Ministry. My prayer life began by asking God to find a way to prove my innocence. He did that using the good police work of my friend Brody over there, and the entire sheriff's department, to reveal the truth. It was only after becoming a free man that I began to pray for a wife. My requirements were simple: that she love God and that she would be willing to join me in the Gideon Ministry. I knew before our first date that she met those requirements, and when I heard her sing, my heart fluttered – and I knew she was the one!"

As the music started, he took her hand, gave her a half twirl away and back again so she was directly in front and very near to him. In that crystal clear, high tenor range he sang "Destiny."

What if I never knew
What if I never found you
I'd never have this feeling in my heart
How did this come to be
I don't know how you found me
But from the moment I saw you
Deep inside my heart I knew
Baby you are my destiny
You and I were meant to be

When the applause died down, Pastor Cooke arose. We took our assigned places and the bride and groom turned to face him. He began, "It is my honor and pleasure to perform this sacred ceremony, joining two dedicated servants of God in Holy Matrimony."

He performed the traditional Christian ceremony and both recited their vows flawlessly. When he pronounced them man and wife, he said, "You may now kiss your bride." Lashawn eagerly complied.

As previously instructed, the four of us faded to the side and the bride and groom took microphones again and sang a gorgeous rendition of a song entitled "The Prayer."

How can I describe it? Impossible! The written word is not capable of conveying the beauty of the sound they produced. I could provide you the words, but they cannot do the moment justice. I suppose it possible for the truly gifted musician to imagine how a coloratura soprano and a tenor, with the capability of reaching the counter tenor range, would sound. Most of us simply cannot do so. I can only recommend you go to YouTube and listen to Andrea Bocelli and Celine Dion sing the song. That just might produce the same feeling I experienced, that of my spine tingling, the hair on my neck rising and goose pimples all over my skin.

Everyone stood, clapping for the couple and in praise to the Lord. A beautiful and very memorable wedding!

It was almost comical to turn and see this huge cow, standing at least six and a half feet tall, holding a sign in one hoof that read, "Eat Mor Chikin," while pointing us toward the food with the other hoof.

I remember hearing it said that life is all about emotional highs and lows. I didn't agree with it then, nor do I today, but I must admit that the thought was becoming relevant to my situation. I was on cloud nine, basking in the sea of adoration and praise, eternally secure, great job, a wife to hold in my arms every night – it doesn't get any better than this!

All that came crashing down with a phone call from Mike Balls' father. "Brody, this is Hugh Ball. I have bad news. Annie has cancer and is sinking fast."

"That can't be! I just talked to her last month."

"I know. We suspected something was wrong then but didn't want to say anything until we knew. Two days after you called, she went to her doctor and got the diagnosis. It's the bad kind, pancreatic, and it has ravaged her. We've been advised to call in hospice. She really wants to see you, Brody. Can you please come?"

"Yes, I'll make arrangements to leave early tomorrow. Can you get me reservations at a hotel or motel nearby?"

"No way, you'll stay in Mike's room – and don't eat before you get here. We have so much food around here we can't get it in the refrigerator. And, don't think about staying until the end because we are not going to have a funeral. She wants to be cremated, and we'll just do a family and friends kind of memorial thing in a few days."

I swallowed the big knot in my throat and muttered, "I am so sorry. I will see you tomorrow."

Calling in to the office to arrange for a vacation day off, Right Arm said, "Just let me put you through to the sheriff." He listened as I explained my need for the day off before my shift change, and answered, "Brody, consider this a pass, not a vacation day. You have earned it."

I turned to my wife and she glided into my arms. "Nothing more soothing and comforting than a loving wife," I thought. We embraced for several minutes before she reminded me with, "Go out there and keep me safe."

The day went well. I decided to stay on schedule and patrol the Belhaven and Pinetown areas and to stop into as many businesses as practical. It was very rewarding to find that almost everybody seemed to recognize me and wanted to talk about one or more of the recently solved cases. That made the day fly by. I do remember Doc calling to express his gratitude for the way Lashawn and I had honored the Lord. That was special.

As we prepared for bed, I told B.J., "I'm packing for three nights, just in case, but I don't expect to stay but two." In bed, she snuggled up to my back with her right arm around me and her hand gently scratching my hairy chest; I almost rolled over to ask if she wanted to reconsider our mutual decision not to practice. There was no need to count sheep to get to sleep.

I left early and arrived at the Ball's house on Sterling Boulevard just a few minutes after noon. When I pressed the doorbell, Sissy came out and ran into my arms. I was holding her while she cried silently, when Hugh got there to make it a group hug. He explained that Annie had been in a lot of pain and the nurse had increased her morphine drip sufficiently to keep her asleep for another hour or two. "Come on in and put your stuff away, then we'll try to do away with some of this food."

In the kitchen, I saw what he meant by an abundance of food. A tray of deviled eggs caught my attention and I popped one in my mouth as an appetizer. Hugh suggested that we fill our plates and meet in the sun room to eat and talk. Without further prompting, I tackled the sugar-cured ham, green beans almondine, pickled beets, and potato salad. I popped a roll on the plate and grabbed the glass of sweet tea Sissy handed me.

As we sat down, Hugh explained that hospice had made an evaluation the night before that Annie's body was already shutting down. In their opinion, it would be cruel to try to feed her, as her body wouldn't be able to process food. They didn't expect her to last more than two or three more days.

With that news, the conversation dwindled and the formulation of a prayer became more difficult. My food was becoming more difficult to swallow. Finally, Hugh, pushing the last bits of food around on his plate, said, "Brody, we were never religious people, but several weeks before her diagnosis, Annie got saved, and I think that's what she wants to talk to you about. I hope she can do it, because she really wants to. It didn't seem to bother her at all to receive such bad news just days following her confession of faith. But I'm angry at God."

"I understand that, Hugh, and at the moment all I can think to say is, I will pray for you. I do hope the scripture that says, 'All things work together for good for those who love and trust Him,' will come to be reality for you."

"If He can use this to work out good for me, indeed He'll be a miracle working God. I'm so depressed; I just don't know how I will be able to go on without Annie; we've been together thirty-five years."

"Whoa, stop right there! Please don't even start thinking like that! You can go on; you must go on. Sissy's very future is dependent upon you, now, more so than ever. You will do it just like everyone else does it, one day at a time, step by step. You have friends who will be glad to help you, and I will help you any way I possibly can. Come visit me. We'll go fishing – whatever – but you have to keep on keeping on. The one thing I know for sure is, it will be easier if you let God lead the way. There are many ways to find God, but there is no surer way than through His Word. Try reading a portion of scripture each night and each morning, if you can. I believe you'll be astonished at how quickly things will seem better for you."

A nurse poked her head into the sun room and said, "She's awake and asking for Brody to come to her room." As I rose to go, Hugh said, "Be forewarned: she looks bad. Try not to let her see the shock you'll feel." I could only nod.

Annie had her eyes closed when I entered as silently as possible. I was kneeling beside the bed when she opened her eyes. "Hi, Momma."

"Oh, Brody, those are the sweetest words I could ever want to hear! Thank you so much for coming."

"How could I not come? You are dear to me!"

"Brody, there are so many things I want to say, and I know there is so little time left for me, so please let me try to get it all out as quickly as possible. I hope it will make sense and you'll be able to carry out my wishes. You and I are both young Christians and we still have a lot to learn; but I believe God has chosen you as His child, and He's given you to us to be our child for the time left here on earth. So, I beg you to do everything you can to be a son and a brother to Hugh and Sissy. Be their spiritual leader and guide them to Christ; help them see that the only way they will be able to see me again is to be where I will be, in heaven. Promise me that you will pray them toward Jesus. We both know if they will give Him their hearts, He will never fail them. Will you do that?"

"I promise you, they will always have priority on my prayer list, and I will do everything I can to lead them to trust Christ."

"Good, good! I knew I could count on you for that. Now I have a task for you that you may find more difficult. The most difficult thing I've had to face these-past few weeks has not been cancer and the devastating effect it has on my body – it has been how I can be obedient to God's Word. Luke 6: 27 tells us to love our enemies and to do good to them that hate us. It has haunted me until I had no choice but surrender to its true meaning. I've flushed out the hate in my heart towards the one we know as Ali Baba, and I've replaced it with a choice to love him. The hardest thing I have ever done is to deal with that hate and expunge it from my body and my thoughts. I want you to know, I've been praying for the salvation of that man's soul for the last two weeks. I will continue to do so as long as I have that ability. Brody, I'm asking you to do it, too."

"I don't know, Momma. You've laid some heavy stuff on me. I'll think about it. I do know I'll have to pray for myself before I can pray for him."

"Yes, you are right, but remember, God never asked us to do anything He hasn't already done Himself. Jesus died for the Ali Baba's of the world. Brody, the world will know we are Christians by our love, not our hate."

Then she drifted off to sleep, so I kissed her cheek and went out to be with the others.

As soon as I sat down, they wanted to know how it went. "I think she got to say all that she wanted to say. She laid some heavy stuff on me about getting rid of the hate I have for Ali Baba, and I promised to try to deal with it. I'll have to keep you posted on that. I called her 'Momma,' and that really pleased her. I'm so glad I thought to do that."

"Yes, I am too," Hugh answered. "Brody, I need a favor."

"Of course, what can I do?"

"Annie's sister is coming in from Los Angeles at five o'clock. Could you drive Sissy to Dulles airport and let her go inside to meet her aunt? You can wait for them or drive around the circle if they make you move."

"Yes, sir, I'll be glad to do that."

On the way to the airport, which is only about five miles away, I learned that Annie and her sister, Betsy, were not close, and only saw each other a couple of times a year. But Aunt Betsy had never had children, so she'd always been very generous in her attention to both Ball children, with a leaning toward Sissy as her favorite. She lived in Burbank where her artist husband, Thomas Jewell, worked for Universal Studios. We had checked the airline schedule and knew the plane had landed before we left the house, so the wait wouldn't be long. But I was asked to move the car twice before I saw them coming out. I got out to greet Aunt Betsy for the first time, and was surprised that she rushed to give me a big hug. She said, "Brody Edwards, I'm so glad to meet you. You're not going to believe this – I think this is one of the weirdest coincidences I have ever heard of – my next-door neighbor in Burbank is Johnny McQuaig, your high school classmate. I told him I might get to see you, and here we are! Wow!"

I put her bag in the rear of the Escalade and noticed a black Mercedes pull up in front of me. As I started to close the rear door, a sense of darkness came over me, and I froze. And it was good that I froze, because I was hidden from view behind the car door. Replaying it now, I see it in slow motion – the figure walking out the airport door and straight to the Mercedes, was Ali Baba himself.

No way – it's not possible – he can't be here. But he is.

"**What the hell is that raghead doing in our country***?"*

"I don't know, Rage, but you can bet he isn't here for good."

I waited until Ali Baba handed his bag to the driver and got into the Mercedes before I moved. When they pulled away I followed at a safe distance.

"Listen carefully, ladies, this is very important: Help me keep sight of that car in front of us. I have to find out where it's going. I glanced in the mirror, caught Mrs. Jewell's eye and said, "If you think living next door to my high school classmate is weird, wait until you hear this. The man who just got in that car is the man who killed Mike; that is Ali Baba himself. I could never forget that face. Plus, I saw that his right middle finger is missing, where I shot it off."

The Mercedes exited the airport onto Route 28 heading toward Sterling, and turned right onto Sterling Boulevard. When they passed the Ball's house, I said to Sissie and Aunt Betsy, "I wonder if he knows he's passing the boyhood home of the man he killed?" The car turned right onto Route 7 East, and we followed, allowing two cars between us. We crossed out of Loudoun and into Fairfax County and soon Sissy commented, "They're probably going to that Islamic Mosque up past the Route 193 turnoff." She called it right, and we saw the huge iron gates swing open as we passed. Sissy told me, "You can do a U-turn up at Utterback Store Road." We did, and as we slowly passed the Mosque again, we saw Ali Baba being given what looked like a royal welcome.

I got back to the house as fast as possible. When I rushed in and told Hugh the news, he told me, "This may be your lucky day. You never asked where I worked, and I never told you, so I wouldn't have to kill you. Let me see what I can find out." He made a call, while telling me he knew "We have a plant in that Mosque. We've suspected them of fanning the flames of radicalism for some time. We just might be able to pick up on what he has in mind."

I heard him relay the necessary information to whomever, and then he added, "Look, this is personal. We're talking about the son-of-a-bitch who cut off my son's head. I want to know who he is and why he's here – and I want him taken out. I don't care how it's done, just do it. Text me as soon as you know something, no matter how late."

Annie was lucid long enough to realize her sister was there and to thank her for coming. That evening the four of us sat in the living room. It was obvious we were all dealing with emotions, each in his or her way. Sissy began to pace the floor and then stopped and demanded our attention.

"Can you all stop talking for a few minutes and listen to me? I feel like I'm going crazy! I need to make some sense out of this . . . this mess! There are so many weird things going on that it can't be coincidence. I mean, it's like someone is writing a drama and we're all puppets in the play. How can it be?

"My brother gets killed by some idiot halfway around the world, who thinks God wants him to be judge, jury and executioner of anyone who won't accept his religion. My mother finds God and commits to trust Him for her eternal salvation and immediately has to deal with the worst form of cancer.

"My brother's friend from Choctaw – "Choco-hannity" – Podunk, USA, comes to visit my dying mother and she wants him to stop hating the man who killed her son! We go to the airport to pick up my aunt who lives 3,000 miles away, and we find out she lives next door to your classmate from high school. In the next instant, we witness the arrival of the man who killed my brother, and we're able to track him to a place where Dad can find out what he's doing here. Impossible! But we all know it's real – so real that it really hurts!"

She stopped pacing long enough for her dad to grab her into his embrace.

Finally, I was able to say, "I believe that my life is orchestrated by God, and that He is in the business of working out things for His glory. Personally, I cannot wait to see what He has in store for us. I hope you all will begin to look at life with an attempt to see Him at work."

Sissy spoke up saying, "I'll try. But I want to tell you what I heard at school last week. You talk about weird coincidences. We had a substitute teacher who was called in at the last minute who had no lesson plan or anything. And she tells us this story:

> My friend, Janie, was a flight attendant for United Express out of Dulles Airport. Her schedule for the month of September 2001, was all day trips, first from Dulles to JFK, return to Dulles – lunch break – to Knoxville, Tennessee, and back to Dulles to finish the day. She was flying on a twin engine, 19-passenger plane with a crew of three: two pilots and herself. On the tenth-of-September the return trip to Dulles from Knoxville only had three passengers, an elderly couple and their thirty-year-old daughter, and Janie began to chat with them. They introduced themselves as Roy and Joan (last name started with an H but she couldn't remember it) and the daughter's name was Leslie. She asked if they would be flying home that night, and they answered, "Oh, no. The last time we were in the country we wanted to see the World Trade Center, but there was a bombing in the basement and it was closed! So, we're going on to New York tonight to tour it tomorrow, and we'll fly home the next day."
>
> The next morning, September 11th, Janie greeted people boarding to go to JFK, and the same three people from London boarded her flight. The two women were quite congenial, but the man was steamed because their originally planned flight the night before had been grounded for maintenance, and the airline had to put the passengers up in a hotel in Sterling, Virginia.
>
> As the plane approached JFK, Janie noticed that the man had a video camera in his lap. She stopped to let him know they were flying right down the river line, and he would have the opportunity to get a great shot of the Statue of Liberty. "It can be difficult to locate, so if you just look forward until you see the World Trade Center and do a 45-degree sweep to the left, you'll be able to lock on to the statue pretty well."
>
> There was a passenger blocking Janie's view out of the window as they came in, so she saw nothing as the plane passed the two towers and banked left toward JFK.

They landed at 9:02 AM – the second plane hit the second tower of the World Trade Center at 9:03. Late in the afternoon, passengers, pilots and crew were told they would not be allowed to ferry the plane back to Dulles as they had hoped, and they would be put up in a hotel in Jamaica Bay, New York.

The next morning at brunch, Janie saw the very same family from London, and they walked over and sat at the table right next to her. After the meal, the four new friends took a stroll outside. Smoke was visible coming from across the river. Janie said to the man, "I'll bet you are glad now that you didn't get to New York night before last, aren't you?

And to that, he said, "Amen!"

"What do you think are the odds of someone from Sterling, Virginia, and someone from London, England, meeting one day in Knoxville, Tennessee, the next in Sterling, Virginia and the next in Jamaica Bay, New York?"

"Weird, eh?"

We all nodded in agreement and the ladies excused themselves for bed. Hugh and I continued talking until late, hoping to learn more information, but none came in. Just before we made the decision to hit the hay, I was able to get his promise to seek professional counselling for Sissy in the near future. It was just past midnight when I turned off my light.

The next morning, I was the first one up and was fumbling in the kitchen trying to figure out how to get coffee going when Aunt Betsy came in. She immediately took charge, got the coffee going and said, "How do you want your eggs?"

"Fried, over-medium, please."

She fumbled in the refrigerator and said, "Bacon or sausage?"

"Either or both is good for me." (I got both.)

She said, "I'm not much of a breakfast person. I'll just have a cup of coffee with you, if you don't mind." I motioned her to a chair as I stuffed a big bite in my mouth. She told me she called Johnny last night at midnight, our time, but only nine o'clock there. He gave her instructions to tell me to start converting my journals into book form, and he expected to see some results when he came to Chocowinity in June. I chuckled.

Breakfast finished and on my second cup of coffee, I watched Hugh approach with a note pad in hand.

"Here's what we have so far: he's going by the name Faisal Molecki. He is here for revenge on the man who killed his friends, one Brody James Edwards! He intends to see your head on a stake, even if he has to be a martyr to do so. He picked up on you from the Al Jazeera coverage, and he has online access to the Washington Observer, so he knows all about you. Here's the deal. We don't want to blow the cover of the man we have inside, so we can't make a raid on the Mosque. We have to wait and capture Molecki when he leaves. Hopefully, it will be that easy.

He paused. "I need to bring you up to date on Annie's condition. She has entered a comatose state, and the hospice nurse thinks she will likely remain that way until she passes. It could be a day or two from now, maybe three. Brody, I believe you would be best served to go home, live your life, and remember Annie as she was yesterday, rather than to have your last memory of her be as she is today. What do you think?"

I realized he was right. "As soon as Sissy finishes breakfast, I need to talk to you both about what Annie and I talked about yesterday. Then I can leave."

The three of us gathered in the sunroom, and I began to tell them of the conversation between Annie and me. "First, she expressed her concern for the spiritual well-being of both of you. She asked me to continually pray that you would both come to Jesus; I promised her I would, and I'll keep that promise, so you should expect to be prodded toward God by the Holy Spirit. She then shocked me with her concern for the salvation of Ali Baba. That's not the natural response one would expect from an injured party; it could only come from God. Annie testified that her prayers for that man's soul brought her relief as she felt the hatred melt from her soul. She asked me to join her in that prayer. I've not done so yet but I'm going to try to do it today and from now on. I will leave you with this thought: If you want to be with your wife and your mother, in the future, it will have to be in heaven; and the only way you can get there is to believe that Jesus is the Son of God, and put your trust in Him alone."

At that point Hugh excused himself to go check on Annie, and I was glad for the opportunity to be alone with Sissy. I reached over, took her hand and tried my best to be the big brother I knew she needed, though I'd had no experience at all. "Sissy, you are going through some very difficult times now; we can all see the stress you're dealing with. I wish I could be of more help. Even though I'm not your real brother, I want to be as close to one as I can. Promise me, when your dad suggests professional counselling for you, you'll take advantage of it. If it were not for my sessions with Commander Mandino at Walter Reed, I don't know where I'd be today."

She smiled at me and nodded.

"Here's some more brotherly advice. You don't need to be entering any new relationships with boys for a while; you're far too vulnerable and don't need that sort of comforting. But you need a good sounding board, so use your best girlfriend to pour out your heart to. Believe me, it helps to hear yourself talking, and at times you'll be able to tell whether you're being rational. I promise you, if you start journaling daily you'll reap benefits – you can go back and read over your thoughts and correct and expound upon them. That advice worked wonders for me. My final piece of brotherly advice is to get yourself ready for college. Consider East Carolina University in Greenville, which will put you within thirty minutes of our home. Barbara Jean and I will be delighted to have you in our home as often as you can be."

We stood and she gave me a big hug, saying, "Oh Brody, just knowing you and your wife want me near makes me feel better. I promise I will make East Carolina one of the places I consider."

Hugh came back, I got my bag and he walked me to the car. We huddled together in a sweet embrace and I uttered a short prayer for comfort for them and safety for my return home. It was about 9:30 when I headed out.

I had just sat down in the Escalade from having lunch at Ralph's when my phone announced a text message. It read, "No change in Annie. Something up at the Mosque - one bug disabled???"

The rest of the trip home was unsettling to say the least. My mind kept going over the things that would need doing, should Ali Baba get to my home territory.

I stopped off at the shoppe and brought Barbara Jean up to date on everything. When she heard about my conversation with Annie, she exclaimed, "What deep spiritual insight for someone so recently converted!"

I could only agree. Barbara Jean suggested that I go over to Aunt Hannah's to bring her up to date and decide about what the three of us should do for dinner. We decided to have Joe and Tillie join us at Smokey's for Karaoke Night.

At home, I settled back in my recliner and picked up a book I'd been reading about a ministry that is devoted to witnessing to Muslims. I began where I had left off a few days earlier. I was finding it difficult to concentrate until a statement jolted me fully awake: "Statistically, around the world now, the number one way a Muslim comes to Jesus is by a dream or a vision; and I want to declare to you that those instances will increase." Wow! I remembered reading earlier where the author cited the Books of Acts and Joel where the Spirit would give visions to young men and dreams to old men. I began to wonder if God has something like that in mind for Ali Baba.

I needed to think more about what I would do if I did have to engage Ali Baba. It took a while for it to register in my mind that I was staring at his scimitar there on my bookshelf.

"**Maybe you'll get to use that thing on him yet**."

"Stop that, Rage, we don't need your input right now."

Nightmare or Reality? Chapter Forty

I slept late for me. It was almost 8 AM when I opened my eyes. Gosh, Barbara Jean has been gone for two hours already! What a good night's sleep! Whether due to stress, travel, good food, good company, or practice, practice, I don't know; but I felt ready to deal with whatever came my way. I did the morning chores and headed out to have breakfast with my wife, when my cell phone rang.

"Brody? Hugh here. Molecki has definitely flown the coop. He might have scaled the back wall and gone through the woods to be picked up on Route 193, or more likely, he left in the weekly pickup of laundry which happened late yesterday. At any rate, we have to assume he's heading your way. Knowing how these bastards operate, I suggest you get Barbara Jean out of there ASAP. He'll most likely try to get to you through her."

"Yeah, I agree. I'm on my way to her right now."

"Look, I'll have a team of two or three men on the way within two hours. I'm pretty sure the FBI will want to be in on the act, too. You get into the station and bring the sheriff up to speed as quickly as you can. You need 24/7 coverage, now. Wait, don't hang up. I'll have his picture sent to your phone by the time you get to the station. Put a copy in every hotel/motel in the area. Let's try to get him before he can get to you. I'll stay in touch."

As soon as I walked in, Barbara Jean knew something was wrong. She rushed to me with, "What's going on?"

"Ali Baba has escaped the CIA trap, and we assume he's on his way here. I have to get you out of here now to a place where he can't find you" I turned and locked the door and we began to bat around possibilities. We had no family to turn to, but several friends came to mind. Joe and Tillie, our best friends, were our first choice. Still, we contemplated whether there had been any news coverage that would link them to us. We finally decided that there was no way he could know about them; therefore, they were our best option. Tillie was already at work when B.J. reached her on the phone.

"Of course, you are welcome. Come on as soon as you can. I can't leave here before closing time but you can come by and get a key."

I took the phone from B.J. so they could both hear. "Here's what we'll do. We go back home and pack B.J.'s bags for two or three days and then she goes to the station with me. That way she'll be in on all the planning and be able to see the precautions we take. Hopefully that will help her cope with this. We'll have dinner brought in to the station and I'll leave alone afterwards. If Molecki's around he'll follow me. A patrol car can deliver B.J. to you, probably around 6:30." I received a nod from B.J. and a "sounds good" from Tillie, and I hung up.

Back at the house, I watched my wife pack her bag – two pairs of slacks with blouses, pajamas, slippers, robe, makeup, plain cotton underwear, etc. She zipped the bag closed and as we started for the door, I told her I noticed she'd left the blue lacy things out on the dresser. "Yeah, I know, I left them out so you would think about me while I'm gone."

"Not funny."

"Your opinion, not mine," she threw over her shoulder as she swished her cute little behind out to the car.

Our entrance into the station with suitcase caused Ellen to rise and head toward us. "We have an emergency," I explained. "We need you, Donnie and the sheriff to join us in the conference room as soon as possible."

They were all there in short order. I covered everything as succinctly as possible, from what happened in Afghanistan, how Ali Baba had identified me, the miraculous events of my interception of him at Dulles Airport, the CIA's presence at his choice of refuge, to his escape from our trap and his intent to seek revenge on me here. I went on to explain that the CIA would have two, maybe three, assets here in six or seven hours and they were going to brief the FBI, which would probably give us more assets.

I finished up by saying, "My number one priority is to keep Barbara Jean safe. She will be staying with Joe and Tillie Cooke until Molecki is killed or captured. I think it's safe to assume that when he can't find her, he will come after me head-on. I'm not concerned about his being a sniper. I'm confident he'll want to capture me so that I know it's he who is inflicting the revenge he seeks.

"Therefore, we need to keep my schedule as normal as possible. The CIA plant was able to get a camera shot of him, which I have on my phone and am sending to each of you, so we'll all know what he looks like. He used the name Faisal Molecki on his passport, so I would expect him to continue to use that, whether real or not."

The sheriff took over. "Let me see that." He instructed Right Arm to get the photo sent to everyone as an APB to call in when sighted. "Make twenty paper prints to be delivered to every hotel, motel and B&B in the area. Use your notes to prepare a shift commander's briefing to be used with every shift change until further notice. Get Brody to look it over before it's released to each shift commander. Now, Brody, you would normally finish day shift on Saturday and go to days off, then to swing shift, right?"

"Yes, sir."

"I think you need to stay on day duty until this thing is over. Take Sunday off and go about your normal Sunday activity. I think it will be good for him to see you doing that. I recommend that Barbara Jean not go to church, or anywhere else for that matter, until we get this guy. Maybe Joe and Tillie can be persuaded to have home church with you that day. Can you please see if you can make that happen?

Brody, you need to call Aunt Hannah and brief her. Make sure she stays away from you and your house until further notice. We certainly don't want Molecki to know how special she is to you. Also, brief Doc and have him arrange for transportation for Aunt Hannah. Ellen, make sure all shift commanders know they have to have at least one unit within thirty seconds of Brody's 20 at all times. The midnight shift unit can be used to check on Aunt Hannah's residence several times each night. Anyone have something to add? Questions? . . . Then let's get those pictures out there."

When the others left, I knew B.J. was pleased with what she had heard and grateful for having been included. We embraced for a long while and then went to the day room to get a soda and find more comfortable seats. When we finished our drinks, I went to check with the sheriff to see if he was okay with me staying inside until we heard from the incoming assets.

"Yes, absolutely. But I see a potential problem. We don't want Molecki to know we have additional resources and we certainly don't want him to know what they look like. He's probably watching the station now and knows you're here. Call Mr. Ball and tell him to have his people call in about fifteen minutes before arrival. Then you can leave to draw Molecki away. Donnie will be your tail, and we'll call you back in when the assets are inside."

"I like the way you think, sheriff."

I called Hugh and relayed the sheriff's request. "Done."

Back in the day room, I looked at B.J. and asked, "Rummy or Skipbo?" We played Skipbo for the rest of the afternoon. While we played, I told her about the plan for me to leave the station to draw Ali Baba away so the assets could come in unobserved. When the call came in, I took off immediately, and Donnie followed shortly after.

I decided to ride by and check on B.J.'s store. Seeing nothing amiss, I turned back toward town, driving slowly and awaiting an okay to return call. Watching my rearview mirror all the way, I thought, "If he's trailing me, he's good at it!" A few minutes later the call came in for Unit 61 and Unit 6 to return to HQ. B.J. joined us in the conference and the sheriff briefed the newcomers on the plan of action for the next few days. He projected a map of the county and demonstrated how, on Saturday, I would stay relatively close to HQ by patrolling from Chocowinity up to the Pitt County line and down to the Craven County line on Route 17.

"Sunday is a day off for Edwards. Brody, do you want to share your plans for that day?"

I got up and pointed to the location of Joe and Tillie's residence. "That's where I would like to be but can't, but I do want it to be a primary focus of yours – the most precious possession I have will be there." I pointed to the church. "I'll be here from 10:30 until 12:20 or maybe 12:30. I'll probably stop by Hardee's to take home lunch and watch the Nationals game." Pointing out Chocowinity Bay, I said, "I'll go down here to do some fishing around five. B.J. and I often do that on Sunday afternoon, and I try to get down there on Wednesday or Thursday evenings. That's all I have for now."

B.J. and I ordered Chinese for dinner, and I left the station at 6 PM, again taking a turn around the store to see how things looked. Nothing wrong that I could see. "Heading home," I reported. A TV dinner of spaghetti by Marie Callender satisfied my appetite, and then I watched the game shows, Wheel of Fortune and Jeopardy, which satisfied my desire for entertainment. I took the precaution to double check every window and door to ensure I was locked in, and then went up for a fitful night of sleep.

The next morning, I awoke at 7:30 and was dressed and downstairs by 8:00. I started the coffee and texted B.J.

"I'm up and having breakfast."

She called back in less than a minute. "I hope you slept better than I did. I missed being held by Superman!"

"I missed you, too. I didn't like being separated from you but, it was for the best – the house creaked, a shadow moved across the room and I darn-near shot a hole in the door before I was fully awake."

"You're kidding."

"No. I had my gun in hand ready to pull the trigger."

"Maybe it is a good thing I wasn't there."

"When you get back, the gun will be in the safe where it usually is."

We did the goodbye thing, I gulped down my coffee and headed in for the shift briefing. It was weird being the central focus of the morning briefing, but I also sensed that everyone there was concerned about and committed to keeping me safe. The day went smoothly, and I actually enjoyed spending more time stopping in at as many businesses as I could – it gave me the opportunity to show Molecki's picture around and ask people to call in if they spotted him. Signing out for the day, I found that no one had reported seeing him, and all the motels, etc., had negative reports. At home, I backed the cruiser into the single car garage, knowing I would not be using it until Monday. As soon as I unlocked the kitchen door, I sensed something was not right. I put my back against the back wall, pulled my weapon and called for help. In a matter of seconds one unit arrived with flashing lights, and within just a few more minutes there were at least a half dozen more responders. I made the decision to have two of us enter the front and the back simultaneously while two others would stay outside at the front and back. Going around front to use my key, I shouted, "Let's go."

In the living room my sense of assurance increased. I could smell him. We gave the house the most thorough search possible but we found nothing. I could feel the confidence my guys had in me waver. I could almost hear them thinking, "Is his PTSD kicking in due to stress, or what?"

At that moment, I realized what was wrong. I pointed to the bookshelves. "It's gone – the scimitar – it's gone!"

Donnie knew exactly what I meant because he'd seen it there on several occasions. We dusted for fingerprints, checked every possible place of entry but found nothing. That night the sheriff directed a doubling of the guard to cover both front and back entrances. I finally got to sleep.

I sensed it was early morning, even though I couldn't see the clock. I could, however, feel the coldness of the steel pressing against my throat. I opened my eyes to see Ali Baba standing over me with a big grin on his face. Finally, I was able to get the words out, "How did you get in here?"

He just shrugged and said, "Sit up, Corporal Edwards, there is no need to scream. It will all be over before anyone can help you."

The thought hit me, "I'm not going to get to hold my babies!" Then the horrible sound of swoosh came to my ears and I screamed, "No!"

Now fully awake, sweating and shaking, I turned on the lights, picked up my walkie-talkie and keyed in "I'm okay. It was just a nightmare!"

Sunday morning, I was talking to my wife as I fixed coffee and toast, and when I related the nightmare to her, she started crying. "Please don't cry, honey, I'm all right, and I have two guards following me everywhere I go."

"How much longer will this last? I can't take too much more."

"I don't know sweetie; I have put some thought to that myself. We're obviously dealing with a well-trained person. Anyone who can break and enter without a trace is so good, I can see him wanting to play cat and mouse; by the same token, he may see himself as so good he will want to get it done just to prove his superiority. On one hand, we are at his mercy whether we like it or not; on the other, I can sense the Lord has something to say about all of this. Either way, God is in control. Have no doubt about that."

"Are you going to church?"

"Of course. I need to do that. Hopefully Doc will have a message that will get my mind off this mess."

"I hope so, too, baby. By the way, Joe said he has a lesson for Tillie and me that will show that there could have been two good preachers in the Cooke clan, if he'd chosen the ministry."

With a chuckle, I said, "What a nice way to end our conversation. I love you."

"Me too, kiss, kiss."

About fifteen minutes before time to leave for church, my phone rang. It was Hugh Ball. He choked out, "She's gone," and he began to cry.

"Oh, Hugh, I am so sorry. But now she isn't in pain, and she is with Jesus."

Then I asked him if it was okay for me to pray, and I did. It was only after we hung up that it occurred to me that Hugh may have been surprised I didn't pray for Annie, but instead for him and Sissy. I thought, "I hope he'll figure out soon that her future is already securely in the hands of the Lord, and she needs no further prayer."

If my life depended upon it, I could not tell you much about the church service that day – the hymns sung, scriptural text, the poetry of Doc's typical message – nothing comes to mind. What I recall now are things leading up the service. It was nice that, once inside, I could greet Aunt Hannah properly. We stood in front of our pew, talking to Doc. She had her left arm around my back while patting me gently on the chest with her right hand. We were telling the pastor about Ali Baba and the surrounding incidents, when I thought to tell them both about Annie Ball's going home to be with the Lord this morning. My last memory of the service was the pastor asking the congregation to pray for me.

On the way home, I stopped by Dairy Queen and ordered a shrimp basket with fries and coke. I downed those promptly, went back to the counter to get a pineapple sundae and took it outside to a table with an umbrella. A fine, beautiful spring day to be eating ice cream. Yes, thank you Lord!

Almost home, I saw the Hardee's sign and remembered that I had intended to get a couple of country ham biscuits but had pulled into the Dairy Queen instead. "The pressure must be severe to get my mind off country ham biscuits," I thought. I changed into grungy jeans and a tee shirt, and slipped on a really old pair of deck shoes, no socks. I decided to add my 38 snub-nose pistol and ankle holster to my ensemble and to clip my handcuff case to my belt. I stood in front of the TV – a Washington Nationals game, or mow the lawn? Unable to picture myself sitting still, I chose the lawn work.

I picked up my walkie-talkie and advised the tail that I was going out to cut grass. I grabbed the cadet key hanging by the back door, went to the garage and fired the tractor to life. I ran the mower faster than I should, watching the clippings flying out from under the mower deck. Twigs that should have been raked snapped under the blade. The exertion of spinning that steering wheel relieved the tensions that had gripped me all morning. Making a mental note to call Big John to give the yard some better attention than I intended to give it, I went to my recliner and keyed in, "nap time."

At 4:00, I communicated, "I'm ready to go fishing." I heard the following: "Special one, we are ready. Special two, we are ready. Unit 16, in place. Unit 32, in place. Birdman awaiting instructions." Then it was the sheriff's voice. "Okay guys, if by some chance he does get to Brody or at the first sign of his presence, I want to hear the signal 'Red Alert.' If you hear that, make sure your exits are blocked. No one gets in or out without a thorough check. Birdman, you do have a sniper onboard, right?

"Affirmative. Let's roll."

I parked the Escalade, got out my tackle box and pole and started across the street to the prearranged dock. Seeing Donnie at work in the yard closest to my car and knowing he had a rifle hidden in the bush closest to him, gave me the feeling that this was going to turn out right.

As soon as I got my worm on the hook, I swung the line out as far as I could and immediately saw the cork start trembling. I watched intently, hoping to see it go under, but nothing happened. I thought, "Just a little one playing with the bait," and moved it to another location. This happened several times before I heard what sounded like rapid gun fire coming from behind the house where Donnie was posted. I heard Donnie yell, "Get down, Brody!" and I put the pole in a holder on the railing and did exactly as he commanded. I heard the distinct sound of a Harley-Davidson cycle coming toward us. From my prone position, I looked up, while reaching for my leg holster, and saw Donnie draw aim on the cyclist. As if on cue, the cyclist stopped and the motorcycle began to backfire. Suddenly – a tremendous flash of light, intense pain – and my last conscious thought was, "Have I been hit by lightning?"

I learned later that Donnie sounded the Red Alert signal and yelled out, "He's gone! Brody has disappeared into thin air! I looked away for what couldn't have been more than a minute, and he was gone. Move, move, guys – Birdman, I need you now! Anybody see anything suspicious?"

The sheriff broke in, "He has to be in the creek. Donnie get your ass in that creek now and give me a report. Hurry, man."

Maybe two minutes passed before Donnie came back to the dock. "It's useless. I can't see down there. I felt around on the bottom as best I could, but I don't think there is a body down there." He climbed up on the dock to retrieve his cell phone and walkie-talkie and called to Birdman, "Do you see anything?"

"No, sir, no cars moving. The only one I see outside is three doors away, and there's a man grilling out back.

"That must be in the Friedl yard," and Donnie took off running."

At the Friedl's gate, he yelled, "Joe, we think someone abducted Brody Edwards. Did you see anything?"

"No – I heard all those fire crackers going off, and I saw a man on a motorcycle trying to get it running, but I didn't see anything else. Wait. I did hear a powerboat leave from out front right after that."

"By golly, I heard that, too, but I thought it was you and Betty leaving for your usual Sunday night dinner at the Waterfront."

"No, it wasn't us. Betty isn't feeling well."

Donnie ran back toward the dock, yelling into the microphone to Birdman. "Go directly across to the other side of the Pamlico. Look for a powerboat that left here about six or seven minutes ago."

Seconds later Birdman reported, "No moving water traffic. I do see one speedboat docked – umm – looks like a couple of scuba tanks in the boat."

"That has to be the way they got him out. Birdman, run the route into town, look for anyone speeding, and get an ID if possible. Attention all units: I need a road block on River Road as close to the city limits as possible. Now, move!"

I have no idea how long I was unconscious. But I can tell you this. When I awoke, my head felt like someone had buried a hatchet in it; I had difficulty focusing my eyes; they seemed to be rolling around, under someone else's control. It soon became clear that I was in the back seat of a moving vehicle with my hands bound behind my back. It took a few more minutes for it to dawn on me that I was probably handcuffed with my own cuffs. I thought, "It's a good thing these seats are leather; I'm dripping wet – oh, wait – that means he hit me in the head and drug me into the creek . . . But how did I get here?

After three attempts, I was able to reach a sitting position, and saw Ali Baba driving a Nissan Pathfinder.

"Welcome back Mr. Edwards. I was beginning to think I hit you too hard, and cheated myself out of the pleasure of cutting off your head."

"May I assume you intend to do that with your own scimitar, which you stole from my house?"

"That would be a good assumption on your part."

"Does it bother you that I am not afraid?"

"You will change your mind about that in just a few more minutes."

"No, I will not, because God is on my side, and I cannot lose; if I die, I'll be in heaven. I think you are the one who should be afraid. Remember what happened in Afghanistan, when God wiped out all your friends with a lightning strike? Look over to the left. There's a storm rolling in from the coast. Do you see the lightning? I bet one of those strikes has your name on it."

In the rearview mirror, I could see the worry on his face. He was swallowing repeatedly. "I'm getting to him," I thought.

Sirens – must have been three or four cars heading our way. Ali Baba did an immediate right turn, and the police cars passed, heading in the direction we had come from. His little evasive tactic seemed to give him reassurance, so I started at him again.

"Do you remember my friend that you killed in Afghanistan?"

"Yes, of course, I remember."

"Well, his mother passed away this morning. I visited her in Sterling, Virginia, several days ago, and she told me that since Jesus had saved her, she knew she was obligated to forgive you for killing her son. It was the hardest thing she had ever done, she told me, but as she began to pray that God would forgive you and save you, she was able to do it. She prayed for you for the past two, almost three weeks, and she asked me to forgive you and pray for you also."

I saw a change coming over him. I can't explain it, I just know that something within him seemed to soften.

"And have you done either of those things?"

"I have prayed for the salvation of your soul. As for forgiveness, the jury is still out on that."

He made a quick right turn, and I recognized the parsonage, which is to the west side of our church. He pulled into the church parking lot and brought the car to a stop directly across from the front door. "Oh, so this is where you have planned to do the dirty deed."

"Yes, I thought it would be a nice touch to have them find your body leaning against the door, with you head in your lap, when they come to open the church for tonight's service."

"**You bastard!**"

He must not have heard Rage, as he made no comment. He just slammed on the brakes, grabbed a backpack off the front seat and opened my door. He dragged me out of the car to the front of the church and kicked me behind my knees, forcing me to kneel before him.

Seeing the sunset casting a shadow of the cross from atop the church onto the parking lot, he exclaimed, "Ah, the perfect spot for your beheading: Beneath the shadow of the cross." Placing the backpack on the ground between us, he unzipped it and extracted his scimitar.

He rose to his full height and stood with the scimitar tip touching the ground and both hands on its hilt. "This would seem more real if he were wearing a turban," I thought. We looked at each other, and both of us shifted our gaze briefly toward heaven. I don't know what he said to Allah, if anything, but, I know exactly what I said. "I could sure use another miracle right about now. Please, God."

I did not hear a thunder clap nor see a lightning strike, but I did hear a loud whack and saw a baseball hit Ali Baba in his left temple. "He went down like a pig at a hog shoot, straight down, as if dead; not at all like a Hollywood production," I thought.

C.J. came running up, and I yelled, "Get these cuffs off, quick! Keys are in my right front pocket!"

Once free, I grabbed him in a huge hug, then directed him to call 911

"Tell them to come in quietly and that everything is under control." He ran toward the parsonage, and I cuffed Ali Baba's hands behind his back. When he regained consciousness, I helped him to his knees and took the same pose in front of him that he had taken in front of me several minutes before.

"What happened?"

"Your life has been spared. It seems as if God has plans for your future."

"I don't understand. What do you mean?"

"Hopefully, you will in a few minutes; but first let's talk about those dreams you've been having."

"Wait. How do you know? You can't possibly know about my dreams."

"Oh, yes, I do. I know that God has been trying to get your attention. The man in white has been calling for you to come, hasn't he?"

"Yes. I have dreamed once or twice over the years, but in fact almost every night for the past few weeks about a man in white, waving me to come. He has an aura about him that makes it difficult to see his features, but his hands have holes in them."

"Those are the nail scarred hands of Jesus, calling you to believe in Him."

"I do believe in Jesus; he is a great prophet."

"He's more than that. Do you have a copy of the Quran with you?"

"Of course. In the bag, there."

I took his copy of the Quran from the bag, noting that it looked new. Relieved to see it was in English, I opened it to chapter 3, verse 47, and read:

"Lord," she said, "How can I bear a child when no man has touched me?" The angel replied, "God creates whom He will. When He decrees a thing, He need only say: Be, and it is."

"Now my question to you is, who caused Mary to get pregnant?"

"Why, God did, of course."

"The One who causes a woman to get pregnant is universally known to be the . . . ?"

"Father, of course."

"And the male child is known as the Son, right?"

"Yes, that's right."

"The Quran always refers to Jesus as the Son of Mary; but, in accordance with your own words, Jesus is the Son of God. Do you believe that is true?"

"Yes, I think so, but I am not sure I understand that."

"Okay, that's fair enough. Let me try to explain it better. The Son ship of Jesus has nothing to do with the fact that He was born of Mary. It has everything to do with the fact that He is eternal, always has been, and always will exist. Remember, the Quran tells you the Old Testament and New Testament are books that come from heaven. In the Old Testament, the prophet, Micah, foretold that the birth of the Messiah would be in the little town of Bethlehem.

"Out of you will come this One who was from everlasting to everlasting,' meaning that Jesus existed before He was born as a baby, and that He always will exist. His death on the cross was the substitute for your sins and, indeed, for the sins of all of us. It's important that you see and understand this so you can believe in Him correctly. So, I ask, do you believe it enough to ask Him to be your Savior?"

"Yes, I want to do that."

I reached in my pocket, unlocked his cuffs, and tossed the scimitar behind me. I fell to my knees, and we embraced.

"Because Jesus has forgiven you, so do I."

Proof that God Works in Wondrous Ways! Chapter Forty-One

I learned later from Pastor Cooke that when he and C.J. rushed out of the parsonage, they saw that I was in charge of the situation, in that Ali Baba (as they knew him) was in handcuffs, and I now had the scimitar. So, they came discreetly into hearing range and witnessed the whole conversation between the two of us. They waited to reveal their presence until we were both laughing and crying as if we had experienced a miraculous event. (Which, in fact, we had.)

I had just asked Pastor Cooke to talk to Faisal, to determine to his satisfaction that there had been a real conversion experience, when the rescue team rushed onto the scene. Six cars, light racks fully flashing but without sirens blaring, all slid to a stop around us. I held one hand down to assist Faisal from his knees, and extended the other hand to slow my team down.

"Everything is under control here, so put your guns away."

Undeterred, the two FBI agents rushed forward, re-cuffed Faisal's hands behind his back and secured him in the back seat of their SUV. I spent the next several minutes relating to them everything that had transpired, from the time I had regained consciousness until they arrived. I did my best to express the importance of what had occurred; that a life had been changed, that Faisal was now a different man than the one who had intended to kill me. With the exception of the sheriff, I don't think any of them thought what I told them made any difference at all. They were all tired and hungry, and it was evident to me that my defending Faisal was not producing results. So, I looked toward the sheriff.

He immediately said, "Okay, men, let's get him back to headquarters and into a holding cell so we can get some dinner and a rest." He looked at his watch and added, "Let's meet in the conference room in two hours."

I gave him a look that I hoped expressed my gratitude, then walked over to the SUV and told Faisal I would visit him before the night was over. I picked up my set of handcuffs and the scimitar, looked at Donnie and Doc and said, "I need a favor from each of you, please." I handed my car keys to Donnie and requested that he get someone to drive my car back to my house and leave it in the backyard.

I turned to Doc and asked him, "Will you please take me to Joe's to get Barbara Jean, and then take us home?"

They were both glad to do so, and it really warmed my heart to know that friends so willingly stepped up to meet my needs when I asked.

While I watched my team pull away and Doc head back to his house to get his car, I hit speed dial. When she answered, I simply said, "It is over." She calmly answered, "Thank You, Lord."

I almost was offended that she was so calm, until I realized she didn't know any of the details of what had occurred, and could not grasp how close I had come to death. So, I just said, "Pack your things as quickly as possible, tell Joe and Tillie 'thanks' and be ready to leave ASAP. Doc is going to take us home to get a quick bite to eat, and I have to be back at the station in two hours." Doc heard me tell her that last sentence and he interjected, "Tell Joe and Tillie I'll take you two home and come back to give them the details as soon as I can."

As we drove the short distance to Joe's house, Doc said that he knew Faisal had experienced an encounter with God. Just before the FBI guys re-cuffed him, he told Doc, "I feel as if a load has been lifted off my back, and, although I know I will be facing difficult days ahead, I believe God will get me through it all."

What a nice beginning, to have calm assurance in God! I thought that this just might be the beginning of something big.

Upon arrival at Joe's house, Barbara Jean came running down the steps and almost caused us both to fall to the driveway as she tackled me into an embrace. She was sobbing and kissing me with little pecks all over my face. Finally, I leaned back and said, "What happened to the calm assurance I heard over the phone?"

"C.J. called Joe and I heard over the speaker phone that Ali Baba had actually captured you and would have cut off your head if C.J. had not beaned him with a baseball! I had no idea what you had been through when you called me!"

In an attempt to calm her, I told her that I believed God had answered Annie's prayers and had visited Faisal in his dreams almost every night for the last three weeks. He was so ready for God, I just had to get him to see Jesus as both God and man. By the time I reiterated the story, she had her hands raised and was whispering, "Thank You Lord," over and over. I will keep that picture in my memory bank for many years to come.

At home, we found the Escalade in the backyard with the keys in the cupholder, just as Donnie had texted me they would be. Inside, I asked Barbara Jean to fix me a grilled cheese sandwich and a glass of milk, while I took a shower and made myself more presentable for our meeting.

Back at the table I found everything ready for me, and I sat down to give thanks. This time, there was no hesitation on my part to pray aloud. Thank You, Lord, for my safety, the fact that Faisal had struck me from behind and not in the front part of my head, for life and an opportunity to serve and hopefully make a difference, for my dear wife, whom I love with all my heart, and "Thank You, Lord, for the experience of witnessing Your love and power to Faisal. Thank You for saving him. And Lord, I look forward to seeing You work out things for his good, that he might be able to make a difference for You in the Muslim world. I believe You have great things in mind for that man, and I promise to praise you every day as I see those things happening. Let it be so! Amen."

"Oh, Brody, that was so beautiful. I love hearing you pray. Eat up. You need to hurry to make it on time. What do you think will be the best possible results of this meeting?"

"I have no idea. I just plan on letting the Lord lead me to do what He wants to be done. That's all I can do. Please pray for us during the meeting that the right outcome may be reached for His glory."

"I promise I'll be praying the whole time," she said.

As I walked toward the car, I thought, "Faisal needs a Bible." So, I dialed Lashawn Johnson. He answered on the second ring. When I explained what I wanted, he replied, "I have several cases of hotel Bibles I'll be using this week to replenish my three locations. I'll be glad to give him one if you can arrange it."

"I could stop by and pick it up if you like."

I could sense his hesitation. He explained that they were supposed to present the Bibles in person rather than through a third party. "Can you meet me at the sheriff's office in a few minutes?"

"Yes. I'll be there in ten minutes."

I waited for Lashawn in the back-parking lot and asked him to stay by the door until I got approval. I entered from the rear, to avoid the conference room area, and tapped lightly on the sheriff's door. When I explained what I wanted to do, I asked if we needed to get the FBI to approve Lashawn's visit.

"No, this is my territory, and I decide who can visit and who can't."

I got Lashawn and we entered the cell block area together. Faisal jumped up and came to the front of the cell, sticking his arms through to greet me like a long-lost brother. It's impossible to explain the camaraderie we both felt with one another since his conversion experience. I introduced him to Lashawn as my friend, and Lashawn wasted no time in explaining the Gideon ministry to him. He also exclaimed, "I was saved while in prison and reading a Bible like this one, which I bring as a gift for you on behalf of the Gideon Ministry. This is yours to keep. I know it will serve you well if you'll devote yourself to letting it guide your way."

Faisal acted like a kid with a new toy as he clutched the Bible to his chest. Lashawn asked the jailer if he had time to say a short prayer and was allowed to do so. I whispered that I had to get to the meeting and would check with them both later. I left the cell block area, lifting up my silent prayer as I hurried to the conference room.

The meeting opened with the FBI leader asking me to recap the whole story from the time I first saw Faisal at Dulles Airport until now. I did that as succinctly as possible, which took about ten minutes. When I finished, I was encouraged to hear him say, "We have no jurisdiction or authority over what was done in Afghanistan, but we can certainly prosecute him on some very serious crimes he's committed since being in this country."

He began by ticking off counts on his fingers: "One, we have an audio tape of him boasting he intended to kill you. Two, we have him for assaulting you. Three, we have him for kidnapping you. And four, we have him transporting you, against your will, from one jurisdiction to another – county versus city. I think we have enough to put him away for a long time, even if the Defense Department lays no claim to him."

"Yes, but this is a man who's just had a life-changing experience, one which, I guarantee, has changed him to the extent that he would not make those same decisions now. We should contemplate what a valuable asset he could be in the fight against Radical Islam, if we handle this correctly. He obviously knows the inner workings of the Taliban in Afghanistan, and maybe other countries. He probably knows the way they communicate, including their codes. He might even be able to identify some moles or informants who are leaking valuable information back to them.

At that point, the CIA agents began to speak up in support of pursuing my suggestions. Seeing my words were making an impact, I couldn't help but add, "What happens if I refuse to press charges against him?"

"You can't do that!" the FBI leader snapped.

"Oh, but I can, and I think I just might do so."

"Well, you may be able to make the assault and kidnapping charges disappear, but we still have the recording on which he states his intent to kill you."

"You have the tape, but we all know that getting it introduced in court as evidence is extremely unlikely, because it was obtained by unauthorized means and without his knowledge or permission."

As the truth of that statement slowly penetrated his brain, the FBI leader sagged to his seat. The sheriff quickly called for an end of the meeting.

"This has been a long and trying day. Let's try to finish up tomorrow morning. Nine o'clock sharp, okay?"

Evidently, no one objected, because we all got up and began heading for the exits. I watched them leave, expressed my gratitude to the sheriff and made my way back to the holding area to see Faisal. He looked up from his reading and came forward to stick his right hand through the bars.

"This is one fascinating book. Let me tell you what happened when I first opened it. I was sitting on the bunk giving thanks for my salvation and asking for guidance to better understand Him and how He works. When I opened the Bible, I looked down and saw it was opened to the book of Romans. Why I did not automatically begin to read in chapter one, I cannot explain, but my finger went to chapter two, and the first thing I read was:

'Therefore, thou art inexcusable, O man, whosoever thou art that judgest another, thou condemnest thyself; for thou that judgest doest the same things.'

"I read that verse over and over and a shame so deep came over me, I fell to my knees and begged God's forgiveness; for I realized that is exactly what I had been taught to do even though it's the direct opposite of God's teaching. I made a commitment to the Lord that I would use the rest of my life to help free people from the evil teachings of Islam. It seems so clear to me now, that I wonder how can so many be blinded to the fact that a Holy God would never tell an unholy man, even Mohammad, to execute judgment on other people."

"Wow! All that in just a few hours of reading, I wonder what God has in store for you, Faisal." I told him the gist of our meeting, making sure he understood that if he used his knowledge judicially, and I refused to press charges against him, he could be free to pursue a productive life without jail time. He was amazed that I would consider not pressing charges. I felt inadequate, but did my best to explain that true Biblical forgiveness is the same as if it never happened.

* * * * *

EPILOGUE

I called Buzz Latham and requested his help in the ensuing meetings. He graciously accepted and was instrumental in working out a conclusion with which we were all happy. To make a long story short, the FBI agreed to withdraw from the case, I agreed not to press charges, the CIA agreed to accept custody of Faisal and work with the Defense Intelligence Agency in debriefing him and preparing him for a new life here in America. He was returned to the Washington, D. C. area and placed in a safe house where he was debriefed and given what was basically a new life. He and I talk on the phone weekly and I am pleased to tell you that he plans to enter Washington Bible College in Lanham, Maryland, next semester to pursue a degree in theology and apologetics.

Lashawn, Joe and I are now Gideon's and our wives serve in the Auxiliary. Lashawn has taken on the role of Scripture Chairman for the camp and oversees the distribution of Bibles in every place that will give us permission to do so.

Barbara Jean and I began filling up the back seat of the Escalade with the birth of twins, Hannah Jean and Joseph James Edwards. Aunt Hannah has gone to be with her Lord Jesus, but not before she realized the dream of rocking our babies. One of my most treasured possessions is a photo of her rocking both of them in that old green and white glider on my front porch.

Johnny McQuaig did read my journals and persuaded me to convert my notes into a book. You are reading the results; I hope you enjoyed my efforts.

I leave you with a truism, which I found on a sticky note in Aunt Hannah's Bible. It was attached to the 23rd Psalm.

"Satan always gives you his very best first. Not so with God. It just keeps getting better and better."

"God is good all the time!"

"Psalm 90:2b From once upon a time to kingdom come. You are God. Psalm 90:2b"

"Rage, you have finally gotten it right."

"And all God's people said . . . ?

"Amen!"

ACKNOWLEDGMENTS

To my wife, Betsy, for her editorial skills; without her help the job would not have been completed.

To my brother-in-law, Dr. Tom Nettles, for introducing me to the wonders of sermons by Charles Spurgeon, for his proofreading and insightful input.

To my grandson, Jared Mihill, for many hours of drawing my concept for a book cover only to find out later that the publisher uses only photographic art.

To my daughter, Julie Mihill, for early editing and helpful suggestions that improved the product.

To my daughter, Stephanie Hall Wedan, and her husband, Steve, for their hours of fine-tuning and editing to bring about the final manuscript.

To our friend Esther Haugen for her many suggestions and corrections to the manuscript. I am very appreciative of the time and effort you put into making this a more acceptable product.

To Simon Riemersma, my golfing buddy, for taking the time to proofread this book.

To Suzanne Leonhard for sharing her experience with publishing, and for her generous offer to help convert my manuscript to eBook format.

To family, friends, and co-workers who contributed to the content herein and for making my life a fantastic ride.

To those who read this book, know that several of the stories contained herein are from real life experiences. The snake and the albino stag stories are events from my childhood, and the restaurant owner who got shot was really my father. The 9/11 story is one that happened to me during my time as a flight attendant.

About the Author

Geoffrey Cratch was born and raised in Beaufort County, North Carolina, where he graduated from Chocowinity High School in 1953. He attended Chowan Junior College from 1953, to 1954, and enlisted in the US Air Force in January1955, where he served until December 1959. He entered the Civil Service in January 1960, and retired as a member of the Senior Executive Service in August 1992. He and his father were investors in real estate and together owned and operated the Sterling Park Dry Cleaners from 1970, to 1982. During his career in the Pentagon he served under thirteen Secretaries of Defense. As the Director of Budget and Finance for the Office of the Secretary of Defense he appeared before House and Senate Appropriations Committees on many occasions in support of important defense programs. He continued his education while working, earning a Master of Public Administration Degree from The American University in 1979. In 1989, he was awarded the Secretary of Defense Medal for Meritorious Civilian Service.

He married Betsy Roebuck Cratch in 1961, and they raised three daughters while living in Sterling, Virginia. Now, 55 years later, they are proud grandparents of 23 grandchildren and 6 great-grandchildren.

In addition to his government career, he served as a Deacon and an Elder in his church and was an active member of the Gideon Ministry for many years.

Made in the USA
Middletown, DE
24 July 2017